Beyond the Waves

A story inspired by real events ...

'With courage, nothing is impossible.'

Sir William Hillary,
founder of the Royal National Lifeboat Institute
in 1824

Beyond the Waves

A story inspired by real events ...

C. J. Bateman

EHB

Edgehill Books

Also by C. J. Bateman:
A Dreadful Trade, Edgehill Books, 2017
If The Cap Fits, Tony Williams Publications, 1993
String Fellows, Matador, 2010

ISBN: 978-1-9998037-1-1
First published in 2019 in the UK by Edgehill Books,
Edgehill House, Hawkhurst Road,
Cranbrook, Kent TN17 3QD
colinjbateman@hotmail.com
(00 44) (0)1580 712366

Design and layout by Amanda Helm
amandahelm@uwclub.net

Printed and bound in Great Britain
by Short Run Press, Exeter EX2 7LW
www.shortrunpress.co.uk

Cover images:
Front: River Rother estuary at Rye Harbour:
photo © C. J. Bateman
Back: Conrad Gries, Alderney Museum

For Max

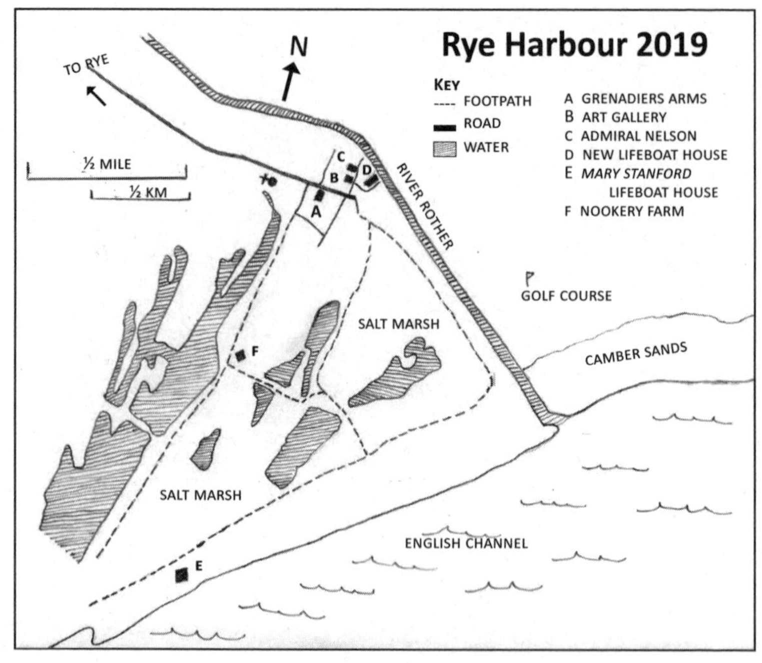
Rye Harbour 2019
N
TO RYE
KEY
FOOTPATH
ROAD
WATER
A GRENADIERS ARMS
B ART GALLERY
C ADMIRAL NELSON
D NEW LIFEBOAT HOUSE
E MARY STANFORD LIFEBOAT HOUSE
F NOOKERY FARM
½ MILE
½ KM
RIVER ROTHER
GOLF COURSE
SALT MARSH
CAMBER SANDS
SALT MARSH
ENGLISH CHANNEL

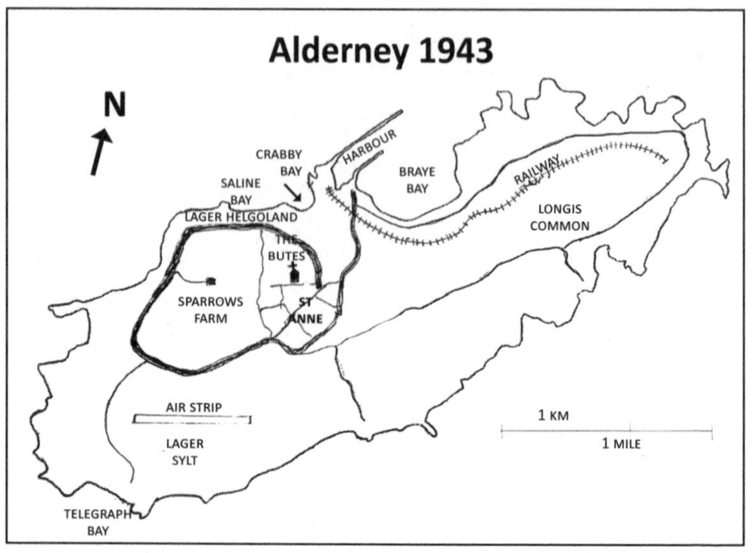
Alderney 1943
N
CRABBY BAY
HARBOUR
BRAYE BAY
RAILWAY
SALINE BAY
LAGER HELGOLAND
LONGIS COMMON
THE BUTES
SPARROWS FARM
ST ANNE
AIR STRIP
LAGER SYLT
1 KM
1 MILE
TELEGRAPH BAY

1

Present day. South Coast, England.

Be brave. Do something. Don't be a wimp all your life. Well, that's all very well if you are a super-hero striding through a movie swatting away the bad guys. But when walking alone on an exposed coastal path, chivalry is a less attractive option.

I could do the right thing and say something: step in, tell them off, and hope that other right-thinking members of the public might back me up if things turned nasty.

But, as usual, I said nothing. I watched, keeping my head down, muttering to myself about the youth of today.

Fortunately, nothing did turn nasty. The three boy-racers on their fancy bikes did a couple more wheelies as an encore to their little show and pedalled away into the wind, laughing and shouting as they went.

One of the two teenage girls, who had been walking arm-in-arm huddled into their shiny padded jackets before the troublesome trio had started circling them, stuck up a middle finger at their backs as they rode off. Perhaps the girls could have handled themselves anyway. No need for a chivalrous intervention at all. Just as well I kept my counsel like the rest of the weekend walkers and joggers out on a sunny Saturday morning.

The wide tarmac path appeared to stretch forever

between the stony dunes on the left and the salt marshes on the right. Families with young children, dog walkers, pensioners determined to stay fit, lovers entwined in each other, and lycra-clad runners clutching water bottles were out in force.

I felt out of place – a middle-aged man walking alone holding a map of Rye Harbour Nature Reserve in one hand and a pair of Zeiss binoculars in the other. I was not sure exactly what I expected to see with them, but as they had been a recent extravagant purchase, I thought it best to bring them. I could not tell an oyster catcher from an avocet if truth be told, but at least I looked the part.

The map said the lump of land in the hazy distance was Fairlight, and that I was heading for Winchelsea, where there should be a road and a bus stop. I didn't fancy the return journey on foot, even though the relentless wind would be behind me on the way back to my latest billet.

The English Channel chuntered to itself out of sight behind the stone ridge that was dotted with driftwood and brown clumps of wiry grass stubbornly holding on in the tough environment. There was a sandy beach beyond the shingle but that was covered by the morning's high tide.

The last time I had walked along this coast, I had discovered the floating body of a young man. It was only a couple of years ago, but it seemed like an eternity. My life had done several somersaults and back-flips since then and here I was, walking alone again, still looking to make some sense of where my mid-life was heading.

Where I was going in the immediate future began to creep into view over the mounds of pebbles. It lay a few steps off the tarmac path and most of the promenaders carried on their way without giving it a second glance. It was a featureless grey stone building isolated on the shoreline a mile from the nearest inhabited house. Its slate roof was patched here and there with bits of old tin. At the gable end facing inland were large wooden double doors, remnants of red paint flaking off, the rusty hinges and padlock suggesting they had not been opened this century. The window-less sides of the building were daubed with graffiti. 'Refugee Rapists' had been sprayed in lurid blue next to 'Mind the GAP' which was painted in red. The front gable end facing the sea had also once had large double doors but these had been replaced with breezeblocks. A crumbling concrete slope led down from the front of the building between what remained of wooden breakwaters onto a shingle beach.

This is what I had come to see although, in truth, it was not much to look at. I walked around the outside of the building twice. It was about four times the size of a domestic garage. I tried pushing the eight-foot high double doors but they did not budge. There was not a crack nor a key hole to peer through, but even if there had been, I was not sure what I had expected to see. It was almost certainly totally dark inside. Its tragic past had been buried long ago.

The Admiral Nelson was packed. Not a spare seat to be seen anywhere despite the little pub going back a deceptively long way around its wooden partitions and nautical paraphernalia. Bloody tourists. In my month here, I had gleaned that the locals liked to refer to them as 'piles'. It took me a while to work it out but then I got it: they came down in bunches and were a pain in the backside.

What I had come to regard as 'my corner' tucked away in the front bar had been taken by a middle-aged couple in motorcycle leathers who were engrossed in the menu. They were leaving no time soon.

Even the seats outside and the grassy bank in front of the lifeboat station were strewn with trippers, some down for the day from London, no doubt, others holed up in the holiday cottages that mingled with local homes in Rye Harbour.

I decided to try the Rother Art Gallery, which nestled behind a low stone wall next door to the pub in what was once the harbourmaster's cottage. The conservatory at the back had been turned into a small tasteful café. Hopefully the tourists had not discovered it as well. Sure enough, it was empty apart from one other couple.

I sat at a table near the open double doors. The breeze was a blessed relief from the August heat radiating through the glass roof. I pulled the newspaper from my backpack. It was crossword time.

'Hello Mr Kidd, how nice to see you again.'

Lizzy White was the gallery owner. A cheery woman who always seemed to be happy with her life, whether anyone was spending money in her gallery or not.

'Please, Lizzy, you've known me for a few weeks now. It's Tom. How's business on this busy weekend?'

'Oh not so bad, can't grumble. Sold one nice piece this morning, and a few postcards, but generally the day-trippers aren't here to buy art. I just about tick over, it's more a labour of love keeping the place going.' She sat down opposite me. 'How's that book of yours going, made a start yet?'

'I haven't really. It's still in, what us authors like to call, "the research stage".'

'Sounds intriguing. How many have you done before?'

'Well, let me see … to be exactly accurate: none. I've written thousands and thousands of words, but none actually in book form.'

'But I thought you said…?'

'Yes, I am here trying to write a book. I've tried several times before but never got it done. But the book writing is in my spare time, my main job, if that's what you could call it, is doing pieces for the *South Coast Gazette*. I'm a freelance journalist and I do bits for them most weeks. So any tittle-tattle you hear, let me know.'

'I'll keep my ear to the ground. Now, what's it to be? Have you had time to look at the menu?'

I placed my order and looked down at the untouched crossword again. Time for some mental gymnastics to keep the grey matter ticking over.

5 Across. Everyone on a cruise is confused (3,2,3).

Pen poised to fill in the little squares, the mobile rang. 'Bugger'. I said it quietly. I don't think the other couple in the conservatory café heard. I saw the name on the screen. It was Katie, my ex-wife, whose life seemed more chaotic by the month despite her still having the anchor of living in what was our family home in south London with our daughter Alice.

My index finger hovered over the red button but my conscience told me to take the call, just in case there was a domestic crisis.

'Yes, Katie. What is it?'

'Tom, I need you to talk some sense into Alice.'

'Why?'

'Because she's announced she's going on holiday.'

'So? It's August. It's the school holidays. Seems a reasonable time to take a holiday if you ask me.'

'Don't be so bloody facetious, Tom.'

'Whoa, keep your voice down, Katie. I'm in a very nice art gallery and I have you on loudspeaker.' I lied.

'Well switch me off loudspeaker, you fucking idiot,' she hissed.

'Dear me, your language has not improved since you met Fergus, or is it Brutus?'

'It's Angus. You know it is. Don't be such a prick.'

'My point exactly.'

There was a pause. There had been a time when silences between us were meaningful or tender. Now they just radiated hostility. I was sad about that, but she was the one who had wanted a divorce a couple of years ago, and she was the one who seemed to get more irritated with me when her lovers decided to move on.

'So Katie, tell me about this holiday that Alice wants to go on.'

'She's been invited to go Spain next week by her friend Beth. Her parents have a holiday villa out there.'

'Sounds like a nice opportunity after all the work she put into her GCSEs. What's the problem?'

'The problem is that Beth's boyfriend is going to be there, and his mate. Another boy.'

'I can see your concerns. What do Beth's parents think

about it? I thought you always said they were nice, decent folk?'

'Oh, they are. They'll be there too. They spend half the summer there.'

'So what's the problem if the parents are going to be there?'

'Christ, Tom. She's sixteen. I remember what I was like at sixteen at the sight of a young male in budgie-smugglers.'

'You shouldn't judge everyone by your own standards, dear.'

She did not bite on the last remark. I doubt she even processed it.

'What's more, Beth's parents have a very liberal attitude to teenagers drinking alcohol. I wouldn't be surprised if they smoked weed as well.'

'Now you're letting your imagination run amok, Katie. Look, Alice is a sensible girl … a young woman, actually … you should show some trust in her, and then you might get some back.'

'What do you mean by that?' The decibel level was going up again.

'Exactly what I said. You complain about her not telling you everything, but if you stopped treating her like a kid and…'

'Oh you've no fucking idea have you? Here I am living in London with a teenage daughter, I have to deal with her day-in day-out while you're drifting around the country wanting to be the next Ernest Hemingway, dropping into her life once a month.'

'That's not fair. Anyway, it's William Boyd.'

'What's William Boy?'

'It's Boyd, with a D at the end. You should read him. Brilliant writer. That's who I'd like to be like if you must know. And I see Alice more often than that – and if it makes you happy, I'll have a word with her about the holiday. But I think she should be allowed to go and let her hair down before she starts on her A levels, or whatever they're called these days.'

There was silence at the other end. I could almost sense Katie compiling her next complaint, so I spoke next.

'Is she on the pill?'

'What? No, of course she's not on the pill. She's only sixteen!'

'But you just told me what you were like at sixteen.'

'But that's different.'

'Is it?'

'Oh you can be such a smart-arse at times, Tom, playing with other people's words. That's all you get off on, isn't it? Look, just talk to her.'

The line went dead. Thank goodness for that. It was perfect timing too as Lizzy White arrived with a tray bearing a pot of tea, toasted sandwich and slab of fruit cake.

'Oh, I didn't order the cake, Lizzy.'

'I know Tom, but I thought you might fancy it, build up your strength, you know.'

'Does it need building up?'

'Well, I wasn't eavesdropping, but I couldn't help gather that wasn't just a social call.'

'Ah yes. No, you're right. It wasn't. My rather fractious ex giving me grief about our daughter. It'll blow over.'

'A daughter? How old is she?'

'Sixteen.'

'Sixteen going on twenty I suspect. I remember what my Zoe was like at that age: all worldly-wise and love-bites, leaving a trail of forlorn boys in her wake.'

'How old is she now?'

'She's thirty-two – and now there's not a boy nor a man in sight in her life, which is such a shame because she's a lovely young woman. You must have seen her around.'

'Is that the lady I see in the gallery sometimes?'

'Yes, that's Zoe. She helps out here a few days a week when her work allows. She's a keen artist too, like me, but probably not good enough to make a living out of it, also like me. Some of her work's in the gallery, on the wall opposite my desk.'

'I'll have a look on my way out. I could do with a painting or two to brighten up my place.'

The bell rang on the front door. 'Customers, perhaps. I'll leave you to your lunch.'

I was not really into art. The walls at my rented first-floor flat in the village were certainly bare, but it hadn't crossed my mind to adorn them with paintings when I had a view of the moorings from my window. It would be best to look interested, though, and on the way out after lunch I mooched around the gallery, that was spread through the front two rooms of the quaint white-walled cottage.

Most of the pictures were seascapes by local artists trying to make a few pounds out of the summer tourist trade. I soon identified the daughter's work which took up one wall. Each one was finished with an extravagant black Z in the bottom right hand corner. Her style was, to my untrained eye, abstract with big bold slashes of thick acrylic paint. One depicted what I supposed to be a sunset over the wind-turbine farm on the other side of the estuary. I spotted the war-time pillbox on the headland in another. Scenes of breakwaters and the bleak shoreline filled the others. I also worked out that the grey and silver mound in another was the local Martello Tower.

Another wall contained more orthodox watercolours of fishing boats, sunsets over the sea, gulls and wind-blown sheep on the marshland. In the smaller room local pottery was displayed on tables and shelves beside ornaments made from pebbles, shells and what looked like bits of driftwood. The wall space was given over to dramatic photographs of angry skies and foreboding seas, both in colour and monochrome prints. Very few items were priced at under three-figures. This was clearly a business worth getting into.

Postcards, maps and local guides filled a rack beside the desk where Lizzy was sitting. Behind her on the wall was a washed-out watercolour, yet another seascape of waves crashing on to rocks. The frame, dotted with woodworm holes, had seen better days too. It was the only item without a yellow price-tag stuck in the corner. That didn't surprise me.

The picture, though, did flick a switch on a light bulb at the back of my brain.

5 Across. Everyone on a cruise is confused (3,2,3).

'Got it,' I thought as I pulled the crossword out of the back pocket of my jeans and filled in the little squares – *'All at sea.'*

The Channel Islands. Summer 1943.

The sharp crack of the single shot ricocheted around the steep edges of the cliff and the stacks of jagged rocks that rose out of the restless sea in Telegraph Bay.

A heap of rags lay in the coarse grass on the cliff top. The emaciated body was motionless apart from blood leaking from a hole in the side of the head. The toe of a gleaming black leather boot prodded the corpse just to make sure the job was done.

'That's what happens to thieves,' Max Hegler told the row of grey-faced prisoners as he slipped the Luger P08 into its leather holster at his waist. 'You, you and you,' he addressed the three nearest to him. 'Throw the body over the cliff.'

Heads bowed, eyes emotionless, they obeyed. The frail corpse was heaved off the edge, bounced twice on its way down and landed on the black rocks below, before the white waves rolled over it and bore it away.

'Take them back to the quarry.' Hegler strode off. It was his lunch time.

Two people had watched the summary execution from a safe distance. Neither had thought to intervene. If they had, they might have suffered the same abrupt end.

Jens Weiss knew not to cross Hegler, an SS lieutenant at Lager Sylt, the concentration camp housing a thousand prisoners at the wind-blown south-western tip of this tiny island that his countrymen had occupied. They had called it Adolph Island, but the few remaining locals knew it as

Alderney. Weiss was sitting behind a cliff-side mound, chosen originally to give him shelter from the wind, but which also kept him out of sight of prying eyes.

It was not that he was not allowed to be here. As an officer, albeit a minor one, in the occupying German Army, he was entitled to wander freely to do his work. Weiss, however, concluded that it was better not to attract the attention of the SS, particularly Herr Hegler. He would not approve of such a frivolous pastime as sketching.

Weiss watched the ragged line of prisoners, some of them barely out of their teenage years but walking stooped like men of sixty, stumbling along the coastal path with heavy shoulders as they headed past the telegraph tower towards the east. 'Poor wretches,' he said quietly to himself.

He looked at the charcoal drawing in the exercise book propped up on his knees. The scene was of the bay below with the foaming waves pounding the ancient rocks. It was far from finished, but he was in no mood to carry on. It was time, anyway, to head back to his office in the town. His work was never done, even in this desolate, miserable island.

Giselle was the other observer. Her father did not like her straying far from the farm but she loved this wild corner of the island, especially on a summer's day like today with the white clouds bustling in from the English Channel, across the Alderney Race bound for France. She had been resting in the long warm grass, looking up at the sky and wondering what it would be like to be a teenager when her daydream had been broken by guttural German words she did not understand.

She rolled onto her stomach and raised her head slowly. She could see a line of prisoners – 'Bolsheviks' her father called them. They were only about thirty yards away. There were ten. Giselle counted them. Then there were nine as one was ordered out of the row by one of the two guards and pushed towards the other special uniform standing near the cliff edge. The prisoner seemed reluctant to move, and looked around wildly before the butt of a rifle thudded into his back and lurched him forward. The special uniform with the gleaming boots waited until the prisoner was no more than two feet away. He took out his gun and pointed it at the side of the prisoner's head just as he opened his mouth to speak.

Giselle heard but did not see the shot. She had buried her face in the sweet-smelling grass, her eyes screwed shut, her fists clamped over her ears. She had seen death before on the island, lots of it in the last year. She had even seen the naked bodies of men being tipped from the back of a lorry off the end of the harbour breakwater into Braye Bay. Dozens of them, tumbling in a lifeless mass into the water. It still made it no easier to see a man executed at close quarters.

She lay as still as she could. She heard some more German orders and then the clip-clopping of leather boots along the stony track she knew led towards the airstrip where the planes with the black crosses landed, and the Lager Sylt gates and fortified entrance. When she looked up again, the line of prisoners was winding slowly to the east towards Blue Stone Beach. She wondered what they had done to deserve such a hellish existence – although her father had warned her not to ask too many questions. He said that they should do what they were told and the Germans would leave them alone.

There was no sign of the one who had been shot. She crawled to the cliff and looked over. She could not see him but assumed that was where he had ended, down by the crashing water. Then she noticed some movement to her left, slightly lower down, and she flattened herself to the earth once again, her heartbeat thundering in her ears.

She waited for the angry shouts but none came. She expected to hear the crunching of boots but the only sound came from the wind and the sea. Terrified, she ventured to look up again and saw another soldier, this one in a different coloured uniform to the others from the camp, and carrying a satchel under his arm. He was hurrying away from her on the path back towards her father's farm and the town.

✠✠✠

2

Larry Lander was on the phone surprisingly early, particularly for a Sunday morning. Perhaps he had seen the divine light and was off to church. Somehow I doubted it. As he was my one source of steady income, I decided I'd better answer his call rather than roll over and let it ring out into the answering service.

'Hi Larry, where's the fire?' I immediately regretted sitting up too swiftly as the previous night's intake in The Grenadiers Arms coursed around my bloodstream and launched into a drum solo somewhere near the back of my skull.

'Billy, got an invite and a job for you. What you up to today?' Lander, a life-long buddy from our days as cub journalists together in the Midlands, was the last remaining soul I knew who still occasionally used my moniker Billy, as in Billy the Kidd.

'Ok, but what's the hurry' – I focused on the watch on my bedside table – 'at eight thirty on a Sunday morning? The paper doesn't come out until Thursday.'

'Sue's got an old TV colleague down for the weekend and as it's such a lovely day we thought we'd take her out: walk along Camber Sands and then into Rye for a spot of lunch. Fancy making it a foursome?'

There was a pause. I knew what was coming.

'Please Tom. I need some moral support. The woman's all right but she's into all this "MeToo" stuff. And that sets Sue off. All they yack about is the liberties blokes used to take with them in their early days in TV. I could do with a bit of sensible male conversation about the Test match over my pint.'

I liked Sue Lander, she was the anchor on the regional evening news programme and the rock of their marriage, which had survived storms and tempest, usually of Larry's own making. I could imagine he might feel a bit like a punch bag at the hands of two women rightfully indignant about the sexism and worse they probably had to endure when the cameras were not rolling.

'Who's this friend? Do I know her?'

'Denise Rutter. Started off as a weathergirl, then went on to do the sport on breakfast TV for a while. She became quite a celebrity as one of the first women in sport on the box until she had that affair with the old Tory sports minister. Remember that?'

'I do. The red-tops had a lot of fun with her surname in the headlines. Was she quite a looker too?'

'Now you see, Tom, that's exactly the sort of remark that gets her wound up – but yes, she was. Still is. But, please, don't mention her looks, just tell her you're pleased to see her back on the box.'

'Hang on, Larry. I haven't even agreed to this little plan of yours. And, anyway, am I?'

'Are you what?'

'Pleased to see her back on the box? What's she doing now?'

'She introduces the late-night mid-week football

highlights on one of those obscure Freeview channels. And yes, you are.'

With a promise to pay for lunch, Lander gave me a time and meeting place in Rye. He said he would also give me details of the story he wanted following up for the *South Coast Gazette,* the paper he edited with panache, bucking the national trend and actually increasing its weekly circulation with stories that were on nodding terms with the facts.

First I had to clear my head of the several pints of Moonraker IPA that had slipped down a treat on 'Vinyl Nite' in The Grenadiers, where the landlord had played his vast and popular collection of LPs from Bowie to the Buzzcocks long after official closing time. Two years short of my fiftieth birthday, I really should have known better.

The walk to the general store in the village from my first-floor flat in Coastguards Square followed by a fry-up in the Bosun's Bite was the panacea for most things.

The café was on the slipway, opposite the current lifeboat station and next to the sailing club. The three rickety metal tables outside were unoccupied. It was still too early for the trippers. The tide was rushing out of the estuary towards the English Channel, taking a few yachts with it. The sun danced off their hulls and the day smelled off freshness.

I had been in Rye Harbour for little more than a month but I loved the place. Originally it had been just a short-term bolt hole, but I had already doubled the three-month lease on my flat. I was certain that for the first time in more than two years, I could find a place to call home again.

The Sunday morning scene could not have been more serene, yet even on a day like today, I'd been warned that danger lurked in the currents and hidden sandbanks just half-a-mile away where the gentle River Rother merged into the sea. The tragedy that had happened off this coast would never be forgotten.

I looked at the Sunday paper crossword: *1 Down. Noah's Ark? (8).*

'Tom, may I join you?' It was Norman. I didn't know his surname but he was in charge of the small gift shop attached to the lifeboat station opposite the café. I had found him helpful when I first started making enquiries about the maritime history on this part of the Sussex coast, but he was one of those kindly yet persistent souls who was difficult to shake off once they knew you.

I looked around at the other empty tables outside the café but Norman did not appear to take – or want to take – the hint. 'Of course, Norman, take a pew.' I folded the newspaper.

'Lovely day.' He put his mug of tea and a bacon sandwich down on my table and inhaled deeply. 'Expect we'll be busy in there today. Better open up soon.' He nodded at the shop where puzzles, children's books and soft toys nestled on the shelves alongside maps and DVDs about the work of the Royal National Lifeboat Institution.

I shoved a piece of sausage in my mouth and mumbled, 'Hope so'.

'You know that research you said you were doing for a book? Are you still interested?'

I swallowed a lump of gristle. 'I am. Definitely.'

'Well, after you left the other day, I remembered the name of someone you really should talk to. Got a piece of paper?'

Rye, the handsome big sister to Rye Harbour's quirkiness, was a two-mile walk away. I could have driven, but I knew parking would be a nightmare as the old walled town was more of a tourist trap than the Harbour. The Ship Inn was bracing itself for the Sunday roast rush, and the only tables not occupied were those with 'reserved' notices on them. Fortunately one was under the name of Lander.

I was early. An old habit. It was always best to be in place and prepared when doing an interview. Not that I'd done much of that since being made redundant from my job as a sports journalist on a national newspaper more than two years ago. Since then, my life had been like the little boats moored high and dry in the muddy estuary: buffeted around but not going anywhere.

I had been trying to picture Denise Rutter since Larry had mentioned her but the only weather forecaster I could conjure up was Michael Fish, and he wasn't my port in any storm, whether it came with a warning or not.

Lander obscured my first view of her, his bulky frame silhouetted by sunlight filling the little doorway and briefly casting the pub into semi-darkness. He raised a chubby hand in greeting and squeezed himself between the other diners to our table, his polo-shirt straining desperately to escape the confines of his bright red shorts.

'Where are they?'

'The girls? They're just looking in the estate agents' window next door. Denise is so taken with the area, she's thinking of moving down. Reckons she can commute to London a couple of times a week. I'd take cover, Tom, if that does come to pass.'

'Why's that?'

'She's on a man-hunt, old son. Last bloke ditched her for a newer model six months ago and Sue reckons she's on the lookout for someone to butter her parsnips.'

'Larry, you can be quite crude at times, you know? I hope that's not why I've been invited to this little foursome.'

Lander shook his head and shot a glance at the door. 'Eyes down. They're here.'

Introductions over, Larry excused himself and bustled over to the bar to order drinks. Sue sat opposite me. She was as radiant and confident as ever. We went back a long way, but our friendship had never been anything but proper. She was the wife of my best mate and temptation had never crept over the threshold.

I pretended to remember Denise's work on breakfast television. Unlike most journalists working in newspapers, those who worked on the little box tended to think they had a sprinkling of stardust on them. She was probably about my age, but the subtle application of make-up made it difficult to be sure. She clearly knew she had a fine figure, and could get away with wearing tight white jeans and a deep mauve Ted Baker tee-shirt.

'Were you still on the breakfast show when Morgan Pearce joined? I remember him from his days at the *Mirror*, he used to turn up on cricket tours and could be a right pain in….'

'Oh no,' she interrupted. 'I was long gone by then. It all became about the cult of the celebrity presenter. That really wasn't my style you know.'

I bet it wasn't. I let her carry on.

'What about you Tom? Sue tells me you're an author now. How thrilling.'

'A want-to-be author,' I corrected her. 'I've not had anything published yet but I've got an idea for a book and now I've got the time to write it.'

'Why's that?'

'My last fulltime job just didn't work out. I tried my hand at PR work, as the editor of an in-house magazine in the energy industry, but after about a year I knew it wasn't for me: nice people, nice pay, nice hours and all that, but just not my style. So I'm here now, doing a bit of work for Larry and anyone else who'll offer me some freelance work, but determined to write that book.'

'What about? Do tell. Steamy locker rooms, bonking on the physio's couch?'

'Why does everyone assume I'm writing about sex? No. I'm going to tell a story of bravery and tragedy.'

Denise Rutter looked disappointed.

'Denise is thinking of moving down this way, Tom.' Sue sensed the conversation on our side of the table had dried up. 'Did Larry say?'

'Yup. He did mention it. Bit of a commute for your sports programme.' I looked at Denise, who perked up again.

'Oh, I only have to go to the studios about twice a week, perhaps three times. I can always stay up in town, too, if it's a late finish. No, it seems lovely round here – and so cheap compared to where I am.'

'Really? Where's that?'

'I'm in Lambeth. You know it? The South Bank? Very *de rigueur* these days. Of course, when I bought my apartment it was less than half a mill. Now you can put a one in front of that. I thought I could buy myself a nice snug townhouse here in Rye and still have enough left over to get a sweet little boat, I've always wanted a boat, especially on days like this. Do you sail, Tom?'

'No, Denise. I don't.'

'Well then, perhaps I could take you out on mine once I've learned to steer it, or whatever you do with boats.' She laughed, revealing a set of perfectly regimented white teeth.

'Well thank you, Denise, but I don't think my sea-legs could take it.'

'Bloody hell, Larry. I've got a lot of sympathy for women who complain about sexual harassment in the work place, but if you flirt like she does, it's hardly surprising if a few blokes might get the wrong signals.'

We were sitting outside the Ship Inn with the smokers and vapers. Lunch had been good, Larry had footed the bill as promised and Sue and Denise had announced they were going off to seek more estate agents' windows.

Lander chuckled. 'She can be hard work, can't she? Not your type?' He laughed again, this time following it up with a belch so voluble that it startled passers-by. 'Ah, that's better.'

'No. You know she isn't. Actually, I'm not sure what

my type is any longer. I don't seem to have made many right moves in that direction recently.'

'Missing Jo?'

'Nah, not really. It was nice while it lasted and all that, but ... well I guess it wasn't meant to be. Now, what's this job?' I was keen to change the subject.

He pulled his chair up to the table and leaned over conspiratorially. 'Nice little tale, I think. There's been a series of shed thefts around here – Rye, Rye Harbour and Camber way – you know the sort of thing: ride-on mowers, chainsaws, hedge trimmers, stuff like that which is easy to flog on.'

'Sounds pretty minor. What's the angle?'

'It is small-time theft, and that's the point. So small-time that the police can't be bothered. To be fair to them, they haven't got the manpower to launch a full-scale investigation, but they have to sound concerned because they're under pressure from above.'

'From whom?'

'The local Police and Crime Commissioner. Gail Fawkes. She's been one of those raided and lost a load of stuff. She's also under pressure from the local Neighbourhood Watch schemes to get something done about it. Her old man's a retired copper too, I think. Anyway, she was voted in by a very small majority in 2016 and it's coming round to election time again early next year. She'll be very keen to be seen to be pro-active over this. It's local matters that swing votes, not the bigger picture.'

Lander drained the last of the white wine from his glass. 'I think Gail Fawkes can be a bit of a pain in the arse. My sources at the cop shop say they'll be glad to see the back of her, which may be one of the reasons they're dragging their feet over the shed burglaries. As well as being short of man-power, they wouldn't mind a local issue that damages her chances of getting re-elected.'

'OK, I'll have a word with the locals, and go and see this Gail Fawkes.'

'One other thing: the individual or little gang who are doing this are getting cocky and leaving a calling card after their raids.'

'Really?'

'On the shed doors they spray-paint "Mind the GAP" with the GAP in capitals.'

'Mind the GAP? I've seen that before round here.'

'Well, if they're getting flashy about this, Tom, they'll make mistakes. Have a word in the local pubs, see if anyone's been trying to flog garden equipment on the QT. It's becoming quite a big local issue – and local issues sell papers.'

'That's it. The old lifeboat station.'

'What's the old lifeboat station, Tom?'

'Where I saw "Mind the GAP". It was graffiti sprayed on the wall. It's also given me the obvious answer to my crossword clue.'

1 Down. Noah's Ark? (8). I filled in the answer: *Lifeboat.* 'That's it, completed.'

The two women reappeared on the busy pavement outside the pub, Denise grasping a bulging glossy folder.

'Reading matter?' I asked.

'Plenty of it, and there's one delightful looking dear little place down near you, Tom. I've even arranged a viewing for Wednesday afternoon. Perhaps we could meet up and you can show me around Rye Harbour.'

My heart sank a little. 'Yes, why not?' I gave her my mobile number and address. 'But give me a ring first, Larry's got me working on a story and I may just be busy.'

The plan was to have a quiet evening in. The big lunch in Rye meant I did not need to cook for myself, and an evening off the alcohol sounded eminently sensible. The first-floor flat in a modern weather-boarded house designed to merge in with the 19th Century white-painted terraced cottages in Coastguards Square was perfect for one. The spacious open-plan living room and kitchen was tastefully decorated with wooden flooring and grey walls. A large brown leather sofa took pride of place in the centre of the room in front of a wall-mounted television. I had opened the dining table to its full extent by the window. It was where I liked to read and type. The en-suite bedroom was a mess, but it was my mess and I didn't care.

Slumped on the sofa with Bob Dylan ripping through '*Desolation Row*' in the background, I was mentally planning my week ahead. First thing tomorrow I would start chasing up Lander's story by visiting Mrs Gail Fawkes, the Police and Crime Commissioner, but I was damned if I was going to put my idea for a book to one side.

I needed to visit the parish church, the Church of the Holy Spirit, for a start. I also hoped to hear some seafaring stories from some of the elderly sailors who hung around the Admiral Nelson. There was a run-down boat-yard on the little industrial estate on the edge of the village. That might be worth a visit, too.

It's odd why and when loneliness kicks in. As Dylan slipped into his melancholy *'It ain't me Babe'* it caught me unawares again. The plain walls of my living space were a metaphor for my life: perfectly pleasant but featureless. Self-contained and comfortable. Unchallenging. Perhaps that was how I wanted it after the failed marriage to Katie and the brief liaison with Jo, who was now back in Australia nursing her invalid mother.

Mind the Gap indeed. There was a gap in my life but I was pretty sure Denise Rutter was not the one to fill it. As for the four grey walls that surrounded me, I made another mental note to have a closer look at the work on sale at the Rother Art Gallery.

Alderney 1943

Jens Weiss' dusty, cramped office was on the fourth floor of an old municipal building in a square behind the main street of what had become known to the Germans as 'The Town'. To call it a town, though, was stretching the imagination, thought Weiss. It was little more than a village that had spread itself along the broken, rutted road that curved up the hill from the harbour and Braye Bay.

Weiss knew it intimately because he had mapped it as part of his job for the Army. The Rue de Braye led to the Rue de Rocquettes, which in turn led to the main part of town with its British influences: Victoria Street and High Street. Some of the old road signs still hung from the walls of the buildings now taken over by the German troops. What were once shops, pubs, fine houses and small hotels were now officers' quarters, bars, offices, store houses, a picture hall, a dance hall and a brothel, the latter run by a French madam with her French whores. They attracted good business from the bored German troops who had little else to do in their spare time on this island that the Führer had decided to occupy along with the other Channel Islands.

Weiss, a draughtsman and surveyor by trade, had been found a job in the German army as a surveyor. His weak left leg, the result of polio as a child, had meant he was of little use in the front line, so they had posted him to this island, part of a Channel fortification planned by the Third Reich. He and about three thousand other Germans lived on this slip of land with around the same number of slaves, mainly from Russia and Eastern Europe, shipped in as a workforce and incarcerated in four camps around Alderney. He had heard that the prisoners lived in appalling conditions, but he did not really know. He had never set foot in one of their camps or spoken to any of them. He had merely seen them up close in their work gangs when checking on the progress of the road building and mine-laying that he oversaw.

His office was set in the eaves of the building. One dirty window let in a shaft of sunlight, but still the bare bulb hanging from the ceiling was left on. Leaving it switched on was the only way of knowing if the generator was working that day. He shared the office with Anton List, who was in charge of supplying the material for building five coastal gun batteries, adjoining bunkers and the connecting tunnel network, an altogether more important job. He came from Berlin and was married. Jens came from a small village in the west near Hanover and was single. They did not talk about their past lives much, mainly they just complained about the weather and the food.

On the wall above his desk was a map of the island left behind by the inhabitants when they had fled three years earlier, shortly before the German Army occupation. It showed the town was called St Anne and that there was no other sizeable settlement on this piece of rock five kilometres long by two-and-a-half kilometres across.

In fine red pencil, Weiss had marked where the lines of mines had been laid around the coast. In fine yellow pencil, he had marked where mines still needed to be laid in wait for unwelcome visitors. Precision came easily to Weiss, and he was particularly precise about this job. He could not afford to be otherwise. He was grateful to the English. At least they made good maps that he could trust. It also helped that he could read English. So far twelve thousand mines had been laid. Only another twenty-five thousand to go.

On his desk was a second map. It showed the meagre road network on the island, most of which was little more than muddy farm tracks and narrow cobbled roads, totally unsuitable for the trucks and artillery that rolled off the ships ready for installation around the coast. It was another of Weiss' jobs to upgrade the roads where necessary, it was the prisoners' job to get it done under the unflinching gaze of their jailers.

He tucked the sketch of Telegraph Bay that he had been working on into a drawer and returned to plotting the best route for a road to Batterie Annes, the fortification on the western tip of the island where the guns would have a range of more than fifteen kilometres across the sea.

List came in, sweating, angry and keen to throw off his coarse grey-green uniform jacket. 'How's the road coming along, Jens? We need it done before winter sets in.'

'I was out checking the lines this morning,' Weiss lied. 'If we can get double the number of working gangs and double the amount of hardcore from the quarry, we can get it done by the end of September.'

'Make it by the end of August. OK?'

Although they treated each other as equals in the office, List was a rank above Weiss, and occasionally reminded him. Weiss knew when not to argue. He also knew List was concerned about the lack of a monthly letter from his wife, who had moved herself and their two sons out of Berlin because the British were intensifying their bombing raids.

The tide of the War appeared to be turning, although on Alderney no-one really knew what was happening. They just followed diktats from the German command.

'Any news from home?'

'No,' said List, who covered his eyes with his fingers and shook his head. 'Why are we involved in this? What's it all about, Weiss?'

'I honestly don't know, my friend. You and I, we're just told what to do: told to join up, told to learn to fire a gun, told to make plans, told to hate the English. Do you think it's the same for Churchill's Tommies?'

'Who knows? Perhaps they think they have a higher cause. Perhaps they are different from us.'

'No, I don't think they are. I spent three years in London after my school years. My father said the art colleges were better there than in Germany, and he said I should travel, so I did.'

'Did you like it?'

'Not at first. The food is dreadful, the weather not much better and the women are frigid. But after a while, I grew to like the Londoners: they're just ordinary people like you and me. Some good, some not so good. I learned to draw and I learned to speak English. Oh yes, and I learned to like their awful beer.'

List laughed. Weiss had lightened his mood and he was glad he had done that at least.

'Come on Anton. When we've finished here, we'll go to the beer cellar and then the whore house, they tell me there are some mademoiselle virgins just come over.'

'French virgins? There's no such thing,' List laughed again and thumped his desk, the dust jumping off the angle-poise

lamp over his work.

Laughter in war time was allowed, but you had to be careful who shared it with you.

✠✠✠

3

How the other half live, eh? Down a tarmac drive lined by trimmed box hedges, the bluestone farmhouse with leaded windows sat behind lawns dotted here and there with fruit-laden apple trees. The home of Gail Fawkes. The only drawback to this idyll on the edge of the village was the crunching and clanking from the open-cast stone quarry less than a mile away across the gravel dunes.

A Staffordshire Terrier came yapping up to the five-barred gate as I rested my hand on it. A woman wearing a broad-brimmed straw hat and thick gardening gloves followed to see what the commotion was all about. Introductions done, I was invited in. Anyone elected to the office of Police and Crime Commissioner likes to keep on the right side of the local Press.

The property was no less impressive inside. Cool flagstone floors and tasteful modern furniture mingled seamlessly with the beams and crooked ceilings. Photographs of smiling young people at graduation days were displayed on an upright piano in the corner. On a window table, a silver frame proudly displayed a picture of a high-ranking police officer in uniform presenting a glass decanter to a burly man in a suit, the pair surrounded by smiling colleagues. Logs were piled on either side of the inglenook fireplace beside a wood burner ready for the winter. Mrs Fawkes – please, do call me Gail – served tea from a china pot, offered a plate of flapjack fingers and invited me into the sun lounge at the rear.

'You have to understand, Mr Kidd, that while these thefts from sheds may seem rather trivial, they are very unsettling for the victims, particularly the more elderly ones. We are a remote community here, there has not been a policeman living in the village for as long as I can remember. People can feel vulnerable at times like this.'

'So, can you do anything to get the police in Rye to come out here and investigate?'

'They have assured me they will. My husband was in CID, you know. He's retired from the force now, of course, but he's been trying to pull strings too, and I have warned the Chief Constable that if they don't stamp it out, there are some who may take the law into their own hands.'

'Really? What, like a local vigilante group?'

'Well, I wouldn't like to be quoted using such colourful language, but I do hear that some residents down Oyster Creek have arranged a rota of night-time patrols. There's been at least four thefts on the estate there. My husband has advised them on their rights over making a citizen's arrest.'

'Have you any idea what "Mind the GAP" means?'

'Not in the slightest. Is it something to do with gap years?'

'I don't think so Mrs Fawkes … Gail. Unless we have a gang of students looking to supplement their loans by setting up as part-time gardeners.'

She told me the Oyster Creek neighbourhood watch was headed by Michael Monday. He ran a tyre and exhaust centre on the industrial estate. That was my next port of call.

Two youths in greasy overalls drinking from mugs were sitting in the sun on a pile of discarded worn tyres outside the entrance to the garage, where a Mini was up on the ramps. There was little chance of a quick fit fitting here. The boss? He was in the office, said the female fitter, pointing with a blue rubber-gloved hand holding a cigarette.

Monday was short and wiry, and the only grease he had on him was in his swept back thick dark hair. He was standing behind a metal desk, hunched over a numbers puzzle in a newspaper chewing a pen.

'Business slow?' He looked up, seemingly surprised at being dragged out of his sudoku world. I nodded towards the fitters outside.

'No, it's their tea-break. I'm not a slave driver, you know. And you are?'

When I mentioned the *South Coast Gazette,* I half-expected him to clam up. A whiff of the Press often had that effect on people, but not Michael Monday. He was keen to promote the work of the Oyster Creek residents' patrols.

'If the bleedin' police did their job we wouldn't have to bother but they can't be arsed, can they?' It was not a question to which he expected an answer. 'If we catch the little toe-rags nicking stuff, they'll be sorry.'

He told me five families were running the night rota, patrolling in pairs up to two in the morning. They reckoned by then, even pilferers went to bed. Since they had started their patrols ten days ago, the shed doors of Oyster Creek had remained undisturbed.

'Job done then, Mr Monday.'

'Hardly. I want my bleedin' chainsaw and pole-trimmer back. About eight hundred quids' worth that is, good quality gear. I expect the bloody pikeys have already shifted it on.'

'You know who it is?'

'Not exactly, but you know their sort. Like that bloke who lives in the caravan on the salt marsh with his bit of stuff. What a dump that is. The police are scared to touch 'em because they get accused of victimisation, but I wouldn't mind betting some of my gear has passed through there.'

'Do you think your two mechanics might have heard anything? I think I've seen the girl in The Grenadiers, haven't I?'

'Mary-Lou? You might have done. I think she's sweet on the landlord's son. Help yourself if you think they might have heard anything. The other kid's name is Alex.'

Mary-Lou and Alex said they had not heard anything, but my question did get one positive response: they immediately got up to work on the neglected Mini on the ramps.

The Rother Gallery was busy. That was not to say there were lots of people there. It was so compact that the six browsers moving between the two display rooms made it seem crowded. Uncomfortable around knowledgeable arty-types, I loitered in the café waiting for the three couples to leave.

When they did, I was surprised to see that the woman sitting behind the desk was not Lizzy White but a younger version of the owner. The mop of unruly red hair and freckles on her angular face and neck gave away the family likeness. Despite the August sunshine, she wore denim dungarees over a purple sweater, the sleeves pulled up to the elbow. No wedding ring. Why did I still check on that? She was busy studying the computer screen and did not look up when I returned to the room.

I decided to break the ice. 'Lizzy not here?' What a damn fool question, I thought as the words left my mouth.

'No. Mondays are Mum's day off. And sometimes Thursday. Can I help?'

'You're her daughter. I should have guessed.'

'Should you?'

'The hair.' I pointed awkwardly. 'Well, it's very distinctive.'

She smiled at my embarrassment. 'Yes. It is. I used to hate it you know, when I was at school, but I think I'm getting used to it now at long last – now I'm in my thirties.'

'Ah, I didn't mean to sound rude. Sorry. Let's start again. I was hoping to ask Lizzy's advice. She clearly knows a lot about the local art scene. Certainly more than me.'

'Try me. I know a bit about it too, what sort of thing are you looking for, and, just as important, what's your price range? We start at around £40 for some of the unframed photographs in the next room, up to £800 for some of the work in here.'

I looked at the vivid scenes of sea and sky on the wall opposite. 'Oh, not those,' she laughed. 'That's my stuff. I think Mum priced those between £150 and £200. The posh stuff are the watercolours on the fireplace wall. They're done by two well-established local artists and will definitely hold their value.'

'A few have little red stickers on. What does that mean?'

'It tells us we can negotiate a little on the price, but the artists do put a reserve on them. Basically, everything you can see is for sale at a price. Except this one behind me.' She turned and contemplated the faded watercolour. 'The old seascape is Mum's favourite.'

I looked at it again. 'Don't worry. It's not my sort of thing. I won't be offering a fortune for that one.' I turned back to look at the acrylic splurges of colour. 'I'm not just saying it, but I think I rather like your stuff. Do I get discount for two?'

She laughed. 'Two? That would double my sales this year. Of course we can do a deal, especially as you're a local.'

'How do you know that?'

'We met two weeks ago. I found your talk on journalism fascinating. I hope you didn't find our questions too boring. I'm Zoe, by the way.'

'You should have seen your face. You were the picture of dumb-struck,' she laughed again, this time sitting in the window seat of the Admiral Nelson. Zoe White had invited me for a sundowner after doubling her sales for the year and locking up the gallery a little early. My two bubble-wrapped pictures were propped up beside her.

'I'm sorry, but I just didn't associate you with the creative-writing group in the Village Hall. It was your mother's idea that I go along, she thought the group would be interested in hearing about the art of writing short newspaper pieces – if art is the right word. I was so nervous, though, I tried not to look at the faces. Was it OK?'

'It was great – and very interesting. There we all are trying to think of ourselves as romantic novelists or tortured poets, and you come along and explain what it's like to actually make a living out of writing.'

'It's not much of a living these days, I'm afraid. I'm having to rely on my redundancy money, and that's dwindling fast. That's why I need to get this book done and published. I'm the one who could really do with a few tips about how to write.'

'Why don't you join our group? We don't bite.'

'I guess I might, but I'm a bit wary of things like that. I think novel writing is a solitary trade. Not one to be shared. For me, the catalyst is finding a subject that inspires – and I think I've found it here in Rye Harbour.'

'Sit tight. I'll get two more G and Ts, and you can tell me more.'

I told her it was the story of the *Mary Stanford* Lifeboat tragedy, the biggest loss of life from a single lifeboat since the 19th century around the coast of Great Britain and its islands. Zoe knew it well. I suspected that everyone in Rye Harbour knew the story of that fateful night in November 1928 when the *Alice of Riga*, a Latvian steamer with a cargo of bricks, was in collision with a larger German ship, *Smyrna.*

At five in the morning, with an 80mph south-westerly gale sweeping up the English Channel, the distress maroons were fired to rescue the crew of the *Riga*, which had had her rudder torn off and a hole ripped in her side, and was drifting eight miles off the Sussex coast.

The Rye Harbour crew and boat launchers raced the mile along the coast track to the lifeboat station. The weather was atrocious and the tide low. It took the men and women three exhausting attempts to get the *Mary Stanford*, a heavy, open-topped eighteen-foot wooden vessel, across the shingle before she made it out to sea through the blinding spray and rain, fourteen men pulling on the oars. By now, it was almost two hours after the flares had first gone up.

Just five minutes after the Rye Harbour crew had left shore, the coastguard received a message saying the crew of the *Riga* had been taken safely on board the *Smyrna.* More flares were fired to recall the *Mary Stanford*, but to no avail.

'There's something of a mystery about exactly what happened,' I said. 'It's possible that in such awful conditions, the flares were not seen. Or they just could not react to them. But three hours later the lifeboat was identified by another ship and all seemed well. It was seen again by someone on the *Smyrna,* and there did not appear to be a problem. But an hour later the boat was spotted from the shoreline, capsized. All seventeen crewmen were dead. They were aged seventeen to forty-seven.'

'Yes,' said Zoe. 'The story is etched into village life. Most folk around here know it. There's an annual memorial service and a beautiful memorial grave at the church. It devastated a tiny community like this. Fathers and sons, brothers, cousins. Three families alone lost nine members.'

'Well, I think the story needs telling to a wider audience,' I said. 'There was also some question at the inquest about the seaworthiness of the boat, and the quality of life jackets they were wearing. I want to do those seventeen men justice. To go out in filthy weather in the pitch dark without any of the modern aides they have now – well, that took incredible selflessness and courage.'

Zoe sipped her gin. 'I don't think the old lifeboat station has been used since then. It's a bit of mess now, but there is a plan to restore it and have a permanent display there as a tribute to the men.'

'The first thing they need to do is get the graffiti off the wall.'

'Yes, I know.' Zoe looked out of the window at a cropped-haired youth sitting in the evening sun on the grass bank across the road from the pub. He had a cigarette in one hand and a pint in the other, a bicycle lying beside him. 'I wouldn't be surprised if young George over there knows something about that.'

'Who's he?'

'George Clunes. I used to go to school with his big sister. Thinks he's a bit of a jack-the-lad but really he's just a bored teenager in a little community with few prospects. Rides around with his mates trying to show off to female visitors in the summer. In the winter you'll probably find him at the snooker and billiard hall.'

'I think I might have seen his little gang on Saturday, out on the path to the Old Lifeboat Station.'

The boy stubbed his cigarette out in the grass, stood up and walked back into the pub for a refill, leering at Zoe as he passed: 'Alright, Zoe? Hooked another?'

'What's he mean by that?' I said as George Clunes beckoned the barmaid with his empty glass.

'Just ignore him,' she sighed. 'He's just a kid from a big family. Probably had very little attention at home so he seeks it elsewhere. I think he works at the solvent recycling plant on the industrial estate, so his little world doesn't even stretch beyond the parish.'

Clunes walked back past us, lager slopping on to the floor as he opened the door. 'Going for the older types now, are we Zoe?' He let the door slam behind him.

'Sorry,' she said.

'I've a good mind to....'

'No you haven't. Forget it, he's not worth it.'

I glared out of the window. Older type! My indignation rose behind the safety of the glass. Clunes had been joined by another lad on a bicycle. Both bikes were *Pinarellos*, expensive machines that I recognised from my days reporting on the *Tour de France*. Zoe followed my gaze.

'That's Peter, another of the Clunes clan. There are five kids in the family, I think. They live on Oyster Creek. Come on, let's forget them, shall we? I think it's your round.'

Two hours later, I had discovered that Zoe lived in a rented cottage near the railway station in Rye with a female friend. She worked on the reception at one of the town's doctors' practices two mornings a week, behind the bar or on reception at a hotel three days a week and at her mother's gallery when required. She painted in what spare time she had, mainly on the salt marsh, and had had 'two or three fairly serious relationships' that had not worked out. I did not think it my place to ask for any details. I discovered she also liked her drink.

She looked at her watch. It was almost nine. 'I'd better phone a taxi, there's no-way I'm driving home,' she said. 'And…' she started to giggle. 'I've got my reputation to think of.'

Just as the taxi pulled up, we exchanged mobile numbers. She said she would be back in the gallery on Thursday if I wanted any more advice on investing my money in the art world.

Alderney 1943

Giselle stood on the rolling hill overlooking the farm, the disused old watermill, and Saline Bay, with The Swinge in the distance, where the angry currents never rested. She looked out at the sea and wondered about her mother and Martine, her elder sister, who would have been seventeen now. Her father was with the dog in the lower field attending to a sick cow.

The farm bore the family name: Sparrows Farm. She loved the sound of it and the Englishness of it. They had been taught in French at school before the War, but English had been the language at home. Now she resented the fact that half the island had French names for its roads and districts because France belonged to Germany, and Germany was the enemy.

Back in the low-ceilinged kitchen of the single-storey farmhouse, she put the cornflowers she had picked into a tin mug with some water and placed them on the table. She had duties on the farm but her main one was here in the kitchen, making sure their meagre meals were ready. The chickens had laid this morning, so there were eggs to go with the soda bread and tomatoes today.

Her routine was now set. Up at six for father's breakfast, check the chickens and help with milking the cows. The weekday mornings were schooling time, her father said. He helped her with her spelling and maths, and then she read an old illustrated encyclopaedia that they had hidden behind the woodpile by the stove in case the Germans ever came searching. The book had a map of the world, about a third of which was coloured pink. The heading was 'The British Empire'. The Jerries would not like that, her father had chuckled.

After lunch she had free time until tea and the evening milking. Her father would then do one last check of the stock while she was expected to tidy and prepare supper. Sometimes she had to repair their clothes, which were getting more threadbare by the month. At least for Giselle there were the two pretty cotton dresses Martine had had to leave behind. She was slowly growing into them.

Her father was agitated that evening. He was normally quiet these days since mother and Martine had gone, but he had climbed into the roof space over his bedroom and brought down one of the bottles of cognac, something he normally saved for special occasions or when his teeth were playing up. He had drained his cup of the ersatz coffee they had traded from the German soldiers and replaced it with slug of the liquor that Giselle had never tasted. He had told her she had to wait until she was thirteen, and only then could she try it, mixed with water.

He was sitting on door step looking towards the setting sun, which made everything glow, even the black wooden cow byre, and held the cup to his chin.

'They want more of our land, Giselle.' She knew 'they' referred to the Germans.

'Two of them were round here at lunch time telling me to expect a visit from the surveyor. They want to drive a road across the field down there.' He nodded towards the low fields where their herd of twenty brown-and-white Alderney

Cattle grazed. He sipped from the cup.

'Don't they realise that if we keep losing land, we'll have to reduce the size of the herd, and if we do that they will have less milk to purchase and we'll all lose out? Ignorant Krauts.'

'How is Lulu?' Lulu was the sick cow. They all had names. 'Is it teat disease?'

He nodded. 'Not so good, Giselle. I've got her in a pen by herself. If you milk her in the morning, make sure you wash your hands before you touch the others. She might pull through, though. She's a strong old girl.'

If she did not pull through, at least there would be meat for a while, and plenty left over to trade with the Germans for grain, cheese, oil for the lamp and a crate of beer.

'Why do they want to build a road, father? What's wrong with the track?'

'They're building another fortress, I suppose, up above Trois Vaux Bay. The whole bloody place will soon be one big fortress. As if they expect Churchill to send an invasion force any time soon. The English have got bigger things to worry about, Giselle. We're just an unimportant speck in the Channel.'

'So why do they do it?'

'Dunno, my dear. It keeps them busy, I suppose. Gives them an excuse to flog the Bolsheviks to death.'

She looked to the north where a ring of long low huts surrounded by barbed wire rolls hugged the sloping land just in front of Saline Bay. It was called Lager Helgoland. When the wind was in the wrong direction, the stench of deprivation from the prison camp swept across Sparrows Farm.

As it was a Wednesday, it was bath night. Wednesday and Sunday, that was the routine. Her father used the tin tub on Tuesdays and Saturdays.

'Off you go, Giselle, shall I boil up a kettle?'

'No, don't bother, father. It's a warm night.'

'You get on then, I'll do my rounds and look in on Lulu.'

Giselle had noticed that her father kept his distance these days when she bathed. Perhaps it was because she getting older, although as she stood in front of the mirror in her bedroom, she wondered how you could tell. Her short dark hair sat on strong square shoulders. Her chest was still as flat as a boy's. Her hips were bony and shapeless and there was no hair at the top of her legs. She wrapped the towel around herself and thought of Martine as she went to the kitchen where she had filled the tin tub with six inches of water from the pump by the sink. Her sister had been fourteen when she last saw her. She had had the body of a young woman and had told Giselle about growing up. The secret things only sisters talked about. The sort of things their mother had not wanted to discuss.

'You'll find out soon enough. Enjoy your childhood,' was what she had said whenever Giselle had asked a question about what her mother called 'women's things'.

Giselle gasped as she slipped into the cold water. Summer or not, it was still a shock as the water slapped around in the tub. She scooped up a handful of the water and splashed her face to wash away the tears.

✠✠✠

4

It is all very well having paintings, but you need something to hang them on: hooks. Being only a tenant in my flat and also being as dangerously incompetent with a toolbox as a drunk in a blindfold, I didn't have the means to hammer them in. So my new acquisitions stayed in their bubble-wrap on the sofa.

Radio Four was droning on about another crisis in the Labour Party and the latest car factory to be threatened with closure. My body was nagging for rehydration and I had forgotten to put my mobile on charge overnight. Even the August weather had taken a turn for the worse, the gentle rain forcing me to abandon plans for breakfast on the little balcony.

Collar up, I headed for the Bosun's Bite, deciding to take the riverside path instead of the main road to the slipway. The path led around the back of terraced houses that would all have been flooded at high tides if it were not for the embankment between them and the tidal river.

The little wharf had seen better days, its perimeter wire fence broken down in several places, the concrete posts crumbling and leaning at drunken angles. The mass of brambles and nettles around the fence had become a dumping ground for black bin-bags, beer cans and takeaway containers. The Rother was at low-tide, revealing muddy flats and the ribs of old sunken boats. It was the less salubrious corner of Rye Harbour.

Near the slipway was an old railway carriage, converted into someone's home. It looked cosy and well-kept, and reminded me of my stay along the coast in Shoreness a few years previously. On the stone desert of the Ness, old converted railway carriages formed the hub of the community, one which had closed ranks when I'd started asking questions about a young artist whose body I'd seen floating in the sea at Shakespeare Cliff. I felt no inclination to go back, even though I was living nearby again. It held few happy memories.

The Bosun's Bite was a warm, steamy refuge, its windows plastered in condensation obscuring the weather outside. It offered a socket to recharge my phone and good strong black coffee to recharge me. I turned to the crossword, my daily distraction from tasks I really should be getting on with.

5 Across. Challenge the Gospel? (8,4)

The mobile's klaxon call – I really must change the ringtone – interrupted my thought processes. The screen told me who was calling.

'Hello, Alice. How's things?'

'Hi Dad. Fine ta. You texted me to ring you?'

'Oh yes.' I paused as the waitress deposited my coffee and toast. 'Your mother asked me to talk to you. I'm sure you know what about.'

'The holiday.'

'Yes, the holiday. She's concerned, that's all. You going off for a week – abroad – on your own.'

'Dad, I won't be on my own. I'll be with Beth, and Beth's parents.'

'And two boys?'

'Yes, and two boys. Beth's boyfriend and his mate. And, no, I'm not going to be dropping my drawers the moment he offers to rub sun cream on my back.'

'Alice!'

'Well Dad. I'm surprised you don't trust me enough to go away for a week's holiday with some friends without it turning into an orgy. Anyway. I'm sixteen now.'

'Yes. I know. I'm sorry. I do trust you.'

'Mum doesn't.'

'She's just concerned.'

'Jealous, more like. Because my friends know how to behave and the blokes she hooks up with don't – yourself excluded, of course.'

'Well, thanks for that, Alice. No, I just wanted to say be sensible – and careful, if you know what I mean. Sun and a few glasses of wine can, you know, lower one's inhibitions.'

'Yes Dad. I know. Anyway, I don't even fancy Max – he's the other boy going – so no need to worry. I might run off with a Spanish waiter though!'

'Oh, that's all right then. As long as you get back in time for next term.'

She laughed. 'Thanks Dad. I'll tell Mum we had a chat and you approve of the holiday.'

'Yes, do that. Because I do. Send me a postcard.'

'Promise. Bye, love you.'

And with that she was gone, although it struck me that she might not know what a postcard was. Her idea of a postcard might be a smiley face and a sunshine emoji on WhatsApp.

The white-painted Rother Gallery door, which was also the front door of Lizzy White's home, was closed, which was odd. Protected by a thatched porch, it had always been open during the day in my time in Rye Harbour, come sun or rain.

There were lights on inside, so I knocked. Lizzy opened the door, her normal happy expression replaced by worry lines and red-rimmed eyes. She appeared to have aged ten years since the weekend.

'Come in Tom. Sorry, we should be open by now, shouldn't we? I've been a bit distracted this morning.'

'Is something wrong?'

'It's something and nothing really. I shouldn't let it upset me but it has.' She shut the door on the outside world. 'Come through. Zoe told me you were boosting our sales yesterday. Looking for something else?'

'No, not exactly. I was wondering if – look, it doesn't matter right now. What's happened? You look very upset.'

She sat down in the café area and beckoned me to do the same. 'I've been burgled. Nothing serious, I suppose, they didn't get into the gallery, thank God, but they've made a mess of the store room in the back garden. It's horrible to think people were out there last night while I was sleeping upstairs. It makes you feel violated in a way.'

I touched her hand, which was on the table gripping a screwed-up handkerchief. 'I'm sorry. Did they take much?' As soon as I had asked the question I wished I hadn't. It is what everyone always asks someone who has been burgled and is probably the least of the victim's concerns.

'I don't know really. I haven't looked that closely, but I can't imagine they found much in there. It's just a shed, I use it to store spare frames, a couple of little heaters for the winter, and a few bits and pieces for the garden. Most of the stuff was my father's old tools, I'd just never got round to sorting them out.'

'Would you like me to check it out with you? And have you told the police?'

'I haven't bothered with the police but I suppose I should, just in case I want to make an insurance claim. If you don't mind, that would be nice.' She got up and I followed her through the open French doors into the courtyard-style back garden, walled in on three sides but with a side entrance beside the cottage. The gate separating the front garden from the rear was open, its metal latch broken and hanging off of the splintered wood.

The shed was not obvious at first, tucked behind an overgrown buddleia bush groaning with purple blossoms and with ivy growing over one end and most of the roof. The door was open, a broken padlock on the flagstone path leading up to it. There was a row of four windows down the side of the shed, one of which was covered in red spray-paint: 'Mind the GAP', it said, drips running down from the letters.

'No alarm out here, I suppose?'

'No, I've never thought about it,' said Lizzy. 'I've got one for the gallery, of course, but that's only to keep the insurance people happy. I've never felt it was necessary in this little community.'

'Do you want to go inside?'

She took a deep breath and pushed back her shoulders. 'Yes. Let's get it over with.'

Inside the long dusty shed it was a mess. Tools with wooden handles – chisels, box planes, hammers and clamps – the sort now sold for a few pounds at boot fairs, were strewn on the floor. A wooden tea chest had been tipped over, its contents spilling under the waist-high work benches. Brushes, pencils, small pots of paint, various T-squares, triangles and pairs of compasses were scattered across the floorboards. On the benches, old tobacco and biscuit tins had been opened and discarded leaving nails, screws and washers lying among plastic flower pots and gardening wire. A pile of empty frames stood up on their sides had not been disturbed.

'Oh dear.' Lizzy held a hand to her mouth. 'Dad's things.' Her voice started to crack.

'I'll help you tidy it up. First thing, though, can you notice what's missing if anything?'

She looked around. 'The little electric mower's gone.' She bent to look under the bench beside her. 'And a spare microwave, I had. That was virtually new. I can't see much else. The fan heaters are still here.'

'What about down the other end?'

'That was mostly Dad's old stuff. I've never had the heart, or inclination, to go through it. Most of it was worthless I should think.'

'Do you feel up to going through it?'

'Yes, it'll be good therapy. I'll get a bin bag – a few of them – and we can sort out what's worth keeping. Not much I expect.' She stepped out of the shed and headed back towards the cottage.

I started to pick up the tools and art equipment. Some of it appeared to be good quality but, as Lizzy had said, of little value except perhaps sentimentally. A row of crooked homemade shelves on the far wall were draped in cobwebs. Tins of old products lay on the floor, all of them empty: Cadbury's cocoa essence, Golden Virginia tobacco, Huntley and Palmers mixed biscuits, Terry's butterscotch. I was putting them back on the shelves when Lizzy returned.

'I never ventured up that end of the shed much. I used to do my work down here by the windows for the light. Goodness knows what Dad kept in all those old tins but he used to love being down here.'

'When did he pass on?'

'Let me think – I was eighteen, I had just started at art college, so that was forty-four years ago. Oh my goodness, that does make me sound ancient, doesn't it? He was only fifty-nine. Poor man had a heart attack. At least it was quick, that's what mother said.'

She started picking up the paint brushes, which were dusty but immaculately clean. 'He loved his art, you know. I guess that's where I get it from. He spent hours down here with the radio, fiddling around with pictures, or pieces of wood making bits and pieces for the home.'

'Did he make a living from his art?'

'You know, I don't really know. It sounds awful doesn't it, but I never got to know him that well. He was a private man, never spoke about his life much, just lived quietly in this little place. In those days, children didn't ask that sort of question of their parents, I suppose. Mum and

Dad just lived their life. Mum worked at the local shop for a while, then opened the gallery. Dad seemed happy to keep himself to himself.'

I started sweeping the nails and screws from the work bench into the plastic bag that Lizzy held open, then remembered why I had visited the art gallery in the first place.

'Do you mind if I take a handful of these?' I stooped down to pick up a hammer. 'And borrow this? I need to hang those pictures I bought.'

'Help yourself. It's no use to me.'

An hour later, the only sign that the intruders had been there was the broken padlock on the garden table where we were sitting and the graffiti on the window. Lizzy had made tea and telephoned the police, who had given her a crime number and said they would try to visit later in the week.

'Whoever is doing this likes to leave their calling card.' I nodded at red paint on the shed window.

She shuddered. 'I find it rather sinister.'

'Yes, and it shows a certain amount of cockiness to hang around long enough to spray their tag before scarpering. It's as if they want some sort of local notoriety. You're not the first. Several houses in Oyster Creek have had sheds raided and a couple in Tram Road. Looks like they're working their way through the village.'

'What does it mean? Mind the GAP? I associate that with the London Underground.'

'I've no idea, Lizzy. Perhaps it is some sort of joke. Some of the residents are blaming the travellers in the area, but I wouldn't have thought graffiti is really their style.'

'I'm just glad I slept through it. I don't know what I would have done if I'd heard them. Called Zoe I suppose.'

'I don't think she would have been much help in the middle of the night. She had to leave her car here last night and get a taxi back to Rye.'

Lizzy feigned disapproval: 'Really? She didn't mention that to me this morning when I phoned her. Were you to blame for this?'

I held up two hands: 'Not guilty. It was your daughter who was the thirsty one. Kept me away from my work she did. I was meant to be writing a piece for the *South Coast Gazette* last night on these shed break-ins. I'll have to do it tonight now. Do you mind if I mention you've been raided too?'

She shook her head. 'No, if you think it will help.'

'I wouldn't hold your breath, but you never know. If the culprits are trying to flog the stuff locally, someone might call in. It's all a bit petty for the police to be bothering with although they're being leaned on to show willing.'

The tarmac of the exposed coastal track glistened in the rain and looked uninviting as it stretched towards the western breakwater which was out of sight, enveloped in a sea fret. I opted instead for the narrow path through the nature reserve where reeds grew in the salt marsh and sheep grazed on the raised land between the drainage ditches. It was said their meat had a special quality because of the salty coastal grasses on which they munched.

The path passed the holiday park where more than two hundred caravans hunkered down beside the marshes behind a man-made grassy embankment. The description 'caravan' was stretching a point. Most of the mobile homes appeared to have become long-term bungalows-on-wheels for those living there. The only rule was that to maintain the home's status as temporary accommodation, the residents could not live in one for more than fifty weeks a year, so, every February for two weeks, most of the park was deserted for 'holiday fortnight' as the locals headed for a couple of weeks in the Spanish sunshine or visited family in other parts of the UK.

Unlike at the weekend, the paths were empty apart from an occasional dog walker. The wind rattled through the grasses and wire fences, and the rain stung the eyes. Even the birds appeared to have given up trying to fly.

After half-a-mile, the path took a sharp left-hand turn on to a boardwalk over the mud-flats. It was making a detour around a clump of conifers which sheltered a black corrugated-iron barn. The metal gate said: 'Nookery Farm. Strictly Private. No Thoroughfare'. A thin trail of smoke from the far side of the barn was being whipped away by the wind, but its pungent smell still lingered in the air.

The leeward side of the Old Lifeboat Station provided some shelter at last. The battleship-grey English Channel looked much more menacing than it had in the sunshine at the weekend as the wind whipped white crests on to the heaving waves. I tried to imagine what it must have been like on that November night in 1928 for the crewmen and the launchers – some of them the wives and sisters of those volunteer lifeboat men – as they battled against the elements to send the *Mary Stanford* on its final doomed mission. Their calling was one of true bravery. In the three months following the lifeboat's last launching, sixteen bodies were washed up along the coast but the sea never gave up the seventeenth, that of John Head, at seventeen the youngest member of the crew. He remained beyond the waves.

The breakwaters leading out to the deep from the neglected lifeboat house were now no more than broken blackened stumps sticking up like rotten teeth as the sea careered over them on to the steep pebble bank in front of the slipway.

A cracked wail of a siren sounded in the distance. After what this village had been through almost one hundred years ago, it would cope with the current unrest rippling through its summer season.

For a community that complained about a lack of a police presence, they were certainly making up for it now. There were four uniformed officers and, as far as I could make out, two plain-clothes officers in the middle of the gawping crowd gathered in a circle in Rye Harbour's large free car park beside two police vehicles, their blue lights pulsing. There were also yellow-helmeted firefighters, rolling up hoses and stacking them on the back of the fire engine, which was parked alongside an ambulance, whose hazard warning lights flashed in unison with the police vehicles. It could have been a scene from a TV cop drama, except for the fact that I recognised one of the police officers.

Two of the uniforms appeared to be trying to calm a

young woman, whose face was blackened with soot and streaked by tears. She wore a bra and jeans, and nothing else. She struggled to break free of the police grip, kicking out half-heartedly with her bare feet before slumping back, resigned and sobbing into the arms of Lizzy White, whom I had not noticed earlier.

On the far side of the human circle sitting on the ground behind the other two uniformed police officers was a middle-aged man, a streak of blood running from his nose and angry-looking scratch marks on his left cheek. An ambulance paramedic was on her haunches inspecting the damage. It appeared I had missed the main attraction and just walked in on its aftermath.

'Come on folks, the show's over.' One of the uniforms who had been with the girl started to usher the crowd away. Lizzy caught my eye and beckoned me over.

'Tom, you couldn't lend Dawn your walking jacket could you? Poor girl is freezing to death, as well as feeling a bit embarrassed.'

'Of course.' I slipped off my North Face and draped it around the woman's pale, bony shoulders. She looked up but said nothing, gripping the coat across her with bleeding knuckles.

'Dawn, we need a word. In the car, please.' It was one of the plain-clothes police officers, the one I thought I recognised, and she obviously seemed to think the same about me. 'Sir, do I know you?' she asked as her colleague led Dawn – and my coat – into the back of one of the police cars.

'You look different in clothes, Sergeant Hopps.'

'Don't tell me.' She bit her bottom lip and held up her

right index finger. 'Yes, you were part of that drowned artist affair weren't you, turned out to be a bit of a hero in the end, if a foolhardy one, I remember. It's Mr Childs isn't it?'

'Kidd. Tom Kidd. And you've gone up in the world from desk sergeant at Normanden nick.'

She looked down at her dark blue business suit which would not have looked out of place in a firm of accountants. 'Still a sergeant, Mr Kidd, but now in CID at Rye. And what brings you to these parts, I thought you'd moved away?'

'I had, but I'm back, as you can see – still trying to earn an honest living and keep out of trouble.'

'Well, if you're not involved with this business with Dawn, I'll say goodbye. I do need to speak to her.'

'I don't know the woman, sergeant, but she's borrowed my coat, so I'll hang around if it's all the same to you.'

The police officer looked at the dishevelled woman in the back of the police car. 'Very gallant of you, Mr Kidd. I've got a blanket in the boot, I'll fetch your coat if you wait here.'

As she walked away, I turned to Lizzy White. 'What's this all about?'

She shrugged. 'Not sure, Tom. There's been a fire at Dawn Speed's caravan, I know that. I heard some screaming in the car park and when I came out to see, she was laying into Steve Kain.' She nodded at the bloodied figure heading towards the moorings. 'I do hope Fin is all right.'

'Fin?'

'Fin McEvoy, Dawn's partner. They've been at the

caravan at Nookery Farm for a few years now. He's a bit of a Bohemian, you know? Fancies himself as an artistic type although I don't like his stuff that much. Still, he seems nice enough.' She laughed: 'He's the peace-loving beatnik, while she's the fiery one.'

'Clearly. The police seem to know her.'

'Let's say that she's a bit of a character. She's never slow in standing up for herself that's for sure.'

Detective Sergeant Hopps returned with my jacket. She appeared to be much less formidable out of uniform, but I thought it wise not to tell her. 'Check the pockets, Mr Kidd, but I don't suppose anything's missing.'

'Is Fin McEvoy all right?' asked Lizzy. 'He wasn't in the caravan was he?'

'We're still investigating the fire, madam, but no, the chief fire officer informs me there was no-one else at the caravan. Just a dog, I'm afraid.'

'Oh dear,' Lizzy held a hand over her mouth.

We headed across the car park towards the gallery. I remembered to go through my coat pockets. They had not been touched. I felt slightly ashamed that I had felt the need to check.

When we arrived at the gallery I saw the man Lizzy had identified as Steve Kain sitting outside the Nelson, pint in hand and laughing loudly with three male companions, one of whom I recognised as Michael Monday, organiser of the neighbourhood watch campaign. Kain was a sturdy six-footer with a ruddy complexion under a mane of tousled blond hair. The scratches on the side of his face had dried to a dark brown.

'He looks as if he could swat Dawn away with one

hand tied behind his back. What possessed her to attack him?'

'No idea, Tom. Like I said, she's a feisty little thing. She comes from a family of travellers in Camber, and they can usually look after themselves. The family have a bit of a bad reputation, but I've always found Dawn to be perfectly pleasant.'

'And her partner, Fin? Is he what the locals call a pikey?'

'I don't like that word, Tom. It's very pejorative.' She frowned at me. 'No, I don't think Fin is a traveller, but with his ponytail and earrings, I suspect most of the locals do. They can be very small-minded, you know.'

'I heard someone say they might be to blame for the break-ins to the sheds.'

'What? Fin and Dawn? Never.'

The Green Leaves Retirement Home in Hythe was where I was told I would find Fred Harris. Norman from the lifeboat shop had printed his name on the corner of newspaper I had torn off.

The twenty-five mile drive to Hythe across the marsh to Lydd and Dymchurch and through the eerie windfarms, their giant sails turning silently, brought back memories of my last stay in these parts when I thought my life was mapped out with a new job in the nuclear power industry and a new romance generating plenty of heat. The spark soon went out of both, though.

The sign at the pillared entrance to Green Leaves announced that it was a 'retreat for the autumn years'. The pedant in me puzzled at the aptness of the use of

'Green' in the place's title, but I concluded that 'Brown Leaves' did not quite have the welcoming ring to it.

The visitors' car park was empty. Perhaps most relatives did their visits in the morning or early evening. Or just ignored the elderly residents locked up safely behind the fine façade of the main building that had the look of a once grand Victorian home. A short flight of stone steps and a concrete ramp led up to a portico on pillars either side of two large doors. They were flanked by bay windows and rose beds.

The sign below a bell push said all visitors must report to reception. I duly did and asked for Fred Harris.

'Geordie Fred?' The young woman behind the desk in a white uniform had an East European accent. 'He'll be in the day room, I expect. This will be a nice surprise, he doesn't get many visitors.'

I filled in the visitors' book and followed her clicking heels through the polished entrance hall with high ceilings and parquet flooring into a more modern extension, flooded by afternoon sunshine filtered through net curtains over large full length windows that gave views of pristine lawns.

The room smelled unpleasantly of stale cooking and urine. It reminded me of visits to see my grandmother in her latter years. A tea trolley was doing the rounds of the residents who were sitting around two low tables in front of a vast television screen that blasted out *Pointless* questions, the volume making the cups rattle in their saucers.

'Geordie's over there,' my guide cupped her hand and leaned closer to inform me, pointing to a figure seated at another table pondering a half-finished jigsaw. 'If you want to go somewhere quieter,' she shouted, 'there's the Quiet Room down the corridor.' She pointed again.

'Thanks. Will you do the introductions first please, Mr Harris doesn't know me.'

Fred Harris – Geordie to all and sundry – could not get out of the day room quickly enough, although quick was in relative terms. He was not a tall man, but the years had eroded him even more, and he hunched over his walking stick as he led me slowly away from the reach of the television quizmaster: 'We asked one hundred people to name something you might buy in a butchers.'

'Tripe', muttered Geordie.

He poked his head into the Quiet Room, where two men and a woman dozed, chins slumped on chests, one snoring loudly.

'Bloody hell, man,' muttered Geordie again. 'God's waiting-room in there. Let's go to my room.'

The lift took us to the first floor where the linoleum-floored corridor, its walls painted institution cream, led us to the rear of the main building. His room was called 'Lindisfarne'. It was my chance to break the ice.

'Is that a coincidence? You sound as if you're from that part of the world Mr Harris.'

'It's Geordie, lad. Aye, I'm from Newcastle but not been there for more than sixty years. All the rooms are named after islands around Britain. Most of the residents in here should be stuck in the Scilly Isles if you ask me. Take a seat on the bed.'

The bedroom was five paces by five paces, or ten by ten if you were Geordie. Apart from the single bed, it had one threadbare armchair, where he was sitting, a chest of drawers with a small television on top, and a built-in wardrobe. A red emergency cord dangled beside the bed. There was a sink with vanity mirror and shaving cabinet in a corner by the window, which looked down on the garden where two benches were placed under an oak tree in front of a small aviary.

'Norman sent a message through, told me you were coming, son. Something to do with the *Mary Stanford*?'

'I'm writing a book about the lifeboat disaster back in 1928 and I want to try to put across the bravery of those men, and others like them; the whole story of that night and the impact the tragic loss of life had on the small community.'

The old man's gnarled hands rested on top of his walking stick which stood between his legs. His mottled pale skin hung in creases around his chin. Whoever had shaved him that morning had not done a good job, tufts of grey whiskers sticking out of his jowls. His eyes were fixed on the floor but I sensed there was still plenty going on behind them.

'Aye, son. I was there.'

'You were there? Actually there that night? It was more than ninety years ago.'

'I was. Be a good lad: in the wardrobe, you'll see an old brief case on the floor. Fetch it would you?'

When I handed it to him, he winked and said, 'Emergency rations.'

I had expected him to pull out old photographs, even possibly newspaper cuttings, instead he brought out a large bag of sweet chilli oven crisps, a small bottle of navy rum and two chipped tumblers.

'They don't like us having booze in our rooms but I think the cleaner turns a blind eye. She's Latvian. Good girl she is. If I was fifty years younger …' He chuckled as he handed me a glass, balanced the other on the arm of his chair and carefully shared out the remains of the bottle of rum. I declined a crisp as I sipped the sweet dark liquor.

His larynx lubricated, Geordie Harris put his memory bank into rewind. 'Yes, I was five when it happened. I'm ninety-six now, bonny lad. Defying the odds and cluttering up the place.' He swallowed some more rum and munched on a crisp.

'I was there when they launched the boat that night. A few of us kids always went along for launchings, it was exciting, like. My mother was one of the launchers, and her brother, my uncle, was one of the crew.'

He told me what he remembered: the cold and the wind, the thrill of racing his mates along the coast path in the dark; the shouting of the men as they heaved the boat across the stones to the sea; the clout around the ear he received from his mother for standing too close when she had told him to stay well clear; the cheer that went up from the launchers on the shore when the boat made it through the breakers as the men rowed.

'As a kid, you didn't sense any danger. It was only later, when the men didn't come home that you realised something was wrong – the women crying; the men going out in fishing boats to search for survivors.'

Just how reliable his recall was, I was not sure, but he told a good tale and clearly enjoyed reminiscing.

He said his family had left Rye Harbour soon after the lifeboat disaster and settled in the north-east. As a young man he had joined the Royal Engineers and served as a sapper during the latter stages of the Second World War. When peace returned, he signed up for the Merchant Navy, hence his liking for dark rum, he said. After a few years at sea, he met a girl, fell in love, married and moved back south.

'It's a bit posh-like down here, lad, but my missus was from Kent and she wanted to be near her kin.'

'Well, you've not lost your accent, Geordie.' I stood up and rinsed our empty glasses in the sink, dried them on a towel and put them back in his briefcase.

'Nice pictures,' I said, looking around the little room that was all that was left of Geordie's world. A long, colourful, and perhaps heroic life, reduced to a small utilitarian box with a few sticks of furniture and a handful of framed paintings and photographs hanging on plain pale-blue painted walls.

'Here.' He handed me the empty rum bottle and fished a wallet from his baggy trousers. 'Dispose of this for me will you, and get me another bottle. Just a half bottle – and make sure it's dark rum mind, none of your fancy stuff. This should cover it.' His trembling hand held out a ten-pound note.

'I was also on the lifeboats for twenty-odd years you know. When you come back, I'll tell you about it.'

That evening I finished my six-hundred word piece for the *South Coast Gazette* and pinged it to Larry Lander's email address. I was just filling in the answer to *5 across.*

Challenge the Gospel? (8,4) with some satisfaction: *Question Mark*, when the phone rang. It was Lander.

'Read it already?'

'Skimmed through it old boy, looks fine but there's been some developments today and we might have to tickle it up a bit.'

That phrase set off an alarm bell. I knew what Lander's idea of 'tickling up' involved.

'Go on,' I said.

'My police contact tells me a caravan on the marshland was burnt out this morning. No-one hurt, but the police suspect it may have been arson – and possibly linked to the thefts in the area. Local CID are talking to that little neighbourhood vigilante group of yours as we speak.'

Alderney 1943

There were few things that the three companions liked about their prison island but one of them was the smell of tangy sea air. It blew in through the slats of Hut 7 purging the place of the stench of decay and death, at least for a short while. Georgi, Petr and Alexei had never smelled sea air before the day the German soldiers had marched them out of their Craft School in Orel in central Russia and into wagons on a train bound for the west. 'You are going to work for The Fatherland,' they were told.

Their mothers cried, their fathers raged as the long winding train pulled out of Orel with hundreds of teenage boys and girls locked into trucks. Alexei's grandmother had squeezed between the guards and pushed a tiny silver cross into his hand as the train lurched forward. That was a year ago but it seemed like an eternity to the three boys.

'I'm going down to the sea tonight,' Georgi said as they huddled together watching the last of the summer sun slip towards the horizon. 'The lice are driving me mad,' He scratched at his ribs beneath the shirt he had been given by the Germans when he had arrived on the island. His only shirt. The other two nodded. They were with him.

Petr Roslov was seventeen. He did whatever his brother Georgi, who was a year older, told him. Alexei Tischenko, a classmate of Petr's at the Craft School where they had learned to work the lathe together, nodded in agreement.

The bars at the window did not present an obstacle. Two

loosened slats in the floor allowed them to drop onto the dry earth underneath the hut. Their emaciated state meant they were easily able to wriggle out and wait for the guard to pass the barbed wire between the camp and the sand of Saline Bay. An old cement bag they had used many times before was hidden in a gorse bush. They laid it across the top of the wire and scrambled over. Capture meant a date with the firing squad or, at best, a severe beating, but living with the insatiable lice was an even worse fate. The one thing that got rid of them, at least for a few days, was salt water.

The boys slithered across the sandy hummocks and into the cool water where they lay looking up at the darkening sky as the waves lapped around them.

'Do you think it's night time in Orel?' said Alexei.

'Of course,' replied Georgi. 'And our families will be around an open fire roasting a boar on a spit. The Germans will have been chased out of town and the Russian army will be planning to rescue us soon.' He knew it would not be true, but the two younger boys liked to hear him talk like this.

'C'mon, let's try the rocks.' Georgi rolled on to his stomach and raised his head to check they were not being watched. He crawled on all fours through the shallow water to the rocky outcrop below Fort Tourgis, where the boys had been working that week widening the roads with The Stripes. If anything made the boys feel better it was the treatment of The Stripes by the guards. At least someone else was worse off than them. If a Stripe dropped his shovel or stopped to cough, he was likely to get the butt of a rifle in the back of the head. If he fell over, that would be followed by a kicking.

The Stripes lived in a camp within the camp. Their huts were surrounded by its own wire fence in a separated section of Helgoland. By the exit gate was a pot of yellow paint which was used to brighten the star on the back of their shirts if it had started to fade. Georgi told the other two he thought they were Jews.

They reached the rocks where they knew mussels and limpets were to be found. Their broken hands, blistered by hard labour for twelve hours a day, could never free the shells from their stronghold, but clipped with pebble at the right angle and the molluscs' grip on the rocks could be loosened. The only danger was the harvest created noise and despite their gnawing hunger, the trio always limited themselves to twelve morsels. Four each. Raw, salty and delicious.

As they sat enjoying the moment and letting their rags dry, a lorry trundled up the hill towards the fort, the two slits of light of its headlamps picking out the newly-laid cement track they had been working on. There was the sound of an aircraft out to sea. 'German?' asked Petr.

Georgi cocked an ear skywards and concentrated. 'Uh-ah. Don't think so. Think it's an Englisher.'

'Bomb the shit out of them, friend,' Alexei whispered as he strained skywards hoping to see the plane in the cloudless night sky. But the only lights he could see were hundreds of stars.

The moon shed a silver glow over the hillside, picking out the shape of three low buildings that the boys knew to be the farm where the Germans got their milk and eggs. On their march up to Fort Tourgis, a week before, they had seen the farmer and a young girl in the fields, going about their chores as if there was not a war on any longer. The following day, half a loaf of bread was left wrapped in old newspaper on the stone wall by the road. One of the other prisoners had found it and word quickly spread around the hut. The next day the same thing happened on their march back, and the next day. On the fourth day, however, the prisoners' eagerness to get to the little parcel alerted their guards, who confiscated the bread and took great pleasure in breaking bits off to feed to their dogs.

'Time to get back,' said Georgi. 'Let's try the piggery tomorrow night. The Ukrainians were unloading swede into the store there today. Don't see why the pigs should have it all to themselves, eh lads?' He grinned and nodded as the guard turned the corner on the perimeter path. 'It's clear, let's go.'

✠✠✠

5

Rye is one of those historic English towns American visitors love: buildings older than their country leaning over narrow roads not built for motor vehicles, tea rooms lurking behind leaded windows, book shops thriving and the heritage centre beside the converted tall fishermen's sheds bustling with visitors. Even the police station in Cinque Ports Street has a certain elegance with its hanging tiles, red-brick exterior and flower tubs. I was there to see Detective Sergeant Hilary Hopps.

'A couple of minutes, Mr Kidd, no more. I have more pressing matters than talking to the Press. You really should be doing this through our media department in Brighton.'

'Thank you for your time. Just a couple of quick questions, and off the record, of course. The caravan, was it an arson attack?'

'Our investigation is on-going but, if this is off the record, then, yes, there are suspicious circumstances about the fire at Rookery Farm. We are still talking to the fire authorities about that.'

'What's this got to do with the Oyster Creek Neighbourhood Watch group? I understand you have been speaking to them.'

'We are talking to lots of local people who may be

able to help with our inquiries, Mr. Kidd. The Police and Crime Commissioner is particularly keen we get to the bottom of this.'

'I'll bet she is. And Dawn? Is she being charged?'

'Ms Dawn Speed has been cautioned about her behaviour, but no, she will not be charged. Now, I think I must be getting on with my real work, but I would ask a favour: if you do hear anything during your own inquiries, Tom, I would ask you to bring the information to us. Not to take the law into your own hands as you did before. My card.'

I nodded and took the card. 'Don't worry, I'm not into heroics these days.' I headed for the door then hesitated. 'By the way, why Steve Kain? Why did Dawn think he was to blame?'

'I'm asking myself the same question. It's not something Ms Speed has been very clear about.'

I had felt my mobile vibrating while in with DS Hopps. The messages could wait until I had found somewhere dry that sold decent coffee. There was no shortage of choice, but I had instructions about where to go.

The Fig Café was, Zoe had said, her favourite. The black walls and black tables with vases of fresh flowers gave it a chic feel. Zoe blended in well with her black blouse and matching jeans. I felt slightly out of place among the young mums and pushchairs.

She had commandeered a table beside the window and waved me over. 'Sit down, I'll get the drinks.'

While she was at the counter, I checked my messages. One was from Zoe confirming she had arrived at the café, the other was from Denise Rutter, who appeared to be genuinely interested in house-hunting in the area. My mood darkened a little.

> Hi Tom, got that viewing at R Harbour at 2 today. Fancy meeting up after? You can show me the sights!!! I'll ring. DR x

I had hoped her enthusiasm for becoming a neighbour had just been a weekend flight of fancy fuelled by sunshine and white wine. She was a friend of the Landers on a brief retreat to the countryside from the big city – a television presenter who knew how to make an entrance. I did not need complications in my life. Anyway, I was here to see Zoe.

'Thanks for coming,' she said, placing a tray containing a large cafetière, two mugs and a small jug of milk on the table. 'How do the pictures look at your flat?'

'Really nice actually. They're up now after I borrowed some hooks and a hammer from your mother. How's she been since the break in?'

'Well, that's why I asked you for coffee. I'm a bit worried about her to be honest. She seemed quite upset when I phoned this morning, she didn't say anything but I know her well enough. I wonder if you'd pop round to the gallery this afternoon – I'd go myself but I'm on a split shift today at the hotel behind reception. I'm not sure when I'll be finished.'

It was only then that I realised Zoe was dressed for work. She was subtly made up and her mop of red hair was neatly gathered at the back of her head, revealing the freckles that cascaded down an elegant neck. On her blouse was pinned a name-badge and the title 'Assistant Receptionist'. She reached into the inside pocket of a black jacket draped over the back of her chair and brought out a man's fob watch.

'In fact, I'll have to be off in a minute. The manager's a stickler for time-keeping.'

'That's unusual, don't see many of them these days.' I nodded at the silver watch cradled in her right hand.

'This?' She looked at the watch and smiled. 'It's lovely, isn't it? My Gran gave it to me on my eighteenth, shortly before she died. I think it belonged to her father, and probably his father before that. It needs winding every day but it still keeps good time.'

She slipped the watch back into an inside pocket.

'You heard about the fire at the caravan on the salt marsh?'

'Mum told me. Awful isn't it? Dawn was pretty hysterical I gather.'

'She was. Seems she attacked someone called Steve Kain. Know him?'

'Not well. He runs a couple of fishing boats out of the harbour, also takes tourists on fishing trips. He's one of the volunteer lifeboat crew too, but he's not a local. I think he and Dawn came from Hastings originally.'

'He and Dawn?'

'Yes, they were an item when they moved to Rye Harbour. They lived in one of the mobile homes at the holiday park, but she got involved with Fin and moved in with him at Rookery Farm about three years back.'

'How did Steve Kain take that?'

'I honestly don't know, Tom. He's a big guy, and pretty

tough I should imagine, doing the job he does, but I've never heard of him causing trouble. Look, I must go. Let me know about Mum if you can look in on her later.'

Left alone with half a pot of coffee and a virgin crossword was an opportunity not to be missed as I braced myself for the afternoon visitation of Denise Rutter.

10 Down. Lean on thief to reveal all and make a splash (6-3).

I eased two wheels of my trusted and rusted Audi gently up the kerb and parked beside the village playing field on the outskirts of Rye Harbour.

The field was well-kept but the white goalposts kept a lonely vigil at either end. The absence of children on the grass and in the small playground, where the swings and seesaw stood idle even in the school summer holidays, suggested the Government's persistent warnings about child obesity and a lack of outdoor activity had not hit home in these parts.

My destination was along a gravel path at one end of the field: The Church of the Holy Spirit, the local parish church, which was reached through an ancient lych gate where the names of the fallen from the two world wars were remembered. It was a memorial for other dead local men that had drawn me here, however.

The robust bluestone church with its solid buttresses pinning it down was built on a slight rise just above sea level. One end was barrel-shaped like the stern of a ship, the other end was overlooked by a gothic bell tower rising above the double wooden doors of the main entrance.

Inside, the maritime influence continued with a

striking wooden vaulted ceiling in the shape of an upturned boat. There was a memorial for the crew of the *Mary Stanford* lifeboat who lost their lives in 1928, but it was not the one I was looking for.

The graveyard skirted three sides of the church and in the far corner I saw what I had come for. Against a low stone wall stood the white memorial rising almost twelve feet. On a plinth stood a carving of a lifeboat-man clad in waterproofs and carrying a coiled rope. Above the statue's head was inscribed 'We Have Done That Which Was Our Duty To Do'. Around the large rectangular base of the memorial were individual plaques to the seventeen crewmen of the *Mary Stanford.* The surnames repeated themselves: three from the Cutting family, three from the Pope family, three from the Head family. There were two Clarks and two Downeys. Just five families sacrificing thirteen lives.

I was not sure why a visit to this memorial, the scene of an annual service in memory of the tragedy, had seemed important, but I felt I should see it if I was to write the story of the *Mary Stanford.*

Fin McEvoy was a lot older than I had expected. I don't know why, but I had assumed he would be about the same age as his partner Dawn, whom I had put in her early thirties. The man I saw picking through the charred wreckage of a caravan on Rookery Farm must have been around fifty. He had a slim, weather-beaten pale face. His hair, drawn back into a ponytail, and goatee beard were flecked with grey. The array of earrings looked out of place with the wire-rimmed spectacles that sat on the tip of his nose.

He was feeling through the ash with his fingers and delicately placing small grey twigs into a plastic supermarket bag. The conifers that once screened the caravan were burnt and blackened but the barn beside them appeared largely undamaged apart from the large door, which was lying on the ground in splintered planks. A small Yorkshire Terrier watched from a safe distance, tied to a fence post by a piece of string attached to her collar.

'Mr McEvoy?' He had not heard my approach. He looked up from his position in the middle of the scorched desolation. His dusty face was streaked with tear tracks. 'Tom Kidd. I'm from the *South Coast Gazette.'*

He straightened himself with a grimace and pushed his glasses back up his nose, as if to focus on the intruder on his grief.

'I was sorry to hear about the fire. I just wondered if I could ask you a few questions. There seems to have been a fair bit of what you might call unpleasantness in Rye Harbour. Some of it illegal.'

McEvoy held out the plastic bag in his left hand and said in the softest of voices: 'Kolo'.

'Pardon? I'm sorry, I didn't quite catch….'

'Kolo. One of our dogs. This is her.'

I realised then that the pale grey twigs he had been collecting from the ash were what was left of the bones of a dog.

'She always sat in that corner.' He turned to look inside an imaginary caravan. 'On the end of the bench seat by the window. It got the sun in the afternoons.'

He gazed towards the shoreline half-a-mile away to the south.

'Look, I'm sorry. I'll come back another time.'

He turned back to me, his eyes moist, and shook his head. 'No, what did you say your name was?'

'Tom Kidd, Mr McEvoy.'

'Call me Fin, man, everybody else does.'

'I'm a friend of Lizzy White who runs the gallery.'

'I'm afraid that doesn't come as much of a recommendation to me.'

'Really? Why's that?'

'It's a long story which boils down to artistic rivalry, I suppose. She's on the parish council, and they helped block planning permission for me to have a small gallery and shop here during the summer season. Then she refused to stock my work at her gallery. Said it wasn't to her taste, whatever that means. She's an artistic snob, if you must know.'

His Scottish accent was a soft one, but still distinctive. He tied the top of the plastic bag into a knot and placed it gently beside a tractor that looked as if it had not moved in years, the weeds reaching up past its perished tyres to the red metal seat.

'I'll bury her later. Tea?'

I thought Fin McEvoy was either being bleakly humorous or was slightly deranged in grief, but he shuffled towards a standpipe, rinsed his hands and then headed through the gap, where the door should have been, into the barn.

Inside was a long work bench with a fluorescent strip-light hanging down on chains. An extension lead, its exposed wires stuck into the back of the light switch, ran along the back of the bench to a gang of four plug sockets. I froze for a moment when Fin flicked on the switch with his still damp hands, but nothing exploded in a shower of sparks. He checked the weight of the kettle for water and waved it at me.

'Thank you. That would be nice.'

'No milk, though. That was in the fridge in the caravan. Nor sugar.'

'Black tea is fine.'

While we waited for the kettle to boil, Fin McEvoy told me he had been on the beach the previous morning gathering driftwood for his artwork when the fire happened, while Dawn had been in the village shopping.

'Zola came with me to the beach, she loves it.' He pointed to the Yorkie who was lazily scratching her chin in the yard. 'But her mother, Kolo, is too old for the long walks now, so she stays – stayed, I should say – in the caravan.'

'Do you find much on the beach?'

'Enough to get by. It's amazing what you can do with bits of old wood, plastic bottles, rope and a bit of spray paint. Some of the tourists seem to like my stuff anyway, even if Lizzy White doesn't. I flog it here and there, it makes me a living. What with that and Dawn's shop work, we manage. Or we did manage.' He looked outside at the mound of ash that was once their home. 'I suppose we'll have to move on now.'

'What happened here yesterday, Fin?'

He shrugged and poured the boiled water into two handle-less mugs and dropped a teabag into each.

'The police suspect that it was started deliberately.'

'I know,' he said. 'And so does Dawn.'

'Where is she now?'

'Gone back to her family in Camber, I think. I expect she'll be back unless her family talk her out of it. They never did like me much, what with the age gap and lack of a proper job, as they called it.'

'What about Steve Kain?'

'What about him?'

'Well, by all accounts Dawn went for him yesterday. Blamed him for this.' I looked around the barn, which had not escaped damage. Tools, wood, tins of paint and tubes of glue were scattered on the earth floor.

'She can be a wee bit impetuous. Look, I know she blamed him but I've no idea. Why would he do it anyway?'

'Didn't Dawn leave him for you? Jealousy can drive people to do all sorts.'

'That was a few years ago. I think his pride was hurt at first, what with me being an older bloke and all that, but, man, I can't see him doing anything now after all this time. I think he's found someone else anyway.'

We drank the bitter tea in silence. Through the open doorway I could see the squat shape of the old lifeboat house standing out against the misty horizon.

'Does your driftwood collecting take you out near the old lifeboat house?'

'Yes, most days I go past that way. It's a sad place.'

'Do you know what the graffiti on the side means? "Mind The GAP". Or who did it?'

'No idea. Sorry. Why?'

'No real reason, I guess. What are you going to do here?'

McEvoy sighed. 'Bury Kolo for a start.'

'And after that?'

'I don't own the land and I can't afford another caravan, so I'll probably go. The wildlife sanctuary will be glad to see the back of me. They've regarded this place as a bit of an eyesore for years, but the barn and caravan have been here for ages and legally they couldn't get shot of me. Now, I've nothing to stay for, especially if Dawn has buggered off for good.'

Denise Rutter was hysterical. So hysterical I could not understand what she was saying. She had called my mobile as I was walking back to the village from McEvoy's barn. I had helped him dig a small hole beside the old tractor and he had tipped Kolo's dusty bones into it. I gave him my number and we shook hands, but I didn't expect to see him again.

The calm clear mellow voice that was her stock in trade on television came in discordant bursts interspersed with sobs and gasps. She sounded angry and scared at the same time without making any sense, but clearly she was in some distress.

'Denise, slow down. Take a deep breath. Where are you and what's happened?'

I had to hold the phone away from my ear as the distorted cry came back: 'Rabour. Ramrud. The fucking bastard.'

The only bit that was clear was the obscenity. 'Sorry Denise, I still don't get it. Where are you?'

'Rye Harbour, of course. Tram Road. Tom, please come.'

'Is someone else with you? Are you in danger?'

'Not now he isn't, the slimy bastard. I'm in my car, the doors are locked and he's fucked off anyway.'

'OK, good. Look, I'm about fifteen minutes away on foot. Stay in the car, I'll find you.'

I did find her. It was not difficult. She had told me what she drove and not many people in Rye Harbour owned a silver E-Class Mercedes Coupe. She was sitting in the driver's seat. I tapped on the passenger's window and her head swivelled around, her on-screen smile appearing as soon as she recognised me. I heard the soft click of the lock being released and slid into the red leather bucket seat beside her.

'Oh Tom, thank God you're here,' she leaned across the leather-clad tunnel between the seats, draped her arms around my neck and buried her head in my shoulder. It was only then that I noticed her cream blouse was gaping open to reveal a red bra trying manfully to restrain a deep cleavage. Her olive green skirt had ridden up above a bloodied knee and what was once a high-heeled shoe lay broken in the well of the car beside a muddy, grazed foot.

I gently pulled back from her embrace and held her at arm's length. 'Christ Denise, what's happened to you?'

'The bastard of an estate agent. He tried to take advantage of me.'

'You what? Surely not?'

'Don't you believe me?' She sounded angry. 'How do you think I got like this?' She held her blouse open so that it gaped to her navel, and tears started to roll down her cheeks.

'No. Yes. Sorry. Of course I believe you, Denise.' I pushed her hands together so that she was decent again. 'Come here.' I put an arm around her and tried to give her as reassuring a hug as is possible in a two-seater with a console covered in dials and switches between the two front seats.

Her perfume was subtle and smelled expensive. She wrapped her right arm around my left shoulder and pressed herself into me. It had been a long time since I had been in this situation in a sports car. If anyone who knew me walked by, this would be around the village in no time. Rye Harbour was a small place.

'Come on, Denise. Let's get you sorted out.' I gently prised her away from me. 'This sounds like a police matter. Let's go to my flat and you can clean up and have a coffee.'

'I think I need something a bit stiffer than coffee.'

I tried to put the thought that she was being suggestive out of my mind. I really could do without this. 'I think I've got some wine.'

'I need a gin and tonic, Tom. A large one. Isn't there a pub in this place?'

'Yes, there are two, both just around the corner – but you can't walk in that shoe.' I looked into the well by the pedals.

She leaned forward, picked up the shoe and lobbed it onto the small seats behind us. She leaned forward again, unhooked her other shoe and did the same thing before turning the key, the powerful engine purring into life.

'Right, I'll drive, you just tell me where to go.'

Two minutes later we were in the Admiral Nelson, Denise with a G&T, me with a pint of IPA. I found a discreet corner, but still we were attracting a lot of attention which, I got the feeling, she rather enjoyed.

'Why are they all staring Tom? I get quite a bit of that with my TV work, you know. It can be a little tiresome.'

'I'm not sure it's so much that, Denise. To be honest, they don't see too many black women in this part of the world, particularly glamorous ones in bare feet, with a bloody knee and a plunging neckline.' I smiled and nodded at her blouse, which appeared to have a mind of its own and had swung open again.

She looked down in mock horror. 'Oooh, Tom. I'm sorry. What will they think of you?' She clasped her arms across her bosom. 'There, is that better?'

'You're obviously feeling a bit better. The wonderful effects of gin and tonic, I suspect. But, look, this sounds serious. Tell me what happened. Slowly, from the start.'

Denise said she had turned up for her viewing of a semi-detached three bedroom house in Tram Road at the specified time of two o'clock. The representative of Webster & Kallas Estate Agents had been there to greet her, and charming he seemed too. The property was empty, but furnished. They viewed the back garden and summer house first, then went inside through the back door.

'He gave me all the waffle about Rye Harbour being a desirable place to live with a thriving local community. I have to say the open-plan kitchen-living area was lovely. I was beginning to fall in love with the place.'

'Yes, Denise, but what happened?'

'Well, then we went upstairs and he showed me the master bedroom, which had a big picture window with views across the wildlife sanctuary to the sea. He said you could even see the sea from the bed, and he sat on it. So I sat next to him and that's when he started to come on to me.'

'Really?'

'Don't sound so surprised, Tom. I'm not ready for the knackers' yard quite yet.'

'No, I don't mean that, Denise. It's just that it sounds so unprofessional of him. So risky these days.'

'Well, he took that risk. And when I made it clear I wasn't interested, he wouldn't take no for an answer. Made a grab for my boobs and ripped two buttons off when I stood up.' She looked down and, seeing her bra was on show again, folded her arms across her chest.

'He got angry then, said I'd been leading him on. Called me a prick-teaser and a black bitch, and made a lunge. Tom, I can look after myself, but I can tell you I was really frightened by then – in this empty house, alone with a middle-aged man who was powerfully built and seemed to think he was God's gift.'

'You really should be telling this to the police, Denise.'

'I don't know. You know what it's like on TV, stations hate their people being in the papers for something like this, even if it wasn't my fault.'

'But he assaulted you.'

'Yes, but he won't be doing it again in a hurry. When he grabbed me a second time, I kneed him in the nuts, really hard. He squealed like a pig, fell sideways and banged his head on the end of the bed. Serves the bastard right. I got down the stairs and ran out of the back door – that's where I tripped on the decking in the back garden and broke my shoe. I didn't notice my knee until I got in the car and locked the doors.'

'What happened to the estate agent?'

'He came down about a minute later, still bent half double. He just jumped in his car and went.'

'Did you get his name?'

'Oh yes. At least he gave me a name. I presume it's real. Roland Fawkes.' She drained her glass. 'Another?'

'No, you're driving remember. Come round to my place, you can clean up. I think I've got a needle and thread too, and we'll talk about what to do. We'll give Larry a ring.'

'You're my knight in shining armour, Tom.'

Denise was in my bathroom, doing whatever women do in bathrooms. I had not told her that I knew the name Fawkes. It must be a coincidence that her assailant had the same surname as the local Police and Crime Commissioner Gail Fawkes. Perhaps it was a common name locally. It could not possibly be her husband. Or could it? No one was that stupid, even those who had spent most of their working life in a profession where those in positions of power got their own way.

Denise emerged from the bathroom, glamour restored.

'As good as new?' I asked.

'Almost, Tom.'

She was wearing one of my denim shirts, which was much too large but still looked good on her. She was the sort who could wear a bin-liner and look good. Her hair and make-up was back in place, her knee bathed and her feet clean.

'Is that tea? I'd love one.' She curled her legs under her bottom and melted into the corner of the sofa. 'What lovely pictures, Tom.'

'I only bought them a couple of days ago. Thought the flat needed brightening up.' I poured the tea. 'Mind the leaves at the bottom of the mug, I don't like teabags and I don't have a strainer.'

'This is really very nice – the flat I mean. But I'm not sure I could face living in Rye Harbour now.'

A little sigh of relief seeped out. I hoped Denise had not noticed.

'Denise, I have to ask one question – and please, don't get angry with me.' I sat at the other end of the sofa.

'Oh, this sounds intriguing. Yes Tom, I promise. Cross my heart.' She ran her right forefinger across and down the breast pocket of my shirt that she was wearing.

'Well. No man has the right to do what the estate agent did today, not under any circumstances. That goes without saying. No question. But, Denise, did you flirt with him at all? You know, lead him on. You and I are of a similar age, you know what middle-aged blokes are like if they think they are getting a bit of a come-on.'

Denise put her mug on the low table in front of the sofa and looked at me. 'No, Tom. I didn't lead him on.'

'Good. Sorry for asking.' I thought that Denise's idea of being friendly might be another man's idea of flirting, but I was not about to tell her so. In any respect, if her account was accurate, she had been terribly wronged.

'I just asked because if you do take this further and

report this to the police – and I think you should – you know what lawyers can do. They'll throw as much mud at your character as they can. It can get very messy, especially when it's one person's word against another.'

'I know, Tom. That's why I don't think I can be bothered to make a police issue of it. The publicity will be horrible and could hurt my career.'

'Well, I think you should consider it carefully for two reasons. The first is that this Fawkes bloke might make a habit of this, there might be others out there who have suffered the same thing as you, and there might be others in the future he will try it on with. Secondly, you're a pretty vocal advocate of the "Me Too" campaign, I think staying quiet will go against all your principles.'

The buzzer rang on the front door entry system. 'That'll be the Landers,' I said getting up. I had phoned Larry while Denise was in the bathroom and they had decided they should both come over. Larry would drive the Mercedes home and his wife Sue would take Denise back. 'Come on up.' I pressed the button unlocking the ground-floor door.

It was not Lander's heavy tread on the stairs, however. There was no wheeze and grumble from the visitor who reached the landing outside my flat door.

Alderney 1943

Georgi woke early. The sun of the previous day was now hidden behind a thick grey blanket of cloud that stretched as far as the eye could see, meeting the sea on the horizon. The ever-present wind carried rain and sea spray across the island that, in these conditions, felt more isolated than ever. He had been woken by the cries of pain from the other side of Hut 7.

It was the two men who the previous evening had lit the stove in the corner, even though it was summer. That day on work detail, they had found a stash of acorns in some gorse and that evening had set about crushing the nuts between pebbles, roasting them on top of the stove before making what they declared was 'coffee fit for a Czar'.

'Coffee fit for the rats more like,' Anton Yeltsin had shouted to the laughter of the ring of men watching the odious brew bubble in the tin can. Georgi knew Yeltsin had been on the island since 1941. There was little he had not seen before. He was a survivor. His words were always worth taking heed of. But the two coffee-makers were not deterred. They sipped the dark rancorous liquor in turns as they passed the tin can between them declaring their coffee was finer than anything from Brazil.

This morning the pair rolled on the floor of the hut crying out in agony and holding bellies so swollen they might have been about to give birth. If death did not get them, the guards would.

'Poor souls,' said Petr, who was now awake.

'Arseholes more like,' muttered Georgi. 'Wake up Alexei. Ration day. We need to get on, the queue is already forming.' He nodded in the direction of a ragged line of men outside the canteen door.

The rations had improved this summer. From one loaf of bread a week per man to two loaves. But you had to be near the front of the queue to ensure you received your quota. The stragglers often ended up with less, and complaining was never any good. The last man who had protested about short rations had had his head cracked open by the ladle of the French Negro chef, a giant of a man who seemed to delight in dishing out pain more than food.

The three companions – 'The Orel Boys' they had been nicknamed by their fellow prisoners – were among two hundred and eighty Russians in Hut 7. Hut 6 had a similar number of their countrymen. Hut 5 had the Ukranians, Hut 8 had Poles, Turks and French. Hut 9 had the misfits and dying. It had its own quarantine quarters and was not a place from which many emerged alive. Either you died on its wooden bunks or were transported to Lager Sylt, a camp said to be more brutal and hellish than even Helgoland, and under the control of the SS.

'Stick together, that way we'll survive,' Georgi had told the other two, and they ensured that whenever the prisoners were divided into firms for that week's work details, they were selected together, watching each other's backs.

Today their firm was sent to Crabby Bay, where a row of six small villas stood beside the beach. The once pretty homes were now derelict, ransacked of anything and everything inside, windows smashed, most of the wood ripped out for burning. The problem for the Germans was that the villas stood between the beach and the recently installed field gun. Anyone invading from the sea could use the villas as cover, so they had to be razed to the ground to give the battery clear sight lines.

The shovels and sledgehammers were handed to the prisoners, whose numbers were displayed on a wooden board around each scrawny neck. The number was recorded in a book alongside the type of tool handed out. Failure to return the tool resulted in execution. Returning a damaged tool was just another beating with a rubber hose.

One of the Germans pointed to the villas and swept his hand across the horizon to indicate they should be flattened, before joining his four colleagues, who were sitting behind a wall taking shelter from the worst of the rain that was driving in from the west.

'The far end,' said Georgi. 'We'll start there. OK?' One of the other prisoners nodded as the Orel Boys walked away from the rest of the firm.

'Why that one?' asked his brother Petr.

'Didn't you notice, when we were coming down the slope?'

'Notice what?'

'There's something in the garden, looks like an old greenhouse, and a vegetable patch. It will be out of sight of the guards.'

They picked their way through the villa, their wooden shoes crunching on broken glass, and out into the garden.

'Fancy a little dacha by the sea, boys? Lovely views, fresh air. Perfect holiday home. Going cheap from its German owner.' Georgi always tried to make the other two smile. 'And....' He held up a hand to halt their progress and then

pointed. 'Its own vineyard.'

'What are they?' cried Petr.

'Grapes, brother. You make wine with them – or eat them. Come on.'

In the remains of the greenhouse, the vine had run wild and a few small bunches of soft green fruits hung in clusters. The three had not tasted fruit, apart from the odd wild strawberry found in a grass verge, since they had arrived on the island. It was a feast for which their stomachs were not prepared, but if their incarceration had taught them one thing, it was to live for the moment if that moment contained even a shred of pleasure.

Jens Weiss watched the slow destruction of the villas with sadness. They reminded him of the holiday home by the Baltic Sea he had once been to with his parents and Hans. He wondered if he would see his parents again. As far as he knew they were still alive in Hanover, unlike his younger brother who had perished on the Eastern Front in Russia.

He was sheltered by a single-storey brick building that had once been the powder store for the granite quarry behind him. Now the explosives were kept under guard down at the harbour. The bread and sausage he had brought with him for lunch had at least lined his stomach after the previous night's excess of sour beer and cigarettes.

Two steaming cargo ships were disgorging their loads of cement, railway sleepers and tracks on to trucks on the new harbour wall the Germans had built. The work on the little fortress island was incessant, as gun batteries, bunkers, anti-tank walls, roads and even sections of railway were built in preparation for the day when Churchill tried to reclaim this place for the English. Weiss wondered if it was all worthwhile, but he would never say so out loud to any of his countrymen, although he suspected the more thoughtful among them harboured similar doubts about the Führer's 'masterplan'.

He had hoped the rain would relent, but it showed little sign of stopping. This afternoon he would just have to accept getting wet. He looked at his English map and ran a finger across the bedraggled paper to the site of his next visit: Sparrows Farm.

✠✠✠

6

Zoe White was framed in the open doorway, a bottle of red wine in her left hand. I was holding the door open but she was staring through me to the other side of my lounge, her smile frozen for a moment before it disappeared.

'Oh. I'm sorry. I didn't know you had company.'

She was looking directly at Denise, wearing my shirt and looking like part of the furniture, curled up as she was in the corner of the sofa, her bare feet peeking out from the creased leather. Our tea mugs were on the table side by side, The Stranglers were extolling the delights of 'Golden Brown' on the audio system.

'I didn't mean to intrude on your evening. I'd better go.' She sounded indignant, almost angry.

I slipped my fingers around the door just before she had yanked it closed and pulled it back open again. 'Zoe, please. Do come in. I wasn't expecting it to be you.'

'Clearly.'

'Not that you're not very welcome, of course.' I lowered my voice: 'It's a long story, I'll explain later.'

Denise smiled sweetly as Zoe returned slowly back over the threshold. I had never been sure what hackles were, but I sensed them rising all the same – from both sides of the room.

I did the introductions but left it at that. The course of events that had led to Denise being in my room in a state of undress were just too complicated to delve into right now. What I did do, to try to make Zoe feel more relaxed, was to tell Denise that she was the artist who had produced the paintings she had been admiring.

'You are clever, my dear.'

Zoe ignored the remark and turned to me. 'Tom. My Mother. Did you see her?'

I slapped a hand on my forehead and groaned. 'Damn, damn, damn. No, sorry Zoe, events sort of took over this afternoon. Denise here, well she ran into a spot of trouble and called me. I completely forgot to look in on your mother. Is she OK?'

'Well, I don't honestly know. In fact, I'm getting a bit concerned, which is why I knocked off work early after I didn't hear from you.'

'I'm so sorry.'

'She's not answered her phone since I spoke to her first thing this morning – not her mobile or the landline – and the house is in darkness apart from the security light in the gallery. I let myself in by the back door and had a quick look around upstairs, but nothing seemed to be wrong or out of place, even. It's not like her not to be in touch, especially as I'm meant to be looking after the gallery tomorrow. She normally fills me in on what's what there.'

Zoe realised she was still clutching the bottle of wine. 'This is for you.' She extended her arm. 'It's a little thank you for being kind to my mother over the break-in.'

The entry buzzer sounded again. This time I checked

that it was the Landers before opening the ground floor door.

Larry puffed and moaned his way into the room before collapsing on the sofa, his heavy posterior sinking into the leather having a see-saw effect and making Denise pop up at the other end. Sue shook her head: 'He's getting so unfit, Tom. One flight of stairs knackers the old boy.'

'Drink?'

'Better not, we're both driving. Tea will be fine, won't it Larry?' she said to her husband, who was eyeing the bottle in my hand.

'Well, Tom, if you're about to open that, one won't hurt.'

'Yes it will, Larry. Tom, ignore him. We'll stick to tea and then get this lady home. You can tell me all about it in the car, Denise.'

Fifteen minutes and one large pot of tea later, they were gone, Denise with my shirt, which she promised to launder and return by hand. I told her there was no need, I could collect it the next time I visited the Landers, but I had the feeling she was not to be deterred.

As the door closed, Zoe stood up. 'I'd better be off too, I suppose.'

'No need to rush, how about sampling that red you bought. Really, what you think you saw, you didn't, if you get my drift. There's a totally innocent explanation to Denise being here dressed as she was.'

Zoe looked unconvinced but agreed to one glass of wine. She was driving. She began to relax at last and then I rather spoilt it by asking about her mother again.

'Where might she have gone?'

'I don't know, really. She has a brother: Uncle Stanley. He lives in South Wales with his wife, but there's no reason for her to just disappear there without saying.'

'Is she seeing anyone?'

'What? A man?' Zoe sounded as if the idea was unthinkable.

'It's possible. She's an attractive lady. She's single isn't she? I've never heard her mention your father.'

'That's because we don't. I think he was a brief liaison at a pop festival somewhere back in the late Eighties, when she was thirty. She had me and brought me up on her own with a bit of help from Grandma. I don't think she's been bothered about men since.'

'Well, if she was seeing someone, she might be a bit embarrassed to tell you. It's a possibility isn't it?'

'I don't think so. Mum is,' Zoe started counting silently on her fingers. 'She's nearly sixty-three. Bit late in life to be looking for a bloke.'

'Ah, there speaks a member of the younger generation.'

'I'm not quite sure what to do, Tom. I can't exactly report her as a missing person can I? Not yet anyway. There's no suggestion that something's happened to her.' She put down her empty wine glass and stood up.

'Try not to worry, Zoe. I'm sure there's a mundane explanation to all this. Get a good night's sleep and I'll see you in the gallery tomorrow morning. Have a good check on her suitcases and clothes when you get there, see if anything is missing. What about her car?'

'I forgot to check that. I'm so stupid. I'll drive round now before I go home.'

'Do that. I shouldn't worry. Perhaps she was more upset by the break-in than she admitted and fancied a couple of days away. Give your uncle in Wales a ring too.'

'Thanks, Tom.' She squeezed my hand, gave me a peck on the cheek and left.

There was no point in letting the rest of Zoe's wine evaporate, so I poured myself a tumbler-full and switched on my laptop. Google soon found what I was looking for.

Roland Fawkes did not warrant a mention in Wikipedia. There were sixteen Fawkes listed, the most famous being Guy, but no Roland. He did, however, appear regularly further down the search engine's list in newspaper articles. Detective Chief Inspector Roland Fawkes featured in various crime reports. He had led an appeal for missing three-year-old twins in the Brighton area, who were eventually found safe and well with their father in France. He had received much praise for cracking a paedophile ring in Croydon and tracking down a gang who staged a daring bullion heist at Gatwick Airport. Awards and commendations had showered down on DCI Fawkes before he took his police pension at fifty-five.

Could this be the same man who had allegedly assaulted Denise in an empty house in Rye Harbour?

By the time my glass was empty, I had nothing but admiration for this Roland Fawkes, the husband of local Police and Crime Commissioner Gail Fawkes. Could there be another Roland Fawkes? Time for a second bottle.

I decided to check properties for sale in the village and quickly found the one in Tram Road that Denise had viewed and then left rather hurriedly. The estate agents, Webster & Kallas, were sole agents. I clicked on their website and at the bottom found a list of partners that included R. Fawkes. Perhaps our retired chief inspector had invested some of his police pension pot in the property business.

He cropped up again in various lists: a governor of a fee-paying boys school in Sussex, a board member of a dog sanctuary, and founder of the *The Ruffians,* a lunch-time club for businessmen who raised funds for charity. He was treasurer of a tennis and squash club, and was pictured finishing the Brighton half marathon, although his face was obscured inside a Mr Blobby outfit. This Roland Fawkes appeared to be a pillar of local society, a paragon of the community. Just the sort, I thought.

I went back to the website of Webster & Kallas and made an on-line booking to view the same property in Tram Road, under the name of Tamsin Kidd.

I looked at the second wine bottle. The remaining liquid appeared a little sad, lying at the bottom without its upper half. Best to put it out of its misery while I completed that crossword.

10 Down. Lean on thief to reveal all and make a splash (6-3).

Thief. Perhaps the shed theft did have something to do with Zoe's mother's apparent disappearance. I filled in the answer: *Skinny-dip.*

Alderney 1943

The German staff car pulled up by the gate in the lower field just off Platte Saline Road. It was no surprise to Edward Sparrow. He had heard it coming from a mile off and was half-expecting the visitation anyway. It was not one to which he was looking forward.

Sparrow was in the meadow checking his herd, to see if any of the other cattle were suffering from mastitis. He had isolated Lulu, but the disease was highly infectious. There was a time when he would have called in old man Slade – a butcher who doubled up as a part-time vet – to check her over. But the Slade family had left with the rest of Alderney's 1400 inhabitants when the island had been evacuated to mainland Britain in 1940, just ten days before Sparrow had watched the first of the Luftwaffe planes land at the airstrip beyond the top fields.

Now he preferred to do it himself. The Germans had a vet in town to attend their horses, and, if he asked the Civil Commandant, he would no doubt receive his help. Even Sparrow had to admit the occupiers had treated him and his daughter well. They were nothing like the uncivilised barbaric rabble he had heard about on the BBC broadcasts in the Town Hall at the outbreak of the War. But he was a proud man and he was buggered if he would ask the Germans for anything. There was, anyway, every chance they would suggest Lulu be slaughtered for her meat, and Sparrow was fiercely protective towards his herd of Alderney Cattle, which he assumed were the last of their breed in the world.

The driver opened the rear door of the battered grey staff car for the officer. Sparrow could see it was David Hanlon underneath the chauffeur's cap, pointing the way through the gate and across the field. Hanlon acted as a guide and part-time driver for the Germans, and Sparrow did not really blame him. He was Irish, a neutral in the Germans' eyes, and, like Sparrow, he had decided to try his luck on Alderney with the occupiers. He had left with the others, but only got as far as Guernsey, twenty miles away, where he stayed a month before returning with his herd of pigs to help keep the Germans in sausage meat.

Hanlon got back into the dry of the car, no doubt to have one of the cigarettes he traded off the Germans. The officer closed the gate behind him and spotted Sparrow among the cattle. He waved and smiled as if they might have been old friends. 'Herr Sparrow?'

Sparrow nodded. 'Best get to the house if you want to talk. This rain ain't goin' to ease off.'

The soldier fell into step alongside the farmer. 'What sort of cattle are these?'

'You speak English then? Alderney 'tis what they are. A special cow with a special milk, but when this lot's gone, that will probably be it.'

The squat stone farmhouse with its small windows was built to withstand the westerlies that hurried in from the sea, over the cliffs and across the exposed land. It had four rooms: a higgledy-piggledy large kitchen with a wooden table in the centre, warmed even in summer by a stove in the corner opposite the sink and water pump. The rough plastered walls were dotted here and there with child-like paintings of flowers, birds and a black and white dog, much like the one that dozed on a sack in front of the stove. Off the kitchen was a smaller room with a desk and sofa. Two other doors led to bedrooms.

Sitting at the table peeling potatoes was a girl. 'Put the kettle on, Giselle, be a love,' said Sparrow heaving off his heavy waxed jacket and levering off his boots on a metal fork just inside the door.

The German took the cue, took off his trench coat and cap and offered a hand to the farmer: 'Jens Weiss, Herr Sparrow. Apologies for interrupting your work.'

The German was dark-haired, unlike most of his countrymen, and slightly overweight, also unlike most of his countrymen. He wore metal-framed glasses and had ink-stained fingers. Sparrow had also noticed he walked with a slight limp.

Sparrow grunted, ignored the proffered handshake and beckoned the German to sit down. 'What do you want with us? I can't up the milk quota if that's what you want.' In truth, Sparrow knew exactly what the German was here for.

'Nothing like that. No, I am one of the planners, I think surveyor is the word in English, being instructed by Berlin on what to do for our work here in Alderney, and it seems we need a section of your land down by the road.'

Sparrow said nothing as he continued to wash his hands under the pump.

'We will need to bring your wall in by about two metres. Also, I believe the land on the other side of the road leading down towards Helgoland and the beach is yours too?'

'It is, but I rarely use it. The grass is lean and coarser down there, not much good for my dairy girls. I was thinking

about trying a potato crop on it.'

'Well don't, Herr Sparrow. Because we need that too, I'm afraid. We plan to plant something different down there: land mines. That's the next stage of the land-mine protection plan, so it will be out of bounds. It will be ringed with wire, so there will no mistaking it.'

'And what do I get for handing over another chunk of my land?'

Weiss smiled at the farmer. 'Our goodwill, Herr Sparrow. Our goodwill and continued custom for your splendid milk, for which we no doubt pay a fair price. And, I believe, we help provide you with winter fodder for the animals.'

That much was true. Sparrow grudgingly conceded he was able to live in harmony with the island's new landlords.

Giselle put the steaming teapot on the table with a jug of milk. Sparrow took one chipped mug from the dresser and filled it. The Germans may be his landlords, but that did not mean they could drink his tea.

'And how old are you, girl?'

'Twelve, sir.'

'Giselle, have you finished the potatoes?' She nodded. 'Then get off to the shed and skin the rabbit that's hanging.'

The girl pulled on a brown coat at least two sizes too big for her and ventured into the rain without saying a word.

'You live here, just the two of you?' said the German after the door had closed.

'Yes. She's my daughter. There's no crime in that.'

'No indeed. But is this the best place for a child? All the others have fled to England have they not? I don't know how safe this island will be if Churchill attempts to reclaim it.'

'We'll take our chances. Now, was there anything else?'

'No, Herr Sparrow.' Weiss knew his presence was not welcome. 'The work on the road will start tonight. The slaves will be working through the night on two twelve-hour shifts because we need this done before winter. I suggest you and your daughter stay well away. The minefield will be laid after that.'

He paused and looked at the farmer who was standing with his back to the room nursing his tea as he watched the rain beat against the window.

'Herr Sparrow, I am not here out of choice. We both take orders. I from my superiors, you from us. I'm afraid that is the way it is, and until our masters decide to end this war, I suggest we just get along. If you need anything for the farm, or any cigarettes, cognac, soaps, let me know. I will have a word with the Civil Commandant. You co-operate with us, we will co-operate with you.'

Sparrow turned and nodded. 'I know. Now, I have work to do.'

Weiss shrugged on his coat. 'I will be back in a few days to check the work is going to plan. Until then.' He clicked his heels and offered a hand to the farmer. It was again ignored.

✠✠✠

7

Zoe White was on her knees but not in prayer. She was scrubbing the outside wall of her mother's art gallery. It seemed a little late in the year for spring cleaning but as I got closer I realised it was not grime she was trying to remove from the white-painted stone.

When she heard my footsteps on the gravel path she turned around, brushed her matted red hair away from her perspiring face and threw the scrubbing brush into a bucket, splashing pink water up the wall she had just been working on.

'I give up,' she said, her flushed face a mixture of anger and tears. She flopped back into the flower bed in the border by the wall, crushing the small blue flowers growing there.

Despite her efforts, the object of her toil was still there for all to see, disfiguring the front of the cottage.

NAZI SCUM

It was written in glow-red paint, similar to that used on the shed in the back garden. The ugly style of writing was like that seen in most graffiti. The foot-high letters started on the double window and spread across the wall, standing out starkly on the white-painted stonework.

'Jesus, who's done that?'

Zoe shook her head, picked up the brush again and started scrubbing frantically until I put a hand on her arm.

'That'll do no good. It will scrape off the glass with a blade of some kind, and we could paint over the stuff on the stonework. I'll deal with this later, let's go inside. By the way, is your mother back?' I'd almost forgotten the reason I was visiting Rother Gallery in the first place.

Zoe shook her head again. She seemed almost incapable of speech.

Inside the gallery, I was relieved to see that nothing appeared to have been damaged although there was a curiously unpleasant smell about the place. I checked the soles of both my shoes.

'Dog shit,' said Zoe. She had broken her silence, which I guessed was a good thing at least.

'You sit down, I'll make us some coffee, and then you can tell me all about it.'

Zoe was in the conservatory by the time I had returned. Even at this time of day, the place was getting uncomfortably hot as the morning sun rose above the pub next door and blazed through the glass roof. I opened the double doors that led on to the back garden and noticed a small polythene bag near the broken door of the shed.

'No word at all from your mother?'

Zoe shook her head for a third time. 'I arrived at eight as normal. Still no sign. I don't think she slept here.'

'If it's her day off, could she have gone out for the day, made an early start?'

'It's possible, but her car's still here, over the road. I think she's been away since yesterday, but why not tell anyone? It's just not like her.'

'Have you checked her clothes, suitcases?'

'The suitcase is still here but she has a weekend bag, I can't see that anywhere. And I think a few clothes are missing, plus her mobile phone, although the charger is here on the front desk.'

'Do you think this vandalism has anything to do with it?'

'Well, what else? It was probably there yesterday, but I didn't notice it when I called round in the evening, it was getting dark. It feels very dried on as if it's been there for a few hours. And before you ask, I've no idea why.'

'And the dog shit?'

'That was in a plastic bag pushed through the letterbox.' Zoe screwed up her nose and nodded towards the garden. 'I threw it out there. It almost made me throw up. What sick pig would do that? What's this got to do with Mum?'

She took a sip from her mug. The thought wheels were turning over. 'I'm calling the police.'

We finished our coffee. Zoe telephoned 101 while I rummaged in the shed for some white exterior paint to cover the graffiti. I had yet to ask her if she knew why the graffiti artist might have chosen the particular insult on the front wall. The police took Lizzy's details but it was doubtful they would class a sixty-two-year-old woman of seemingly healthy mind who had been absent for less than twenty-four hours as being in their 'high-risk' category of missing persons. 'We will take appropriate action and send someone to the gallery later', they had told Zoe.

There had been no messages on the gallery voicemail and no emails to Zoe in her in-box. The gallery email address contained nothing unusual, and the office computer history did not offer up any clues. There was the usual float of £100 in the petty cash tin.

'Uncle Stanley in Wales has heard nothing from her since she visited him in June. He suggested I try Emma, she's an artist friend in London, but she'd heard nothing either. This is totally out of character for Mum.'

'Have you any idea why anyone would spray "Nazi Scum" on the wall?'

'I've been wondering about that, of course I have, and no, I haven't.'

'I'll ask at the Nelson if they have a CCTV camera. It might have picked something up. Or they might have heard something. Other than that, I don't know what to suggest except to leave it to the police for the time being – and keep trying her mobile.'

Zoe intended to open the gallery as normal. She wanted to stay there anyway in case her mother rang, or returned. I painted over the graffiti as best I could, scraped the paint off the windows with an old razor blade I had found in the shed and promised to look in later.

The landlady at the pub said the only security cameras they had were inside the pub, not outside. She had heard nothing last night but would ask her locals when they came in. She sounded concerned and took my number.

This week's *South Coast Gazette* had just arrived in the village shop hot off the presses, as they say. My contribution about the shed thefts was tucked away at the foot of page three and was unrecognisable from the copy I had emailed to Larry Lander. Under the headline 'Suspected Arson attack on Caravan', Lander had merged my story with his own fanciful account of the caravan's two residents having to flee for their lives while their pet dog perished in the flames. How he had come to link the theft of a few mowers and strimmers to fire-setting someone's home was not easy to work out, but I had to concede, he was a resourceful and imaginative journalist.

I flicked through the rest of the paper while I was sitting on the wall by the 'For Sale' sign in Tram Road waiting for my Webster & Kallas appointment. I found what I was looking for: the weekly's crossword.

3 Down. Puzzle in game (6).

The answer was coming at the same time as Roland Fawkes. A white BMW X3 crunched up the curb beside the wall, W&K emblazoned on the driver's door. Out stepped an imposing man wearing a tie-less white shirt and grey suit trousers, the jacket hanging off a peg over the rear door. He was at least six inches taller than me, his swept back hair suspiciously dark. He shut his door, opened the one behind it, unhooking the jacket and picking up a slim attaché case from the back seat. He looked up and down the road, brushed back his hair with his free hand and headed for the front door, seemingly oblivious to the man in jeans sitting on the garden wall reading a newspaper.

'Mr Fawkes?'

He spun around and frowned. 'Yes.'

'I've got an appointment. To view the house.'

His mouth opened and closed in silence before he regained his composure. 'Sorry, I think there must be a mix-up. I'm due to give a young lady a viewing at this time.'

'Really? When I booked on-line, it said the three o'clock slot was free today.'

He checked his watch and then unzipped the case, pulling out a piece of paper. 'Yes, three o'clock. But I have a Ms Tamsin Kidd written down here for the viewing.'

'Well, that's computers for you isn't it, Mr Fawkes? You can't trust the things. A gremlin must have crept into the system because my name is Kidd, but it's Thomas, not Tamsin.'

He looked crestfallen, a shadow of the confident bundle of masculinity that had strode up the path a few moments earlier. 'Oh, right. You must be right, I s'pose. You don't know a Tamsin Kidd, then? Couldn't be a relative, or a coincidence?'

'No I don't. Just me. Plain old Tom Kidd. Shall we go in?'

Fawkes showed me around the property without enthusiasm or elaboration, answering my keen questioning with as few words as possible.

'When was the central heating installed?'

'Not sure, Mr Kidd.'

'Do you think there would be problems with getting planning permission for an extension at the back?'

'Probably not, Mr Kidd.'

'What rating does the Energy Performance Certificate give for the house?'

'The EPC will be in the details, Mr Kidd.'

'Do you know if there are plans to expand the holiday park across the way?'

'Not that I'm aware of, Mr Kidd.'

'Did you find Ms Rutter particularly attractive?'

The silence was deafening. We were standing in the master bedroom at the time, admiring the view towards the English Channel. I heard a weak cough and a shuffle of feet behind me before I turned.

'Well, Mr Fawkes, did you? I'd say she's a pretty striking woman wouldn't you? But I guess you know all about striking women.'

His slack jaw closed and his eyes hardened. The knuckles of his left hand tighten as he gripped his case. 'I do not know what you are talking about.' He said the words slowly and deliberately.

'I think you do. You see, Denise Rutter is a friend of mine. She phoned me yesterday afternoon in some distress. Know anything about that?'

The retired policeman of considerable standing in the local community breathed deeply through his nose and pushed his shoulders back. Perhaps it was a pose they were taught at the police training academy to make themselves look more imposing. It certainly worked on me. I suddenly felt rather vulnerable and powerless, alone in this room with Roland Fawkes and not sure what I had intended to do next after confronting him with what I knew.

He took a step forward and spoke with quiet menace. 'Just what are you insinuating, Mr Kidd?'

'Denise says you laid hands on her, tried to take advantage of her in here. Do you make a habit of that sort of thing, Mr Fawkes?' The words came out too quickly and in a slightly higher, squeakier voice than I would have liked. I swallowed hard. 'She was hurt and her clothes damaged. You can't get away with that sort of thing these days, you know.' I was shocked by my own bravado.

'What sort of thing? I think you'd better get your facts straight before making what are very serious accusations, Mr Kidd. The woman in question – trollop more like – came on to me, made a very improper suggestion, and when I made it clear I wasn't interested, she feigned indignation, said I misinterpreted her intentions and tried to act like the wounded party. She tried to flounce out but tripped over the back step, that's when she hurt herself and damaged her clothing.'

He was very convincing. I had to give the former detective chief inspector that, and perhaps, just perhaps, he was telling the truth. After all, I did not know Denise Rutter that well. I felt I had run out of ammunition.

'So you regarded her as a trollop? I'm sure Webster & Kallas wouldn't like you describing a client like that.'

'Trollop? When did I say that, Mr Kidd? You must be mistaken. I don't think anyone else in this room heard me say that.' He looked around the bedroom. 'No, no witnesses to me saying that. Now, I think this viewing is over. After you.' He stood back and beckoned towards the open door and stairs.

As we approached the front gate, Roland Fawkes leaned forward so that his lips were only a few inches from my ear. I could smell mint on his breath. 'Watch your step, Mr Kidd. There's a good fellow.'

The meeting with Fawkes had left me thirsty. Fear

always had that effect. I had checked in on the gallery. My handiwork with the paint brush, contrary to my expectations, looked quite good and it was impossible to see the message that had been daubed on the cottage wall. There had still been no word from Lizzy White nor from the police. Zoe said she was going to stay there the night in case her mother called or returned.

The Admiral Nelson was my next port of call, ostensibly to find out if the landlady – I knew her only as Babs – had heard anything about the graffiti artists, but principally to get that drink I needed. She too had drawn a blank so I took my pint outside to enjoy the late afternoon sun.

The L-shaped jetty jutting out into the shallows of the River Rother was busy with tourists and local children, dangling lines into the water to catch crabs. The little gift shop at the back of the new lifeboat station was busy, and a queue formed at the boathouse entrance to view *Hello Herbie II*, the name the volunteer crew had given to their Atlantic 85 class off-shore boat.

Three cyclists buzzed in and out of the tourists on the slipway, the same trio I had seen before. The one who had been cheeky about my age, George Clunes, was there. I also recognised Alex, the mechanic from the nearby tyre and exhaust centre. Zoe had said the third was George's brother, Peter. They slewed around outside the Bosun's Bite before braking hard, sending a cloud of dust over the outside tables and leaving black tyre marks on the concrete slipway. They then accelerated through startled walkers and barking dogs towards the coastal path, doing wheelies as they went.

By the time I had finished my first pint, I was convinced Roland Fawkes had been trying to bluff his way out of a potentially very damaging situation this afternoon. By the time the second had disappeared, I was having doubts. Was Denise Rutter the predator and not the prey? She could be flirtatious, that could not be denied. She did have a well-publicised and colourful past. That would all be dragged up if she did take the matter to the police.

No, she could not have been acting when she wept on my shoulder in her car yesterday, her confidence and her stiletto broken. I wanted to believe her; I did believe her. But what she would do about it, I had no idea.

The food in the Nelson was good but I had a yearning for a curry. The Grenadiers was the place for that. As I walked back past the Rother Gallery, I wondered what Zoe was going to do this evening, alone in her mother's home. The gallery was shut, but a single window was open upstairs. She was so different from Denise in many ways yet both were women in need of support right now. The problem was, I didn't feel I was the man to provide it.

I rang Larry Lander and told him about my confrontation with Fawkes that afternoon, explained how the retired policeman had a very different version of events, painting Denise as the would-be seducer.

'She seems quite calm about it all today, Billy lad. Took herself off with Sue for some retail therapy I think they call it. God knows what state my credit card will be in by the end of the month.'

'What she says happened is a serious offence, Larry.

It could be hugely damaging for Fawkes, not to mention his wife. They're both bastions of the community.'

'It would probably turn into a long, messy business if she took it to the police, but the bastard shouldn't get away with it. There will almost certainly be other women he's tried it on with.'

'You should have seen the look of disappointment on his face this afternoon when he realised I was a Tom not a Tamsin.'

Lander laughed and then stopped himself. 'I shouldn't laugh. It's too serious for that. Sue thinks she should complain to the estate agents rather than involve the police, that way she could make life very uncomfortable for Fawkes without making it a legal matter.'

I had reached the Grenadiers. 'Well, that's her decision, but you can be sure Fawkes would scrap like a cornered tiger whatever she decides to do. I get the impression he's one of those men who has a sense of entitlement. Got to go Larry, dinner calls.'

The Grenadiers was busy. The late stragglers among the tourists were still around while the locals were beginning to arrive. Roger, the landlord, was thumbing through his boxes of LPs preparing his play-list for 'Vinyl Nite'. The pub did not have the chic kerbside appeal of the Nelson but it was what my old journalistic colleagues would have called 'a good boozer'.

Locals tended to populate the stools at the bar, with its range of fizzy European lagers and real ale pumps. They left the dining area in the extension to visitors and families. I found a corner by the wood burner – thankfully unlit – underneath the horse brasses and shelf of Toby jugs. It was quiet – or it would be until Roger revved up his turntables. If I was a betting man, something by Queen would be his opening track. Always a good ice-breaker.

My Chicken Madras arrived with a mountain of rice. 'Can I get you a drink, Tom?'

'Thanks Sinead, I'd better have a pint of lemonade to start, please. What's Roger got planned for this evening?' I looked at her husband, who was holding a black disc up to the light and carefully wiping it with a microfibre cloth.

'I think he fancies the 80s tonight: Madonna, Police, Soft Cell, Human League, Dire Straits: all that sort of stuff he loves. Takes him back to his single days, daft so-and-so.' As if on cue, The Buggles began to tell us that video had killed the radio star, and Sinead raised her eyes to the heavens and smiled. 'See what I mean. I'll be back in a mo with your pint.'

While I was eating, I finished the crossword in the local paper. *3 Down. Puzzle in game (6).* The answer was a simple anagram. *Enigma.*

The disappearance of Lizzy White and the very personal attack on her property was certainly that. She appeared to be the most inoffensive of women, a well-liked member of the community at Rye Harbour, where she had lived all her life.

The crowd at the bar was warming to Roger's play-list, especially when he slipped on a medley of Tina Turner hits. There were, however, two men at the end of the bar who seemed deaf to the music. They were studying a sheet of paper, their backs to the disco area. They were

Michael Monday and Steve Kain. I decided it was time for a chat. On a circuitous route back from the gents, I stood behind them, ostensibly to order a drink.

While Sinead pulled me a beer, I took my opportunity to interrupt their conversation. 'Steve Kain, isn't it?'

The burly fisherman looked up surprised. The scratches on his cheek caused by Dawn Speed had already started to merge with his ruddy complexion. 'Who wants to know?'

'Tom Kidd. I've recently moved here.' I offered my hand and he shook it with an iron grip. 'I'm writing a book about the *Mary Stanford* lifeboat disaster, and a friend told me you were one of the current lifeboat crew.'

'Yes. We both are. In fact, we're just checking next month's rota. A few of the volunteers are on holiday and we're making sure we have enough cover.'

'Mr Monday too? I didn't realise. I think what you do is fantastic. I don't think I could do it.'

I sensed the two men relaxing as I gently massaged their egos. 'It's a selfless thing to do as volunteers, and you must all be very aware of the legacy of the *Mary Stanford*. Can I get you both refills?'

Their glasses replenished, Monday and Kain were happy to talk about their work on the boat. They were currently not on call, but showed me the pagers they always carried. Most of their work was close to shore and involved going to the aid of part-time sailors, dogs in difficulty and holiday-makers, although that work had eased up since Camber Sands now had its own summer lifeguard team in the wake of several recent tragedies.

The *Mary Stanford* disaster, said Kain, remained like a

scar on village life. Descendants of those who perished in 1928 still lived locally and a few were part of the current lifeboat team, which now included women. There were husbands and wives, and brothers and sisters on the rota but they were rarely on call at the same time these days so that, if the worst did happen, one family did not lose several members, as had occured in the past.

Monday had ordered another round of drinks. I was beginning to lose count, but six pints was usually my limit, and I felt I was getting dangerously close to that. It was time to tread on more personal matters.

'Was that a boating accident?' I indicated to the marks of Kain's face. He ran a finger over his cheek. 'No. Just some mad woman. You know what they're like.'

'Too bloody right,' I said, grinning. My new companions laughed. We were now brothers-in-arms as Dire Straits hit the turntable.

'Dawn Speed,' said Monday nodding at Kain. 'Steve here should've known better. She's the one, too, you should be talking to if you are still interested in the shed break-ins.'

'Really. Has your neighbourhood watch group found out something?'

He shook his head. 'Nothing concrete, but you can be sure she's got a mucky finger in it somewhere along the way. Her family have never earned an honest pound in their lives, from what I hear.'

'But her partner – Fin McEvoy – he seems a decent sort.'

'He is, daft sod,' said Kain. 'Don't know why he got hitched up with her in the first place, but it takes all sorts.

Not much left of their place now, though. Shame about the dog, too.'

'I heard about that.' I let the conversation lull, hoping one of the other two would embellish the tale, but they stared into their pints while Sting told me to not stand too close.

'One for the road?' I held up my empty glass hoping they would say no. 'My round,' said Kain. 'Sinead, when you're free. Three more Moonrakers.'

After Sinead had put the three full pint glasses on the brass beer tray, I ventured one more line of enquiry.

'Have you heard about the vandalism at the art gallery?' Both men looked at me blankly. I told them about the graffiti, but decided to omit the unpleasant detail of the special delivery pushed through the letter box.

Kain shrugged. 'Don't sound nice, didn't know about that. Bloody kids, I expect.'

'Yup,' said Monday.

Alderney 1943

'Looks like we're off to a wedding party,' Petr muttered under his breath. Georgi smiled as the queue shuffled forward to where the French Negro cook was using his ladle to serve out half-a-litre of gruel into the cans the prisoners carried on string around their waists. The warm slop usually contained a few shreds of spinach and some cubes of swede or potato. If they were lucky, they might find a piece of gristle or bone at the bottom of the liquid. But no-one complained.

The work detail for the Orel Boys' firm of thirty prisoners had been delayed. They were told to have some lunch instead while other firms left the camp. The guard had said that they would be leaving later, to work through the night on the road that curved up the hill towards Fort Tourgis.

'What's a wedding party?' asked the newcomer, who had taken a seat opposite the boys in the canteen. He looked frightened and young. He also had the healthy look only newcomers had. That would not last.

The three chuckled. 'You tell him,' Georgi said to his brother.

'Well, it's not cake and dancing and lovely bridesmaids,' said Petr. 'Sorry to disappoint.'

'Don't tease the boy,' said Alexei.

'A Wedding Party is what we call an important job. The Germans will make lots of preparations for it, just like for a wedding party. They'll have plans, bring in lots of gravel

and cement, perhaps even new tools. There might even be a steam road-roller.'

'Oh, I see.' The boy sounded disappointed.

'What's your name, boy. Where's home?' asked Georgi.

'Ivan. I'm from Sochi.'

'How old are you?'

'Fourteen.'

'A word of advice, Ivan: don't think about home, don't think about escaping, eat whatever you can, whenever you can, except the rats,' said Georgi.

'Yes, don't eat the rats, just catch them. A rat's tail will get you one cigarette off a guard, a live rat will get you a packet,' said Petr.

'But I don't smoke.'

'No matter, you use cigs for trade. A packet will get you half-a-loaf of bread off another prisoner.'

Ivan tasted the watery liquid in his can.

'Yes, it's like piss,' said Georgi. 'Probably is piss, the Frenchie's piss, but never, ever, complain about it.'

Alexei decided to weigh in with his year of experience in Helgoland. 'Don't talk to the Stripes, don't damage your shovel or pick when we're at work, don't piss in the hut, and don't have a crap when Weird Herman's around.'

This last remark brought laughter from the rest of the men around the table, who, by now, were all listening.

'Weird Herman?'

'You'll find out soon enough, Ivan. He'll be one of our guards tonight. If you need a shit, have it in the ditch here.'

By the time they were halfway up the hill they were already soaked. Not by the rain. That had stopped, but by the sea mist that enveloped everything like a damp, grey blanket. They met the bedraggled firm whose twelve-hour shift had finished on the road back to the camp, and as the two groups passed each other, the picks, shovels and sledgehammers were handed over, each meticulously recorded in a small black book by a guard sitting on the wall.

'Weird Herman,' whispered Petr, tilting his head in the direction of another guard. A large brown dog with a malevolent look in its eyes squatted at his feet.

They reached the site. Sure enough, it was a 'Wedding Party'. A pile of wooden posts was stacked beside coils of fence wire. There were mounds of sand and gravel, and bags of cement covered in black tarpaulin. Behind a wall that divided the track from a meadow was a line of string neatly stretched between pegs in the ground running parallel to the track. One of the guards told them to erect a fence along the route of the string, then to dismantle the wall and break it up into small hardcore to form the base of the new road, which would then be covered in cement.

'Work steadily until it gets dark,' Petr told Ivan. 'Then we can ease up a little, but never stop unless you want the guards to get out their rubber hoses.'

'But what if I need a shit?' pleaded Ivan, who was sure he felt his bowels moving.

'Don't,' said Petr. 'Or do it in your trousers.'

Ivan didn't know if he was joking.

The work was tedious and hard, particularly for frail bodies deprived of nourishment. The Orel Boys let Ivan join their little gang. Brothers Georgi and Petr swung the sledgehammers to break large stones, and the other two used their shovels to spread the hardcore behind them. In the field above them, in the moonlight they saw a man and a dog ushering cattle towards a low building, their swollen udders banging between their back legs as they walked. It had been more than a year since the three boys had tasted milk.

'What's your favourite meal?' asked Georgi to no-one in particular.

'Pancakes, with my mother's apple jam,' said Ivan.

'Sausage and fried potato with an egg on top,' said Alexei. 'What about you Petr?'

'Grandma's chicken broth with those dumplings in, and to finish…'

Petr's words were halted by a blow from a short rubber cosh across the small of his back, then another to his neck as he arched up before he fell.

'Work, not words,' grunted the guard. 'Unless you want to go to Sylt, that is.'

Ivan went to help Petr, who was lying face down in the mud, a large angry swelling already beginning to appear at the base of his head, but Georgi shot him a warning look, shook his head and swung his sledgehammer on to the next stone.

✠✠✠

8

The electronic alarm felt like a tiny pneumatic drill at work on my ear drums. My desperate attempts to switch it off succeeded only in knocking over the lamp on the cupboard beside the bed, which in turn upended a glass of water on to my clothes, which were strewn on the floor. I finally muted the mobile phone, cursed silently and buried my head into the pillow again. I realised, however, that I had to get up. I couldn't let Zoe down again.

I squinted with one eye at the day outside. I had not drawn the curtains and the bedroom light was still on. So, I realised, was the television on a bracket on the wall opposite, an over-cheerful weatherman predicting strong winds along the south coast with rain rolling in later. I attempted to tell him where to stick his gale warnings, but my tongue appeared to be stuck to the roof of my mouth with a cement-like mixture of Chicken Madras, rice and pale ale.

The mirror in the bathroom confirmed my suspicions. I looked like the stuff that had been pushed through the letter box of the art gallery. I probably didn't smell too clever either. The toothbrush acted like a scouring brush on the inside of my mouth and the shower washed away the grunge of a heavy session in the Grenadiers with my two new best buddies, Michael Monday and Steve Kain. As an act of atonement, I turned the shower dial into the blue zone and stood under the freezing torrent for ten seconds.

A beery belch confirmed that I was not ready to face breakfast yet so I dressed hurriedly, stuffing the wet clothes of last night into the washing machine before I left the apartment, a bottle of mineral water in hand.

I had promised Zoe I would look in on the gallery. She had told me where to find the spare key and the code for the alarm. She had stayed overnight but had planned to leave early for her seven o'clock shift on the reception desk of the hotel in Rye. She would not be able to return to Rye Harbour until late afternoon, by which time she hoped to have heard something from her absentee mother.

When I arrived at the gallery, a stout figure was bending over looking through the letter box. If only he knew what had been through there recently. 'Hello, can I help? I'm afraid the gallery's closed today.'

He spun around and straightened up, although that did not greatly increase his height. It was nice to meet a man considerably shorter than me for a change. His rotund face was red and mapped with tiny broken blood vessels. A few long strands of hair, which presumably normally sat obediently across his bald patch, flapped mutinously in the wind. He wore denim jeans that clung on for dear life below a paunch only partially covered by a sweater.

'I don't know. Can you?' The voice was surprisingly deep and had a Welsh lilt, which made him sound like the actor Windsor Davies reprising his role of Battery Sergeant Major Williams in *It Ain't Half Hot Mum.* He looked me up and down as if I was Gunner Graham.

'Tom Kidd. I'm a friend of the owner, who's away at the moment. That's why the gallery isn't open today.'

'And where's Zoe?'

'Zoe's at work. In Rye. You know the family?'

'I am the family. And joint-owner of this venture. Stanley White.' He held out a chubby hand for me to shake.

I let us both in by the backdoor and offered to make coffee. Stanley White declined, saying he had been on the road from Swansea since four this morning and had drunk enough coffee en-route to keep Costa's shareholders happy for a year.

'Zoe didn't say you were coming down.'

'She didn't know. Doesn't know, in fact. I only decided late last night after she called me again to say there had been no word from Lizzy. I felt a bit useless sitting on my arse in Wales watching the cricket on television. I could tell Zoe was worried so I decided to come. Olivia's getting the train down tomorrow, she had to take her mother to hospital today, otherwise she'd have come with me.'

'Is Olivia your wife?'

'Yes. That's it. And before you ask, yes, we're known to our friends as Stan and Ollie. Bloody hilarious I'd call it. Not.'

'Have you any idea where Lizzy might have gone, and why she didn't tell anyone?'

'Not the foggiest, old son. Bit of a loner is my little sister. But I don't suppose she's come to any harm. She's not exactly a spring chicken any more, can't imagine any bloke abducting her to his love nest.'

I wasn't quite sure what to say to this so I let Stanley spout forth. He was on his feet, looking around the gallery walls at the artwork, hands behind his back.

'Can't see what the punters see in some of this stuff.' He squinted at the price tag on a seascape of storm clouds and a fishing trawler ploughing through the waves. 'Five hundred and fifty quid! Bloody hell! I wouldn't give you five hundred and fifty pence for that. People round here must be made of money or plain daft – or, more likely, both.'

He moved on to the next wall and huffed and puffed some more. 'Looks like someone sneezed on that one.' He laughed at his own joke. 'And wiped their arse with that one.' He laughed some more. 'Two hundred quid for a splodge of paint! What sort of sucker buys that?'

'That's Zoe's work,' I told him, without adding that I had bought two of them.

He looked again at the rich acrylic lines across the canvas. He took two steps forward so that his nose hovered six inches from the canvas, then three steps back to reconsider a picture entitled *Dawn Tide* tilting his head to one side and then the other. 'No, still can't see it. Probably just as well I have nothing to do with the gallery. Lizzy was always the arty one. Took after Mum and Dad.'

He looked past me at the pale watercolour hanging behind the desk. 'I see Mum's old favourite's still here. No-one daft enough to buy it, I expect.'

'You say you part-own the gallery?'

'When Mum died she left the house and business to

Lizzy and me equally. I was settled in Wales by then and I was happy for Lizzy to carry on living here, but I get half of any profits she makes from the gallery – which are barely enough to bother the taxman. She just about ticks over.'

'Did you know about the break-in?'

Stanley White said he didn't, so I took him into the back garden and showed him the large shed with its broken door and graffiti sprayed on the side.

'What's that mean: "Mind the GAP"?'

'We don't know, Mr White. Want to see inside? They didn't take much.'

The place was tidy again, the old tools and drawing equipment stacked on shelves and hooks at the far end alongside the tins. Stanley White edged his considerable frame down the central aisle and picked up a wooden box plane, inspecting its underbelly and gingerly feeling the protruding blade with a thumb.

'Still sharp. Dad always looked after his tools. He loved messing around down here. I don't know what he did all the time, but we hardly saw him as kids. He never played football or cricket with us like other dads, he didn't seem to get involved in school stuff even when we had homework, and I don't remember many holidays.'

'How old were you when he…?'

'Died? I was twenty-one, just finished at University in Bangor. Lizzy is three years younger than me. I don't know why she's kept all his old stuff. I told her it was of no use to me. I couldn't change a fuse in a plug. Olivia does that sort of thing around the house. I'm in the legal business, you know. A solicitor.'

I think he thought I would be impressed. 'That's nice,' I said.

He put the plane back on the shelf. 'It's sad really. Dad didn't have anyone to leave this stuff too. He and Mum kept themselves very much to themselves. There was only Mum, me, and Lizzy at the funeral, and a couple of old war veterans. Oddly, one of them was German. Dad never spoke about the War, never spoke about much really.'

He walked out of the shed and did not appear to notice the blue plastic bag containing dog shit festering in the grass beside the path. I decided not to tell him about the special delivery, it seemed unnecessarily unpleasant, but I made a mental note to clear it up when I next visited.

'Mr Kidd, if you could arrange for the shed door to be fixed, I'd be grateful. I'll pay, of course. There doesn't seem to be much other damage here.'

'There was some other graffiti sprayed on the front wall but we cleaned it off. It said "Nazi Scum."'

'Oh no.'

'What is it, Mr White? Do you think it has something to do with Lizzy's disappearance?'

He shook his head vigorously. 'Why do you say that? No, no. Not at all. I think you're seeing conspiracy theories where there aren't any. I'm sure there will be a simple explanation and she'll turn up over the weekend safe and sound. Look, I'd better try to ring Zoe. Oh, and by the way, call me Stanley, no need for this Mr White stuff.'

His assurances left me more concerned, not less.

I was sitting in the Bosun's Bite contemplating a rather flabby sausage sandwich when the phone rang. No name came up on the screen, just a number I did not recognise.

'Tom Kidd.'

'Mr Kidd. Gail Fawkes here. A little bird tells me you've met my husband.'

This could be awkward. Tread carefully. 'I did meet a Mr Fawkes yesterday, yes. Was that your husband? I didn't put two and two together.'

'Really, Mr Kidd? Well, of course, it is such a common surname, isn't it? And how is the house-hunting going? I didn't know you were looking to settle down around here.'

'I'm thinking about it. How's the crackdown on the garden shed thefts going?'

'Nice try, Mr Kidd, but let's stick to the topic in hand, shall we? My darling husband. Why is a local newspaper freelance interested in him?'

'Oh, our meeting had nothing to do with the *South Coast Gazette*. I was partly checking a house out for a friend who's thinking of moving here.'

'Is this friend female?'

'She is.'

'Go on, Mr Kidd. Don't stop there. What's Roland been up to?'

I could not keep the pretence up any longer. 'Well, if you must know, Mrs Fawkes, my friend feels that your husband made an unwelcome and an unwarranted approach when she was visiting a property. Now, she may have got it wrong, but I wanted to confront Mr Fawkes about it.'

'I doubt it.'

'Doubt what?'

'That your female friend got it wrong. That sounds pretty much like his *modus operandi.*' I heard a sigh on the line. 'A colleague of his at Webster & Kallas said a complaint had been made, and it's not the first time. Why do you think the randy bastard took his police retirement at the first opportunity? The complaints from young nubile WPCs were stacking up. He was diplomatically shoved towards retirement by the hierarchy before it became public knowledge.'

My sausage sandwich was congealing, but I had more than enough to digest.

'I had hoped that, with the approach of his sixtieth birthday, he might lose a bit of libido and keep his wandering hands to himself, but clearly not. The estate agents have had half-a-dozen complaints from female clients, but they're in an awkward position with him being a partner and with them very keen not to besmirch their good name.'

'Very awkward,' I agreed, not sure what else to say.

'Well, he's had enough second chances. If your friend wants to make it a police matter, tell her to do so. There'll probably be plenty of others coming out of the woodwork to back her up. You know how it is when these things go public – look at the Jimmy Savile business. I'm going to step down as Police and Crime Commissioner at the next election anyway, so it doesn't bother me. He deserves all that's coming to him. Thinks he's God's gift, but there ain't much there, I can tell you.'

The line went dead. I'd gone right off my sausage sandwich.

When I walked back past the art gallery, two police cars were parked outside and a uniformed constable stood at the gate, arms folded, looking bored. Blue and white tape flapped across the entrance. 'Police. Do not enter' it read.

'What's going on officer?'

'Do you live here, Sir?'

Typical of a copper to answer a question with another question. Where do they train them these days? 'No officer, but I'm keeping an eye on the place for a friend: the daughter of the owner, who has gone missing – the owner, not the daughter, that is. She's not gone missing.'

The penny dropped while I was gabbling and landed on the alarm bell. 'She's not been found … nothing's happened to her has it?'

'I wouldn't know, sir. CID are investigating a potential crime scene. You can't come past the tape on to the property, but I will let the chief know you're here. What name was it?'

I told him and he spoke into a small plastic grille clipped to his jacket. A metallic crackle came back and the officer looked up. 'If you'd like to wait sir, someone will be out to see you shortly.'

While I was waiting a text arrived on my phone. It was from Alice.

> 'Don't forget the airport run tonite Dad. Need to be at Gatwick N Terminal by 7.30. A xxxx

'Damn.' The police officer looked at me and raised an eyebrow. I hadn't meant to say it out loud. I'd forgotten I'd promised to run my daughter to the airport this evening. She was meeting her pal Beth and the two boys there for their Spanish holiday. I looked at my watch. Driving out of London on a Friday evening would not be fun. I needed to be making tracks soon.

Detective Sergeant Hilary Hopps appeared. 'We meet again, Mr Kidd.'

'This is very full-on for a shed theft. I'm very impressed at the thoroughness of the investigation.'

'Let's get in the car, shall we, and have a chat?' It was not an invitation with RSVP on the bottom. She held open the back door and went around the other side to get in.

'You can close your door, please.' I did as I was told but asked the first question: 'Is there any news of Lizzy White?'

'No, Mr Kidd. Tell me, how well do you know her?'

I explained we had been friends for a few weeks; that I also knew her daughter – and now her brother – and I was helping to keep an eye on the gallery as she was away.

'Well at the moment, the gallery is a crime scene investigation, so I'm afraid you will not be able to gain access to the premises until we say so.'

'Crime? What crime? Surely not simply the shed break-in? You know about the graffiti too, I suppose?'

'We do. It may be related to that, yes. A firearm has come into our possession that we have reason to believe may have come from here. That's as much as I can tell you at present, if …'

Detective Sergeant Hopps halted mid-sentence to look around at what was causing the shouting outside. The constable who had been standing at the front gate was struggling to restrain someone who was already half-way down the path to the front door of the cottage.

Hopps leapt out of the car as another plain clothes detective appeared from the side of the house. Both converged on the pair at the same time, all four tumbling in an undignified heap on the grass. It was only then that the visitor's identity was obvious. Stanley White.

Comb-over displaced again, knees muddied, he spluttered with indignation as he picked his black-rimmed glasses up off the ground and inspected them for damage: 'Get off me you fools, I'm the joint owner of the Rother Art Gallery, I have every right …'

'You have no right, sir, not at the moment,' said Hopps, who was brushing dead grass off her black trousers. 'If you don't get on the other side of that front wall right now, you will be arrested.'

'What for? I know my rights. I'm a solicitor you know.' Despite his protestations, Stanley was on the retreat towards the front gate where I stood, trying not to smile.

'Do you really want me to start listing potential offences? Obstructing the police in their line of duty, assaulting an officer, causing an affray. That'll do for starters. Now, be a good chap and stand there beside Mr Kidd.'

He looked up. 'You're back again?'

'Just passing when I saw the police cars. The police, they've got a gun. Say it came from here.'

Stanley looked incredulous. 'Gun!'

'Yes, sir. If you would sit in the car, we can have a little chat.'

After ten minutes, both the policeman and the solicitor emerged from the car, a state of truce if not *entente cordiale* seemingly existing. 'If you hear anything from your sister, please get in touch,' said Hopps, handing over a card.

'Not heading for the clink then, Stanley? It could have been another fine mess you've gotten into.' I could not resist it.

'Very funny. Not. I've put the young detective sergeant right on a few matters. She's fairly new to the job so she can be excused her over-zealousness, but I think she appreciated my perspective on matters.'

'Which is?'

'Well, for one thing, where am I going to sleep tonight? I was planning to stay at the cottage, but the police say it's out of bounds for the time being.'

'It's the middle of August, Stan, high season. All the guest houses and hotels will be full, unless you're lucky enough to get a cancellation somewhere. There's always the beach,' I said a little too unhelpfully.

'That's what I feared. And there's no room at Zoe's flat. She thinks she can get me into an attic room at the hotel where she works tomorrow evening when Olivia's due, but I'm stuck for tonight and I really don't fancy the back seat of my car.'

I could see where the conversation was going and had no way of stopping it. He looked at me. 'Oh, all right Stanley. I do have a comfy sofa, you can kip down there.

But for the one night only.'

'Thanks old man, I'll be no trouble. I'll even buy you dinner.'

'That would be nice, but I'm out – I've got to run my daughter to Gatwick. In fact, I should be on the road quite soon.'

We headed for my flat in Coastguards Square. It was a short walk but Stanley, carrying a small suitcase from his car, was soon puffing heavily. 'We should have driven,' he said.

'Your car's safe in the main car park, and anyway, parking is very restricted in the square. Permit holders only.'

I let him catch his breath before posing the next question that was sitting up and begging to be asked. 'What would Lizzy want with a gun about the place?'

'I've no idea. I didn't know one existed. I think the police must have got that wrong. They wouldn't tell me where they picked up the gun or how they linked it to the gallery.'

'Do you think Lizzy could have met someone?'

'If she has, she's not told me anything. Zoe doesn't think so. I asked her that same question. Like I said, as far as I know, Lizzy hasn't bothered with men since Zoe was born, and that's more than thirty years ago.'

We arrived at my flat and Stanley's red-face dropped as he looked up. 'Not stairs?'

'Yes, just one flight. C'mon, the exercise will be good for you.'

'It'll bloody kill me.'

South London's traffic on a late Friday afternoon was constipated as usual. No movement. It did not seem to bother, Alice, though. She was full of excited teenage anticipation as she checked her passport and printed flight details for the fifth time between Blackheath and Croydon.

The satnav had given up telling me to do U-turns where possible to take the M25 route. 'OK, go your own way. You're on your own now, loser,' the lady behind the electronic map said as I ignored instructions to take the first exit at the next roundabout. At least, I suspect that's what she would have said had I not muted her.

'Beth and the others are already there, Dad.' Alice looked at a message on her smart phone. 'They're asking how long I'll be.'

'Oh, let me see … if the twat in front learns to drive in the next twenty minutes or so, I'd say by seven.'

'Sure? Ok that's good.'

I crossed my fingers on the steering wheel hoping Alice did not notice and said a silent prayer to make all the traffic in south London disappear.

I had never discussed the subject of contraception with my daughter, except the more radical type when we had a puppy spayed when she was a young girl. I'd left that sort of thing to her mother. Now, seeing this young woman sitting in the passenger seat wearing jeans that had more designer holes than a golf course, I did start to understand her mother's misgivings about her first holiday abroad without either of us being there, and with three other similarly excited sixteen-year-olds.

'Alice, you will take care won't you? Especially if

you've had a couple of drinks. People might try to take advantage.'

'Dad! Don't spoil it for me with a lecture on the way to the airport. Anyway, who are these "people" who might take advantage. My friends?'

'Sorry.' I cursed quietly, partly at my own parental ineptitude, partly at the driver in front who had stopped as the traffic lights turned to amber instead of accelerating through the junction.

'Anyway, it's Mum who's more likely to get pregnant.'

The driver behind leaned on his horn. Looking at my daughter, mouth gaping, wrestling to compute what she had said, I had failed to notice we had a green light and the road ahead was now clear as far as the eye could see. We lurched forward just as amber appeared again.

'What did you say, Alice?' My knuckles were white as I gripped the wheel and contemplated the bombshell she had just dropped into conversation.

She giggled then looked at her phone, which had vibrated again. 'Aw, that's nice. A message from Auntie Fleur wishing me a happy holiday. And a nice selfie of her with Chris and little Rosie.' She held the phone up for me see the happy family. Fleur was my sister, living in Edinburgh with her wife, Christine, and their six-month-old daughter. I had not asked how it had happened, but it was Christine who had given birth. Now, however, I was more alarmed at the thought of my ex-wife doing something similar in her mid-forties.

'Yes, nice picture – now, what did you mean by saying Mum's likely to get pregnant?'

'Well, she's trying. Her and Angus Freud.' Alice pulled

a face and gave a mock shudder. 'Remember him? Jordan's Dad.' I couldn't, but then most of the other parents at Alice's school had passed me by. I did remember Jordan, though, who was in the same drama group as Alice and saw himself as the natural for any romantic lead going.

'You'd better explain.' We had at last thrown off the shackles of Croydon and were making good progress down the Brighton Road.

'Slow down, Dad, it's still a forty limit here,' she said as we sped past a speed camera. I looked in the mirror anxiously. No flash. 'Well, I think Mum's serious about this one and she's started going to an IVF clinic. I think it's quite exciting. I might have a little brother or sister.'

'She's mad. Sorry to talk about your mother like that, but she is. When she had you she vowed never to have children again. Now, at an age when most women are taking up pilates and pasta-making, she wants to be changing nappies again.'

'Dad, you are an old dinosaur. Loads of women have children in their forties these days, some in their fifties, even sixties.'

'I know, Alice, but your mother was never the maternal type when she was in her twenties. I can't imagine she's changed that much.'

'Well, she and Mr Freud seem pretty serious about it. She's always moaning about how much the IVF clinic is costing them. He more or less lives at home too, you know.'

I sighed. 'To be honest, I don't want to know Alice. You did say North Terminal didn't you?' We joined the queue off the M23 onto the Gatwick slip road.

I nursed a bottle of alcohol-free, taste-free, fizzy liquid – probably not the best lager in the world – in the airport bar watching the manic Friday evening race to the sun. Harassed parents with mountains of bags and bored offspring waiting for budget airlines to Spain; boisterous young men dressed as nuns and drag queens, parties of equally excited females in skimpy cocktail dresses and veils wearing L plates all bound for the stag and hen venues in Eastern European cities; coolly-dressed thirty-somethings with soft leather holdalls heading for the BA counter and Southern France or Northern Africa.

Storm Jasper, as predicted by the grinning weatherman on television this morning, was on its way from the west and 'Expect Delays' clicked up all down one side of the departures board as the mass of humanity snaked around the queue barriers shuffling forwards with their trolleys and getting ever more irritable.

The *Guardian* was open at the crossword page as normal: *10 Across. Go away and act the fool (4,2).* That seemed appropriate enough. Alice's three friends – Beth, her boyfriend Dan and his mate Max – had been waiting as promised when we arrived just about on time. They seemed nice kids. Much more mature, if memory serves me right, than I was at their age. I convinced myself she was going to have a great time as I waved them off through the doors to security.

Their flight to Santiago de Compostela in Northern Spain was boarding according to the departures board. Hopefully they would get out before Jasper arrived. I ordered another drink masquerading as beer and thought about what Alice had told me on the journey here: my ex trying to have a baby after all those years of telling me she did not want any more after our daughter had arrived. I wanted to feel disdainful but found I felt a little hurt, even envious. Her demand for a divorce two years ago had come as a shock at the time, but that phase soon passed. I realised we were both happier apart rather than trying to paper over the cracks in our relationship. So why did her having a child now with some other man bother me?

The departures board clicked again as the sign rolled over. Alice's flight had departed. I could go now, safe in the knowledge that her holiday had got off the ground. I filled in the remaining blank squares in the crossword: *Beat it* – and headed for the car park.

Zoe phoned while I was on the journey back to Rye Harbour. She had just finished work in the hotel. I recounted the story of Uncle Stanley and his brush with the law at the gallery, which lightened her mood. She had, she said, managed to free up an attic room at the hotel for the weekend. It was small, but it would have to do for Stanley and Olivia.

'Are there plenty of stairs up to the top floor or do you have a lift?'

'A lift, in that old place? You must be joking. It's a narrow winding staircase to the top rooms.'

'That'll please Stanley then.'

'Well, it'll be more comfortable than your couch.'

'Especially if Olivia's with him too.'

She laughed again but it was strained. 'Still no word,

from your mother, Zoe?'

'No. No text messages, no calls, no emails. Where in the world do you go these days where you can't make contact with people?'

'Parts of Scotland, the Arctic Circle, on a boat – I don't know, Zoe. There must be some places left on earth. What do you make of this notion of a gun being found at the gallery?'

The police had asked Zoe if she knew why a firearm might be found at her mother's house.

'No idea. Absolutely none. I've never known Mum shoot anything except the odd game of pool at the holiday village. I can't believe she'd keep one for security. She always felt very safe in Rye Harbour until the shed break-in.'

'Can you come over tomorrow? Hopefully the police will let us back in the house. We'll have a really good look through all your mother's things, check the computer, the diary, have another go at the police to step up the search.'

The Audi's headlights picked out the Grenadiers Arms and then the left turn into Coastguards Square. I pulled up directly outside the apartment front door.

'I finish at eleven in the morning, I'll be over straight after that,' she said.

'Good. I'd best go.'

The car's headlights were shining into the entrance hall and lit up the flight of stairs to my flat, the ground-floor door was swinging open in the wind, tapping against a small stone trough where the milkman left the bottles. I cut the engine. Something felt wrong. The light was on in the flat but the curtains had not been drawn. The neon light of television pictures flickered off the ceiling. I switched the car lights off and let my eyes adjust to the dark before I got out. Coastguards Square appeared to be as peaceful as ever, the two street lights illuminating the white terraced cottages on each side, the plane trees buffeting in the wind. Even the cats appeared to have gone to bed early.

I got out of the car and closed the door as quietly as possible, instantly regretting my decision to press the 'lock' button on the key, as the hazard lights flashed in acknowledgement of the command, announcing my presence. Still, nothing stirred except the trees.

The ground floor entrance door was not damaged. I closed it behind me and softly climbed the stairs. The door to my flat was also open. I felt my pulse pounding in my temple as adrenalin flooded into the veins as I stood on the threshold. I could hear the television news but nothing else from inside.

I pushed the door as far back as it would go with my right hand and looked in. Nothing had been disturbed, nothing broken. More to the point, no-one was there.

Not even Stanley White.

Alderney 1943

It was almost the end of August and the new road to Batterie Annes was making progress despite the heat wave of the past week that made work unpleasant and the stench from the slave camp even worse. Jens Weiss stood at the entrance to Sparrows Farm and followed the neat curve of the cement track up the hill through his field glasses with satisfaction. Anton List should have no complaints now. His bunkers, gun installations and observation towers could progress at a rapid rate.

The sweat ran down inside his cap and under the collar of his coarse uniform. He would have loved to have removed it and unbuttoned his shirt, but that was not the done thing outside the officers' quarters – or the brothel. His leather satchel was heavy, too, which did not make walking across the hill towards the farmhouse any easier. He could see the cattle huddled beside the byre looking for any scrap of shade they could find, but there was no sign of human life until he rounded the shed and saw the farmer inside, bare-chested, bending a strip of wire into a loop.

'Herr Sparrow, good afternoon.'

Edward Sparrow almost dropped what he was doing and looked up flustered. 'I didn't hear you coming.' The farmer put the wire under the bench and grabbed a rag to wipe the sweat from his forehead and armpits. He nodded towards the house. 'You'd better come in.'

Inside it was refreshingly cool and dark. 'I'll just get a shirt, sit down if you wish.' Sparrow indicated at the table and chairs, where the girl was sitting again, this time surrounded not by potato peelings, but pots of paint and a jam jar of murky water with a large sheet of paper weighed down with a pebble in each corner. The part-finished watercolour was of wild waves around a rocky outcrop, with multi-coloured sails of little boats further out to sea. Weiss thought he recognised it.

'Hello, again. Is that Telegraph Bay?'

Giselle was embarrassed. Father had told her not to talk to the Germans, but this German seemed nice enough.

'Yes, sir. Just over past the airfield. It's my favourite place.'

'I know where it is. I go there myself to draw. Are all these yours?' He swept a hand around the room at the bright pictures that hung on every wall. She nodded.

'They're very good.' He walked towards the wall by the stove to study them more intently. 'That's a great likeness of your dog,' he said looking down at the collie curled up on the sack. 'And that's St Anne's Church, isn't it? Who's that meant to be sitting on the wall, is it you? It's a very pretty dress.'

'No, sir. That's my sister, Martine. At least, how I remember her.'

'Giselle.' Her father walked back into the room wearing a clean collarless white shirt. His tone was disapproving. 'Clear your things away and put the kettle on.'

'You English love your tea, even on the hottest of days. If I may, Herr Sparrow, a mug of water would be fine.'

'I'm not English, I'm an islander.' Sparrow picked a mug off the draining board and filled it from the pump. He handed it to the German. 'Tea for one, then Giselle.'

'I've come to check the work and to inform you that the

mine-laying starts on Monday. I hope it has not caused too much disruption for you.' Weiss sipped the surprisingly cool water and relaxed in a chair. 'May I take my jacket off, it is so hot?'

Sparrow nodded. 'I don't know how many winters that wire fence you've had put up to replace my wall will survive. If my herd gets out, I don't suppose your lot will be helping me to find them again … that's if they haven't been blown to kingdom come by one of your mines.'

'If there are problems, report to the Civil Commandant. I'm sure he will take action.'

Giselle placed a steaming mug in front of her father and offered to top up Weiss' mug from an earthenware pitcher. He held it out and she filled it with a ruby, sweet smelling liquid. 'It's my own blackberry squash,' she said.

'Thank you.' He sipped it. 'It's wonderful. You clever girl.'

Giselle beamed and hurried away.

'May I ask you, Herr Sparrow. Why do you live here with your daughter? Why didn't you leave with the rest?'

'The rest just ran away'. The farmer stared into his mug. His words sounded contemptuous. 'My father and his father afore 'im spent their lives building up this Alderney herd, I was buggered if I was going to desert them for your lot to slaughter. I thought I'd take my chances.'

'And your daughter? Were you not worried about her? This doesn't seem the best place for a girl to grow up in these circumstances.'

'No, that's what my wife thought too. Fat lot of good it did her.' The farmer's voice started to break. He stood up and walked over to the teapot to refill his mug. With his back to Weiss, he rubbed his eyes and added quietly; 'I don't intend

to let Giselle go anywhere again without me.'

Weiss paused. He wanted to ask more, but it was not his place to do so. He was not good at this sort of thing so he opted to change the subject and reached for his satchel.

'Herr Sparrow, if you will permit me?'

Sparrow turned. The German was holding out a plain bottle containing a golden liquid.

'It's cognac. There's no label on it, but I'm assured it is the finest. It was found in the cellar of a chateau in St Malo. Major Zuske had a case delivered last week, he won't miss one. It's for the trouble you have been put to.'

Weiss put the bottle on the table and delved into his satchel again, this time to bring out a pale blue headband with a silver thread running through it. 'And I wondered if your daughter might like this.'

'Oh, it's lovely.' Giselle looked up from the floor where she had been sitting stroking the collie. 'Please father. May I?'

'Where did you get that?'

'I found it, Herr Sparrow. In one of the drawers in my bedroom in our quarters in Drewitt's House. It seemed as if whoever lived there left in a hurry, because there was so much left. It's been in a box since I moved in. I thought your daughter might like it.'

Giselle looked at her father. He nodded and she took it. 'Thank you, sir,' she said in the quietest of voices.

'No-one took much with them, the day they left,' said Sparrow, twisting the cork top off the bottle on the table and smelling its contents appreciatively. He poured himself a measure and offered the bottle to Weiss, who put his hand over his mug and shook his head.

'There was panic, you see, although Judge French did his

best to make it orderly. He organised the evacuation with the authorities on the mainland when we knew you were coming.'

'Summer of 1940?' asked Weiss.

'June. June 23rd to be precise. Everybody was told to be ready with one suitcase and their valuables. That's all. No pets, no animals. People took their dogs to Butcher Slade's to be slaughtered, they didn't want to leave them. Some let their stock go free, others slaughtered them too. You see, they didn't want the Germans getting them.'

Weiss offered his mug across the table. 'I will have a small measure, if you please.' Sparrow poured the cognac into the mug, and topped up his own.

'When the church bells rang out, everyone, about 1,400 of them, went down to the harbour. Those who couldn't walk, the old ones, were carried. About six large steamers were there to take them, plus a host of little boats. Thank God it was a sunny, calm day. The sea was clear, I think they all made it to the mainland, or Guernsey and Jersey.'

'But not you?'

Sparrow sipped from the mug. 'No. Buggered if I were goin'. They tried to make me, mind. Almost ordered me, but they knew I was within my rights. Some of the farmers came back a few days later to collect their stock, said they were going to set up on Guernsey. Tried to talk me into joining them and I nearly did because that's where Marie and the girls were.'

'Marie?'

'My wife, with our eldest Martine and Giselle. I said I'd think about it if I could get my herd across too. There was no room in the boats that day, so they said they'd be back. The

next day your planes bombed St Peter Port.'

Sparrow topped up his mug again. 'Marie and Martine were in the wrong place at the wrong time. They were buying vegetables at the quay market when it happened.'

'Giselle?'

Sparrow looked at his daughter. 'God looked after her, I guess you would say if you were a religious man, which I don't think I am anymore. They hadn't taken her to the market, she had the chicken pox and was in bed at their guest house when the bombs fell on the harbour. Two days later, they brought Giselle back over on the lifeboat thinking I'd change my mind and leave, but instead we decided to stay, didn't we, Giselle?'

Giselle left the dog and stood by her father's side. Neither of them shed a tear as they hugged. They had probably cried too often, thought Weiss.

'I'm sorry, Herr Sparrow.'

'That's war, isn't it? Heartless, pointless. The likes of you and me, we just try to get through it. Giselle here gives me the reason to carry on, though. We'll see it through.'

✠✠✠

9

The overweight man had trouble getting out of the taxi. His right arm was in a sling and he grimaced as he tried to lever himself out of the back seat using his left. Eventually, the driver got off his backside and came around the car to help. I watched this looking down from my front room window.

When I recognised the hobbling figure, a pang of guilt struck home. It was Stanley White, looking about twenty years older as he struggled up the path to the entrance of my flat holding on to the arm of the taxi driver.

By the time I was downstairs, Stanley was sitting on the step and the taxi driver had his finger firmly stuck on the bell push.

'Forget it mate, I'm here. No point in ringing. Stanley, what the hell's happened to you?'

'He can tell you all that later, squire. I've got another pick-up to make. Thirty quid please.' The driver held out his hand.

'Please pay him,' croaked a voice from the doorstep.

'OK. Wait, my wallet's upstairs. Do you take credit cards?'

He did, and, transaction done, I helped Stanley to his feet. 'You've only got a shirt on Stanley, where's your jacket? You must be cold. Where have you been all night?

I thought you'd gone missing too.'

'Let's get in first, can we?'

Slowly and with much pantomime groaning, Stanley made it to the top of the stairs. His fingers were grazed, the elbow of his shirt bloody and the right knee of his trousers torn, revealing more grazed skin.

'You have been in the wars, Stanley. Sit there, I'll make some strong coffee. I'd assumed you'd found yourself a hotel room and buggered off without letting me know.'

Only after the first mug of coffee did Stanley feel like telling his story.

'I've spent the whole night in blasted A and E at some hospital in Hastings. God, you should have seen the dregs they get in there on a Friday night: druggies, drunkards. Somebody had a fit on the floor in front of me. It was disgusting. Two women had a fight and the police had to be called. I had to sit there for four hours before they saw to me.' He half held up his right arm in the sling and patted his ribs. 'They say it's only bruising but I wouldn't be surprised if they're broken. Young doctor didn't look old enough to be out of school – African too, difficult to understand a word she said.'

'I'm sure they looked after you very well,' I said reprovingly. 'Now, start from the beginning.'

Stanley had made himself at home the previous evening as I had said he should. He had an early supper in the Grenadiers and got back to the flat by eight. He was stretched out on the sofa watching some cookery programme when the entry buzzer had rung just after nine. The voice at the other end said he had a delivery for Mr Kidd. When Stanley pressed the entry button, the delivery man said company rules said he could not enter properties. He had to hand it over on the door step.

'So I went down dressed like this – my jacket's over there on the chair.' He pointed to his rain jacket and sweater hanging on the back of a straight chair by the table. 'The delivery bloke had a crash helmet on and as soon as I'd opened the door he punched me in the ribs. I went down and he kicked me. He bent over, said something, then left on a motorbike. There was no delivery.'

'Obviously not. What did he say?'

'It was difficult to make out, you see, What with him wearing a helmet and all. Something like "do your house-hunting elsewhere, Mr Kidd". Does that make sense?'

'It might do. So how did you end up at the Conquest Hospital?'

'One of your neighbours heard me cry out, nice lady from opposite. She was looking for her cat. Anyway, she came over and said if I could get to her car, she'd run me to the hospital. She said it would take forever for an ambulance to get out to a non-emergency case. Non-emergency! I ask you! What's a fractured skull if it's not an emergency?'

'Have you got a fractured skull?'

'Well, no. But I might have. Hit my head on the ground with a real crack, I did. Seeing stars, I was. They gave me an x-ray though and said nothing was broken, just bruising.'

'And the arm?'

'They think I sprained my wrist when I put my hand out to break my fall. But it's bloody painful I can tell you.

The pain killers they gave me are beginning to wear off, too. Have you got any?'

I didn't. I said I would go to the shop immediately. 'You'd better get your neighbour some flowers too, as a thank you for taking me to hospital, you understand? She couldn't stay, of course. I didn't expect her too, but I did expect them to run me back in an ambulance. That, it seems, is even too much bother for the National Health Service these days, so I had to pay for the bloody taxi back.'

'I paid for it Stanley. Yes, I'll get some flowers as well as painkillers. Anything else?'

'Wouldn't mind a *Daily Mail*, if they have one.'

By the time I'd returned from the village shop, I had thought through the events of the previous night and was convinced the attack was to do with Roland Fawkes, hence the message about house-hunting. It was clearly not Fawkes himself under the crash helmet or he would have realised it was not me opening the front door. I assumed it was a friend doing his dirty work – quite possibly an old colleague from the police force. Word was getting around about Fawkes' wandering hands and his wife may well have confronted him with what I had told her about his lunge at Denise Rutter. He was probably trying to put the frighteners on me, but I suspected that he was the frightened one right now.

Stanley White was under the impression he was the victim of a simple mugging by someone who knew my name from the nameplate on the outside doorbell. I did not disabuse him of the theory, or point out that for a mugger, the assailant had been remarkably happy to scarper without going through his pockets.

Larry Lander telephoned while I was boiling eggs and making white toast soldiers for Stanley, who was sitting feet up on the sofa with the *Mail* spread across his lap and a mug of coffee in his left hand.

'Larry, I've got strict instructions that these eggs have to boil for four minutes and thirty seconds, so don't distract me for too long.'

'Sorry, didn't know you had company, old boy. Denise will be disappointed.' A chuckle came down the line.

'It's male company Larry – and it's a long story. What is it?'

'The police have made progress with "shed-gate." A lot of stolen items have been picked up being sold at a boot-fair at Manston Airport, and some were identified as being from Rye Harbour. The police won't officially confirm this for fear of being accused of being judgemental about certain members of our society, but I know for a fact that the goods have been traced back to some travellers in the Camber area.'

'The thefts do seem to have stopped in this village, that's for sure.'

'Yes, I think they know they've been sussed out, so they'll lie low for a while, and that'll suit the police because it will get the Commissioner off their backs.'

I checked the timer. 'Only ninety seconds left, Larry. What about Denise?'

'She's off back to London tomorrow. She is still undecided about making a complaint against Fawkes, although Sue did take matters into her own hands and contacted someone at his estate agents about it. I think he's for the high jump whatever happens. Now, the thing is, Tom, Denise is very keen to meet you again. Can't think why, but how about supper at our place tonight?'

My brain was desperately trawling through the filing cabinet marked "lame excuses" when the egg-timer went off. Saved by the bell. 'Got to go, Larry, eggs are ready. I'll get back to you on that one.'

Storm Jasper had arrived with a vengeance. The waves were pounding the western breakwater sending plumes of spray over the red and green marker posts that lined the entrance to the channel to the harbour. Walking into the wind on the coastal path, which had been partially covered by pebbles thrown up by the waves at high tide, was like trying to walk with a ball and chain on each foot. Wisely, Stanley White had decided to stay indoors with his newspaper and bruises.

I had wanted to stand on the shoreline and experience the sort of conditions the seventeen crewmen of the ill-fated *Mary Stanford* might have confronted on that winter's night in 1928. If I was going to write this book, I felt authenticity was important. They say the wind can take your breath away, now I knew it was true. Even standing still, it was difficult to catch a breath. Tops of waves were whipped off by the gusts, sending spray back towards the deep before the breakers crashed and rolled over the sentry line of black broken wooden posts that had once been breakwaters near the old lifeboat house. The roar of sea and wind was incessant. The thought of pushing an open-topped rowing boat out into the deep in the dark was difficult to imagine.

When I arrived back in the village, one end of the blue and white police tape that had been run around the front garden wall of the art gallery was snaking wildly across the road. The constable who had tried to restrain Stanley the previous day, was slowly winding it in around his wrist.

'Have you finished here?'

'You'd better check with DS Hopps, sir. She'll be out in a minute. But I think we're through. How's that other chap?'

'Him?' I realised the policeman was referring to yesterday's minor tumble in the gallery's garden, not the kicking Stanley had received as a result of mistaken identity last night. 'Oh, he's fine. His eggs were cooked to perfection, so he's happy.'

Detective Sergeant Hopps arrived, her normally restrained hair flapping in the wind around her face. She peeled it back and smiled. You really should let your hair down more often, I thought but did not say.

'Almost finished here, Mr Kidd. You can return to the property whenever you like. But we are still keen to talk to Ms White.'

'So are we, detective sergeant. So are we. Can you tell me anymore about this gun you found?'

'Sorry, Mr Kidd. Not at present.'

She spoke to the constable and left. I headed for the side entrance and the back garden, where the spare key was secreted behind the water butt. The little blue plastic bag of dog shit still squatted in the grass. Clearly police forensics had not been that thorough.

I found a cane in the shed and gingerly picked up

the bag by a loop, carrying it at arm's length like a ticking time-bomb towards the plastic bins at the end of the shed. General Waste? Garden Waste? Recyclables? Whatever it was, I could smell it from here. The recycle bin was empty. I angled the cane downwards, allowed the fetid bag to drop in and shut the lid.

As I walked back to measure the size for a new shed door, I realised something had been not quite right. The bag when it dropped should have barely made a sound. Perhaps a soft squelch on the plastic base of the bin, possibly a dull plop, but definitely not the hard clunk I had heard.

There was nothing for it. I had to know. I found some old cracked leather gardening gloves in a pot in the shed and picked up my cane again. The bag was easily hooked up, like fishing for plastic ducks with a ring in their heads at the fun fair. I lifted it out wondering what my prize was. Radio-active waste could not have been handled with greater care. I put the bag in an empty black plastic seed tray on the bench inside the shed, found some secateurs and snipped the knotted top off. I could feel breakfast rising in my throat so I ducked outside for some fresh air.

After a few moments, I returned to the shed, picked up the seed tray and put it outside on the grass. This operation was better done in the fresh air. On my knees, with the end of my cane, I started prodding at the foul contents of the bag. There was definitely something hard there, something even the largest of dogs would have had great difficulty in passing. It had sharp corners, and looked metallic. The only course of action was to pick it out with my fingers.

Trying hard not to retch, I felt tentatively with gloved thumb and forefinger hoping desperately that the shit would not seep through the old leather. I found the object and lifted it out. It was square in shape, about two inches across and certainly made of metal.

A dousing under the water butt tap revealed its identity.

It was an Iron Cross. The most recognisable of all pieces of German memorabilia from both the Great War and the Second World War lay in the palm of my glove. Its distinctive black curved arms were piped with white beading and at the centre was a small swastika.

I laid it carefully on the back door step, collected the seed tray with the foul plastic bag still in it and the cane, and dropped the lot in the general refuse bin followed by the gloves.

I found the house key behind the water butt and let myself into the kitchen. What I was looking for was under the sink. I put an inch of disinfectant in an old jar and, using kitchen towel, picked up the Iron Cross and dropped it into the liquid. Five minutes should be enough.

Just to be sure, I left the symbolic piece of metal in the liquid for twenty minutes while I made myself a coffee. I tipped the disinfectant and medal into the sink, rinsed it and, gingerly holding it between thumb and forefinger, gave it a sniff. No essence-of-canine remained. The small chunk of German metal was surprisingly heavy. I slipped it into a small zip pocket in my shirt. I took another look around the gallery just to confirm all was well and left, reprogramming the alarm that the police had deactivated.

There was a different nurse on the reception desk at the Green Leaves Retirement Home but the routine was the same. Visitors' book completed, he led me into the day room where a DVD was playing an old Norman Wisdom film to an audience that had fallen asleep through boredom or necessity.

My guide – I'd placed him as Polish – scanned the room then turned to me and shouted: 'Of course, it's Saturday afternoon. Geordie will be in his room for the football. First floor, do you know where it is?' I nodded, thankful to escape the latest mishap to befall little Norman.

When I knocked on Lindisfarne there was no answer, but there was excited chatter from the other side of the door. I knocked louder and tried the handle. It was unlocked. Geordie Harris was sitting in his armchair, his bony hands gripping the threadbare arms, a newspaper resting on his lap. He was staring into the middle distance carried away to somewhere exciting as he listened to the football commentary coming out of the radio on the windowsill.

He looked up and beckoned me in. 'Come on in, lad. Nearly half-time. The Toon are letting me down again.'

I sat in silence while the Irishman on the radio contorted his tonsils around a series of foreign names, his excited babble increasing in volume and speed until another home team attack ended with the ball sailing into the crowd at the Gallowgate End. It was half-time.

'Bloody useless.' Geordie slowly levered himself up

and reached for the volume switch.

'Your team – Newcastle?'

'Who else, son. If you come from Newcastle you can only support one team. It's not easy, like. I can't remember the last time we had a decent side – probably Kevin Keegan's days. I wouldn't mind so much, but they're ruining my bet too. They're the only team in my accumulator not winning.'

'How much?'

'More than thirty pounds if they can pull their fingers out in the second half and beat Everton. Bloody Everton! I ask you.'

'Well, this might cheer you up if they don't.' I put my backpack on the bed beside me and delved inside. 'One half bottle of best navy rum, as promised. And you get some change.' I put the coins on the arm of his chair.

'Bonny lad. Get the glasses will, you? They're in that old briefcase.'

He poured two healthy measures and sniffed appreciatively. 'I never say no to a drop of whisky, I don't mind a brandy if I'm offered it, but you can't beat rum.' He closed his eyes, sipped and tilted his head back so that his face was looking up at the ceiling. For all I knew he was back on board a merchant ship with his mates in the 1950s.

'You said you were on the lifeboats at one time, Geordie.'

He looked at me. For a moment I think he'd forgotten where he was: a 96-year-old man, a widower alone in the world inside the last bedroom he would ever sleep in. He swallowed what was in his glass and held it out for a refill.

He told me he had been one of the crew and maintenance engineer first with the Margate lifeboat and then at Rye Harbour after he and his wife moved to the village. He had given up the Merchant Navy to keep his wife happy. She didn't like him being away so much, but he could not give up the sea forever, and so volunteered for lifeboat service. He found a job as one of the greenkeepers and as a general odd-job man at Camber Golf Club, but came alive whenever the call went up and he and his mates scrambled for the boathouse.

'More often than not it was something and nothing, some posh idiot in a yacht who didn't know how to sail, but we had our moments. It could be hairy, like, but you didn't think about that at the time. You all had your jobs to do, and we all depended on each other. Our lives were in each other's hands, you see, son. I think that's why there's a special bond among lifeboat crews. Those moments when we set off, not knowing exactly what we were going to find or do, well, they were the moments you really felt alive.'

His rheumy eyes were fixed somewhere out of the window. His voice was quiet, but strong. Then he started singing quietly. *The Blaydon Races*. All five verses and choruses in a dialect that might just as well have been Mandarin to my ears.

'I didn't understand a word of that, Geordie, but it sounded good.'

'There was no finer sound in football than when the whole Gallowgate End sang that before kick-off. I was a nipper sitting on me Da's shoulders in them days. Now, where were we?'

I topped up his glass. 'You were telling me about your days on the lifeboats.'

'Oh, aye, well they were grand days, but you'd never think about the danger until you got back, and then it might hit you. I guess it was the same for those poor buggers on the *Mary Stanford*. God rest their souls.'

'Tell me more about that time, Geordie. You said you were five when the tragedy happened in 1928. You said you were there that night, so how come you grew up in Newcastle?'

'After the tragedy, my parents decided they had to get away from Rye Harbour. My Ma lost her brother on the boat and I think my Da felt so much guilt because he was not one of the volunteers. He suffered terrible seasickness, you see, he could'na face going out on a boat, even on a duck pond. He would've been useless, hanging over the side all the time. But in a community like that, well, some families lost three or four men, and my Da felt bad about it. I think some of the other kids picked on me at school too, that's what I was told. Calling me a coward's son – but it wasn't like that.'

He levered himself unsteadily out of the chair and, grasping the edge of the bed, made it to the sink where he filled his glass with water and took a deep drink.

'Anyway, we went to Newcastle and I'm glad we did. Da got a job down the mines and we had a good life, until the War came along. That's another story, though.'

'Well, you certainly sound like you're a Geordie now. What happened to your Sussex accent?'

'As a southern nipper in a Newcastle school, you soon learn to sound like them if you wanna survive. Simple as that. Anyway, I s'pose I picked it up naturally. That was my home, like.'

He slumped back in the chair and checked his watch. 'Bloody hell, they'll have kicked off again. Turn it up a bit, son.'

While he listened to the match – Newcastle were still losing – I looked at the pictures on the wall. There had been something about them that had seemed familiar when I had first seen them four days earlier. One was a scene of a small harbour with fishing boats crowded up against the quayside wall. Another showed a large Victorian fort on a headland illuminated by the setting sun. The third was of a small house in a field that stretched down to a sandy beach, dense dark storm clouds hovering overhead.

Then I realised what was familiar. In the bottom left-hand corner of each watercolour scratched in the paint was JW.43. I was certain I had seen that before in the faded seascape hanging over the desk in the Rother Gallery.

'Geordie, where did….'

He held up a hand to silence me. 'We've got a penalty. Just a minute, lad.'

The roar from the old radio drowned out the commentary, but told Geordie that Newcastle had scored. 'That's better, come on bonny lads, finish them off now. What's it you were saying Tom?'

'These paintings, where did you get them?'

He looked at the pictures as if he had realised for the first time that they were hanging in his room. 'Those? An old friend painted them.'

'Only there's one very similar in style and with the

same initials – JW – in the gallery at Rye Harbour.'

'John and Elle's place? Is that still going?'

'You know it?'

'I did. We were quite good friends with them back then. Elle was very kind to Mary, my wife, when she was poorly just before the end, and John was with me on the lifeboats for about ten years. He didn't mix much, but we seemed to get on all right. I often had a beer with him in his shed on a Sunday when the two women went to church. He did those paintings.'

'The gallery is run by Lizzy White, were John and Elle her parents?'

'That's right. John and Elle White, but they're long gone now.'

The commentary on the radio was rising in a crescendo once again. Geordie held up a hand for silence and shifted himself to the edge of his armchair. The Irish voice was breaking with excitement and then subsided as the roar of the crowd became a groan.

'Bugger. Useless Frenchie.' Geordie slumped back in his chair. 'Do you like the pictures?'

'Er, yes. They're very…' I struggled for a non-committal suitable word, 'authentic. Are they of the coast around here?'

'No, son. They're scenes from Alderney in the Channel Islands … YESSSSSS. Get In!'

Newcastle had scored. Geordie kicked over his empty glass in excitement and knocked his walking stick across the carpet. 'Better fill that up, Tom. I'm about to celebrate a nice little win. Happy days.'

The tastefully converted barn where the Landers lived was a short drive from the nursing home. I had left Geordie a happy man. His team had come in, his bet had come in and I had promised to return in a couple of days with another small bottle of rum. We had done considerable damage to the one I had brought him and I was not altogether sure I should be driving.

I negotiated the single-track country lanes with exaggerated care. My old Audi had been here so often in the past, it could have made the last few miles on autopilot. Quite possibly it had taken over the navigation.

A dinner invitation from the Landers was always welcome, even though the room-dominating presence of Denise Rutter made me wary. What is it Larry Lander had said? 'She's on a man-hunt again.'

'Thanks for coming, Tom, Larry's feeling a bit outnumbered, the poor dear.' Sue had opened the old oak door and welcomed me with a hug and kiss on both cheeks.

She looked fantastic as usual. Elegant and cool in white tee-shirt and jeans, she was the polar opposite to her deconstructed husband. As the anchor on the regional evening news, she had to look good, but the smile was as warm off-camera as it was on it. We had been good friends since Sue and a female friend had hooked up with the Kidd–Lander axis at a barn dance more than twenty years ago. My part of the deal had long departed the scene, but somehow, Larry had clicked with Sue and their marriage had survived despite – or perhaps, because of – their differences.

'Denise is upstairs putting her face on and the old boy

is slaving over a hot barbecue out back. By the way, I take it you're staying over: I've prepared Mull for you as usual. Denise is in Skye.'

The Landers had named their bedrooms after the Scottish Islands they had visited on their honeymoon. Odd that I had been in Lindisfarne this afternoon. I wondered what Geordie Harris would make of this place.

The cathedral-like lounge went the two-storey height of the building, revealing the 18th century beams above a polished oak floor and full-length windows that offered spectacular views across the rolling farmland.

'Come through, we're having a little sundowner on the patio.'

Lander was hunched over a gas-fired barbecue resplendent in blue and white striped chef's apron, tongs in one hand, a long glass of something pink in the other.

'Tequila, soda and pink grapefruit cocktail, Tom? It's got a hint of nutmeg in it too.' Sue offered me a filled glass, not waiting for my reply.

'I'll have one of those too, please.' Denise appeared from the kitchen dressed in flowing full-length red cotton dress with a deep V-neck that appeared to plunge almost to her navel. Bits of silver jewellery twinkled here and there, and purple toe-nails peeped out from the hem of the dress when she walked bare-footed out of the French windows to join us. It was some entrance.

The steaks were cooked to perfection, the salad exquisitely dressed and the deep-red French wine perfectly matched the meat. Denise radiated happiness as she and Sue swapped tales of television studio mishaps and careless comments when microphones were still open. The subject of the brief encounter with Roland Fawkes was not broached, nor was the progress or not of her house-hunting in the area.

The late August sun dipped behind the far trees and the evening grew chilly as the two women cleared away the plates and announced they were retiring inside for dessert.

'Beer, Tom?'

'Sounds like a good idea, anything cold and fizzy will do at this time of night.'

He returned from the kitchen with two bottles and sat down. 'While they're inside, I can tell you.'

'Tell me what?'

'About the break-ins and that gun that came from the gallery. The police have confirmed they traced most of the stolen stuff back to a small travellers' site near Camber. It had been nicked from all over Sussex and Kent and was then being shifted through a family there, who sold it at various boot fairs or to second-hand shops that didn't ask too many questions.'

Larry took a long pull from his bottle to lubricate the tonsils. 'The police raided the site and found the gun. That's when the investigation became a lot more serious. The travellers claimed they thought it was a replica and were quick to shift the blame to the youngsters who nicked the stuff. They said it had been found at the Rother Gallery.'

'The gallery owner's been away, you know, since the break-in. Seems to have just gone missing,' I said. 'I find it hard to believe she would keep a gun – and in her shed of all places. If she had one for protection, she'd keep it in the cottage, surely?'

'Perhaps she didn't even know it was there. The kids who did the raid told the police they found it in some old tins they'd stolen. Anyway, the cops are less stressed about it because it turns out it had been de-commissioned. It was beyond use, and even if it hadn't been, there was no ammunition with it. It was an old Walther pistol from the Second World War, a German gun. Probably some sort of souvenir. A lot of soldiers brought them back. Another one?'

When Larry returned with two more frosted bottles, I put the Iron Cross on the table.

'What's that?'

'What's it look like? It's a German Iron Cross. It was posted through the gallery letter box in a bag full of dog shit.' Larry, who had been about to pick up the medal, recoiled in horror. I told him the story of the special delivery and the 'Nazi Scum' graffiti on the front wall of the gallery.

'I'm beginning to wonder if Lizzy's father had been something of a collector of Nazi memorabilia, or as you say, had a few souvenirs from the Second World War. I don't know if he fought in the War, he would have been the right age, I guess.'

'Well, only your Ms White will know the answer to that – and she's nowhere to be found.'

'No. And I must confess, I'm beginning to get a bit concerned now, Larry. It's three days without so much as a text message or an email.'

Sue popped her head out of the French windows. 'Dessert!'

'C'mon. It's getting chilly. You'll need Denise to warm you up later.' Larry gave a theatrical wink that would not have been out of place in a Carry-On film.

The evening became more bacchanalian than ever, as Larry produced an expensive bottle of Australian dessert wine followed by his best malt whisky. We tried to play a word game that Sue had been given the previous Christmas, but failed hopelessly, beset by giggles whenever the answer had the slightest hint of a *double entendre*.

Denise draped herself on the leather sofa beside me and announced it was all too erudite for a mere weathergirl. 'I think I'm off to my place in the Skye, Tom. I'll leave you to Mull over your options.'

Alderney 1943

The midnight raid on the piggery had never happened. At least for the Orel boys it didn't. The night before they had planned to wriggle over the barbed wire border and deprive the pigs of a few swedes, three Poles had decided to do the same thing. Unluckily for them, their noise or their smell had alarmed the porkers, and in turn their squeals had alerted the dozing German guards. The Poles were beaten on the spot, then dragged half-alive back to the camp and tied to posts in the parade ground. There they were left for three days as the rats finished them off, their screams ringing out as a warning to others. What was left of their corpses was put into sacks by other prisoners and loaded on to the back of a truck. It was said they were dumped in Braye Harbour.

It was a dangerous time. The heat had made the German guards even more irritable. The lice and the fleas swarmed through the huts feeding on prisoners who had not bathed, shaved or had their hair cut for more than a year. The rats ran riot at night, and each morning, prisoners were found dead on their wooden bunks, the bodies being dragged out and prodded with a pickaxe, just to ensure they were not malingering, before they were thrown into the sea or buried on Longis Common, where the Germans had made a rudimentary cemetery.

Just before the end of August, the camp commandant decided he had had enough. He ordered every prisoner to be taken from the huts and lined up. The ranks of pathetic human specimens watched as the guards boarded up the windows of the huts. The Orel Boys saw tins decorated with skull and crossbones and the words 'Cyclone B' taken into each hut where they were set alight before the doors were slammed shut by guards hurrying out holding handkerchiefs over their faces. Within seconds, pungent, dark smoke started seeping out of crevices and cracks in the boarding. Even the lice didn't stand a chance.

The boys were herded on to the back of a truck and driven into the town, a place they had not seen since their arrival. Georgi noticed it had changed a great deal. The main cobbled street was still pot-holed, but the damaged buildings he had seen on his first day were now largely repaired. German flags hung from poles jutting out of the grander building, and electric lighting cable was strung from property to property.

The truck swung right by a small chapel into a narrower street and rattled up a hill passed a broken green wooden sign that said 'The Butes.' A large circular sports field stretched before them. Down one side, German vehicles were parked in a row against a stone wall. The ground sloped away to the north to give panoramic views across Braye Bay, while to the south, the spire of a large church rose above the town. It was a scene Giselle knew well. She had come here in years past for the annual island fête, bonfire night and, her fondest memory of all, to sit with her sister watching her father play cricket while her mother helped in the pavilion with the teas.

These days, she often cut through The Butes if she wanted to visit the town and her old school, but today her progress had been halted by the arrival of a convoy of German trucks that emerged from Serpentine Road, skidding across the outfield of the cricket ground sending up plumes of dust before coming to a halt. Alarmed, she ducked behind what was left of the old scoreboard, propped up against what had been the groundsman's hut, and once again found herself watching, transfixed, horrified.

'Out. Now,' shouted one of the privileged Russians who acted as policemen for the Germans. Georgi wondered how one of his own countrymen could be in the pay of the Nazis and inflict such cruelty on his fellow Russians.

'Strip and leave your clothes by that can.' Fifty to sixty emaciated naked creatures did as they were told and lined up. It was the first time sunshine had touched their bare torsos since they had left Russia. Petr looked down at himself and then at his brother, who was no longer the strapping, proud youth who had once boasted he would be boxing champion of all of Russia. Petr felt no shame because he had no feelings left inside him. The only instinct he had was survival.

They watched as diesel was poured on their rags and set ablaze, the heat scorching their skin and the dark, putrid smoke spiralling up towards the azure sky.

Giselle clamped her hand over her mouth and nose, and almost forgot to breathe. She had witnessed the execution on the cliff at Telegraph Bay. She had seen the slaves being marched along the road near the farm. She had even left slices of bread wrapped in paper on the wall for them, but she had never seen them up close. With their long ragged hair, beards and hunched, dark skeletal naked bodies, they looked like creatures from the past.

They were formed into a long line across the field towards what had been the pavilion, and, one by one, they were daubed with an oily yellow liquid by a man in a white coat with a thick brush. In groups of ten, they were made to sit on a wooden bench while they had their hair sheared to the skull. The hair clippings were swept up and thrown on to the burning pile. Before they left the bench, they were each given a small green cube of what looked like soap and corralled into a circle by the wall at the end of the row of trucks. For a moment, Giselle thought they were about to be executed. Instead, a laughing German turned a hose on the creatures. They were then marched back towards the trucks where piles of fresh clothes had been thrown for them to fight over.

As the scramble started, the guards began to shout and their dogs barked, straining on their leashes. Amid the cacophony, one prisoner took his chance. He rolled under the truck and out the other side. Giselle saw him before the guards did, but they were not far behind. The naked body scrambled over the wall as two shots spat off the stone work either side of his buttocks.

Alexei found himself in the back garden of a large house. Most of its windows had been broken and a door lay open. He could take refuge inside, but that would be the first place the Germans would look. He heard shouting from the other side of the wall and headed for the overgrown garden, broken glass and thorns ripping the soles of his bare feet as he ran towards the far wall, this one almost twice his height. He was aware of soldiers at the top of the garden, and heard some shouting in the derelict house. There was ivy on the wall in front of him. It was his only option if this was not to be burial place. He reached up and grabbed the thickest stems he could find, hauling himself up. They did not give way as he summoned what strength he had in his feeble arms and pulled himself to the top of the wall. He could see three soldiers stumbling through the undergrowth towards him. A rifle shot cracked off the wall somewhere behind him and he looked up to see a soldier taking aim from an upstairs window in the house.

Before the second shot arrived, Alexei had thrown himself into the narrow cobbled lane the other side of the wall, his left shoulder hitting the stones with a jarring thud. He tried desperately not to cry out, but could not hold back, the numbing pain forcing a scream through his clenched teeth.

There was another wall in front of him. This one was lower than the first, but he was not sure he could get over it. His left arm now felt useless as it hung by his side. He headed downhill before coming to a junction. Right would take him back towards the field, so he turned left and, looking up through the trees, he could see a church ahead, squat and solid with a machine gun pointing out of its bell tower.

The shouts and clatter of boots on cobbles grew louder behind him. He would take his chance and hope the gun was unmanned, or the soldier on duty was asleep. He ran passed a row of empty small houses towards his sanctuary under the eyes of God. A flight of eight steps took him into the graveyard and still no shots were spitting down from above. Somebody was looking after him.

There was no sign of an open door on this side of the church. Some of the stained-glass windows had been broken, but they were too high to reach. He could hide in the overgrown graveyard but his pursuers and their dogs would certainly find him. He hesitated for a second and then bolted for the buttress at the right-hand side of the building. It was the correct choice. As he turned the corner he saw the church's main door, and it was open. Soldiers were sitting outside on wooden cases, seemingly unaware of the chase that had been going on.

Alexei ran past them into the cool dark cavernous interior suddenly feeling self-conscious of his nakedness in the House of God. Down each side of the aisle, the pews had been pushed aside to make room for piles of boxes and barrels, crates and sacks. It was like a giant storehouse, but the altar in front of Alexei was still obvious. He ran up the aisle as the soldiers entered the church, stumbling up the four carpeted steps of the sanctuary, the pipes of the church organ, long silent, rising high to his left into the vaulted ceiling. A tall stained-glass window ahead showed the Crucifixion scene.

'Thank you, God,' whispered Alexei standing up and turning to face his pursuers, arms outstretched.

Three shots rang out, echoing from wall to wall.

Alexei crumpled to the floor, the tiny silver cross his grandmother had given him the day the Germans had taken him away from Orel still gripped tightly in his right hand as his blood ran down the sanctuary steps.

✠✠✠

10

I woke up in bed on the right island. I hoped Denise Rutter would not be offended by my choice of bedroom. The previous night, as I had walked softly along the atrium landing overlooking the lounge with Larry's leery encouragement from the sofa below, I had hesitated briefly outside Skye. Denise was a charming woman, and any liaison with her would, I was sure, come without strings attached. But I was still not ready for any kind of romantic involvement.

I slept as soundly as the alcohol content in my bloodstream would allow. Funny how I always seemed to wake up at the Landers' place in a similar dog-eared state. The hot–cold shower routine did its trick and I felt ready to face the day – and one of Larry's mountainous bacon sandwiches, which I could smell wafting up the open-tread staircase.

The other three were sitting at the granite-topped breakfast bar munching on doorsteps of bread when I arrived in the state-of-the-art kitchen.

'Hello stranger,' said Denise. 'Come and sit here.' She patted the stool next to her. I did as I was told, Larry collecting my sandwich from the hotplate on the range, Sue pouring coffee from vast cafetière into the remaining empty mug. Sunday newspapers and their array of supplements were splayed across the breakfast bar, *The Sunday Times* propped up on a book stand where Larry had been sitting.

'Help yourself, the games sections are somewhere.' Larry looked at the mass of newsprint. He knew I liked to read the sports pages first.

'I think I need the coffee before I can focus.'

'Have a bit too much last night, did we?' cooed Denise.

'I think we all did.'

'Well, don't worry. I won't be leading you astray again, at least not for a while.'

'Oh?'

'I've decided to drop my plans to escape to the country for the time being. My opinion of your estate agents has gone down a little. And, lovely as this rural way of life is, I think I'd miss the bright lights too much.'

'So you're not moving?'

'Didn't I just say that, Tom?'

'What about what happened to you? The assault, I mean. Are you taking it further?'

Sue frowned. 'She should do. We've told her that.'

Denise shook her head. 'No,' she said. 'The estate agents know all about Roland Fawkes' reputation, I think they're ending his involvement with them, but I don't want the publicity of a police investigation and possible court case. I know the TV company wouldn't like it either.'

I was ready to tackle the devilish Sunday crossword. *4 Down. Strip show for soldiers? (8,2,6)* by the time Larry had loaded the dishwasher and Denise had loaded her suitcase into the boot of her Mercedes.

'Now, Tom, you will get in touch next time you're up in the big, wicked city, won't you?' Denise was standing in the open doorway, car keys in hand.

I stood up and I promised I would, and I meant it. I liked Denise and, sometime soon, I might prove it to her. But for now, a kiss on both cheeks was as intimate as it got. She held her handbag over her head, smiled and turned to make a dash through the rain before diving into her sleek machine.

'One down, one to go,' I said to Sue. 'I'd better be heading off too. Zoe White texted me earlier, she said the police had some news about her mother – good news, sort of. I'm meeting her and her Uncle Stanley for lunch in Rye. Can I take the crossword with me, I've barely started it?'

'Of course you can, Tom. And take Denise up on her offer when you go up to London again – I think she's really quite sweet on you, and underneath that bravado, she's a very nice girl.'

The fish bar by the quay at lunchtime on a Sunday in August was not the best place to meet. There were two queues: one made up of families looking to get a takeaway, the other comprising mainly older couples lined up to get a table in the restaurant area.

'Whose idea was this?'

'Yours, Stanley,' said his wife Olivia severely. Zoe smirked and winked at me behind their backs.

'Come on,' she said. 'I know a little fisherman's café the other side of the level crossing. It's pretty plain, but it won't be busy with tourists.'

On our way there, we continued our conversation. 'So, where's your mother been since Wednesday?'

'That is something the police don't know and, to be honest, it doesn't seem to bother them. They just said they had checked the ports and airports again yesterday afternoon and her name had been flagged up on the computer. She'd taken the Saturday morning flight from Southampton to Alderney in the Channel Islands.'

'Why Alderney?'

'No idea.'

'Stanley?' I looked at her uncle, who was walking behind struggling to keep up. He shrugged his shoulders and shook his head.

Zoe continued. 'Seems one of the three police officers on Alderney tracked her down – I think it's only a pretty small place – and spoke to her. They're happy she knew nothing about the gun they found and happy that she's not in any danger. So the file is closed as far as they're concerned.'

Olivia was studying the hand-written menu sellotaped to the inside of the steamy café window. 'This'll do.' I got the impression Stanley had little say in such matters.

Zoe was right: the place was half empty. Three of us ordered sandwiches, Stanley wanted the full English breakfast, which the blackboard behind the tea urn said was available all day, but Olivia told him he would have a jacket potato and baked beans.

'I don't understand why she should take herself away suddenly for a holiday and not tell anyone.' I tossed the question into the lake hoping to cause some ripples.

'Perhaps it's not a holiday,' said Olivia. She was a

diminutive woman, but one who gave off the aura of a person who rarely doubted herself. She had been a primary school head, and I felt sure her fellow teachers would have been as much in fear of her as the pupils.

'Go on.'

'Well, perhaps she's with someone. A man?'

'Stanley?' I looked at him. Again he shrugged, but offered no comment as he shovelled a forkful of beans into his mouth.

'She's never mentioned anyone to me,' said Zoe. 'I don't see why she would keep that a secret.'

'Have you got a name of the guest house or hotel where she's staying? We could give it a call.'

'The police wouldn't tell me. They said it was up to Mum to decide if she wanted to get in touch. They did tell her we were worried, but they said she was entitled to privacy if she wanted it.'

'Bloody ridiculous,' said Stanley.

'Bloody inconsiderate, if you ask me,' said Olivia.

'You know the picture above the desk in the gallery? Is it of somewhere in Alderney?' I looked at Zoe and then Stanley.

'No idea,' said Zoe. 'It's just one of Mum's old favourites for some reason. Don't like it myself.'

'Stan?'

'Me? No idea, I don't know anything about it.' He sent a wedge of steaming potato in pursuit of the beans.

'Well, I think it's by your grandfather, Zoe. Have you noticed the signature scratched in the corner? JW.43.'

'Can't say I have, but JW were his initials – John White. How amazing I'd never thought of that before.

That must be why Mum treasured it so much. She'd never sell it. I never knew Grandad, he died long before I was born, but I'd heard he was interested in painting. Is that right, Uncle Stanley?'

Stanley still had a mouthful. All three of us looked at him in silence while he chewed and then swallowed. 'What?' he said.

'The picture of the cliffs and sea in the gallery. Do you know if it's by your father?'

'I think it might be, but I'm not sure.'

'Telegraph Bay.'

'What is?' I looked at Zoe.

'I'm sure that's what the painting's called,' she said. 'It's hand written in ink at the bottom of the frame. The letters are pretty faded but that's what they say.'

I took out my mobile and punched 'Images of Telegraph Bay' into the search engine. A series of photographs came up. I scrolled across and found what I was looking for.

'That's it.'

'What is?' said Zoe.

I handed her the phone. 'Look across the images. I think it starts with a Telegraph Bay in Hong Kong, then one in Canada then two in the Channel Islands.'

She gently pulled the images across the screen with her forefinger. The first two showed bays with built-up shorelines, the third was a beautifully sandy expanse in Guernsey and then she stopped at the fourth: a dramatic, rocky seascape, a series of jagged mounds rising out of the water.

'That's it,' she whispered. 'That's the painting in the

gallery. Look, Uncle Stanley.' She held the phone up in front of his face.

'Oh yes, it could be.'

'Could be? It is, I'm sure. I wonder why my grandfather painted that.'

'It's not the only one he painted, Zoe.'

Now it was my turn to be looked at by the other three seeking an explanation.

'Yesterday, I went to see an old boy – he's 96 – who used to work on the lifeboat in Rye Harbour. He knew your grandparents, he said he was quite friendly with your grandfather and used to have a drink with him in that old shed of a Sunday. Well, he's got three paintings in his room at the old folks home where he lives, and they are all scenes from Alderney, all marked JW.43.'

'What's his name?' asked Stanley.

'Fred Harris. Aka Geordie Harris.'

'Mr Harris! Bloody hell's teeth. Is he still alive … well, obviously he is, but I'd never have guessed it. Last time I saw him was at dad's funeral in 1975. He was one of the old veterans I mentioned to you.'

'Why's he got Grandad's paintings?' asked Zoe.

'He said they were good mates, that's all I know. The point is, his three paintings, and the one in the gallery, they're all of Alderney, which is where your mother is. It's one pretty big coincidence.'

Silence fell on the table apart from the steady slurp of Stanley's chewing. Olivia dropped her severe persona and giggled, then looked embarrassed.

'Sorry,' she said, putting her hand to her mouth as three pairs of eyes stared at her. 'But you have to admit it's a bit like one of those *Midsomer Murders* mysteries.'

'Except no-one's died, auntie.'

'No, Zoe, but you know what I mean.'

'Tom, I know this is asking a bit much, but, if we've not heard from Mum by the morning, would you mind going to Alderney? I'd go, but I have work commitments at the doctor's and the hotel – and anyway, being a journalist, you're used to snooping around after people.'

'I'm not sure how to take that.'

'We'll pay all your expenses, won't we Uncle Stanley?'

'What? Will we?'

'Yes, we will,' said Olivia. 'Good idea, Zoe. I'm sure you'll be able to find Lizzy if it's such a small place, Tom. The police might point you in the right direction too if you turn up at their station looking lost.'

'You could go too, Uncle Stanley. She's your sister, after all.'

'Um, no, it's all right. I'm sure Tom here is quite capable on his own, aren't you, Tom?'

I spent the afternoon at my flat. There was no real reason to turn down Zoe's plea. I had no work for the *South Coast Gazette* at present, and there was nothing to do on my book that could not wait for a few days. Hopping on a plane was not part of my lifestyle – or within my budget – these days, but as I would not be paying, that was not an excuse either.

Booking the trip on-line was easy enough. I was on tomorrow's 10.15am direct flight from Southampton to Alderney on Aurigny, who appeared to be the only carrier with a direct service. All the other options on the booking site took me via Guernsey at vast expense.

I thought I should do a little on-line research into my destination. Alderney had only the one town, St Anne, right in the middle of the island, which was about three miles long and one mile across. It should not be that difficult to find an English woman with a mop of red hair wandering around on her own.

Jersey and Guernsey were Alderney's bigger, more popular sisters in the Channel Island chain. It was always possible Lizzy could have moved on to one of them by tomorrow, or even flitted over to France, which was less than ten miles away. The island had had a chequered past, particularly in the Second World War, but was thriving now as a niche holiday resort and destination for those wealthy enough to own second homes.

I had not booked a return flight and I packed just a weekend bag, reasoning I would not be there for more than two days. I paid another visit to the gallery to check all was well, half expecting to see Stanley and Olivia there, but it was closed up and the curtains were drawn. Stanley's plan had been to stay at the cottage but Olivia was having none of it, especially as Zoe had moved heaven and earth to get them into an attic room at her hotel.

Stanley had not seemed his usual opinionated self at lunch time. He had offered little to the conversation about the paintings and had not shared any thoughts as to why his sister might have flown, in every sense of the word, to a small rocky outcrop in the middle of the English Channel. I put his reluctance to set the world to rights down to the presence of his wife Olivia.

He had, however, known Geordie Harris and

confirmed he was a friend of his father. Geordie also had paintings of Alderney, which somehow held the answers. I needed to pay the old man another visit with another bottle of rum before I went to my hotel at Southampton Airport tonight.

The car park at the Green Leaves Retirement Home in Hythe was busy at a Sunday tea time. Must be the popular day for visiting the elderly relatives. The front door was open, and loud singing reverberated along the wooden floor of the hallway to greet visitors before they even arrived at the stone steps.

A nurse in white uniform was sitting on the front desk rather than behind it, her feet tapping on the floor as she clapped her hands in time to *Never Mind the Why or Wherefore*. She almost jumped out of her pinafore when I tapped her on the shoulder.

'Oh, sorry, I got a bit carried away, I didn't hear you coming what with the music an' all,' she said, hurrying around behind the desk and smoothing down her uniform. I was surprised that the accent was more East End than East European.

'That's perfectly all right. Gilbert and Sullivan?'

She ran a manicured fingernail down a list of names. 'Sorry, I'm new 'ere, but I can't find anyone of that name. It was Sullivan you said, wasn't it?'

'Gilbert and Sullivan – the music, it's by them. From *HMS Pinafore*.'

'Oh, blimey. Silly me. Sorry,' she blushed and giggled. 'I didn't know. There's some society 'ere giving a sing-song for the old dears. Nice innit?'

'Lovely, but I doubt if who I'm looking for is enjoying it. I'm here to see Fred Harris, he's in Lindisfarne – that's the name of his bedroom.'

'OK, let's see.' She ran the crimson nail down the list again. 'Oh yeah, Mr 'arris. That's right. He's 'ere. You'd better sign the visitors' book.' She turned the book around to face me. 'Car reg too, please, don't wanna make any mistakes this being my first week an' all.'

I filled it in and presented it back to her to show I had not missed anything. She checked it through. 'That Mr 'arris, he's a right popular bloke, Three visits in three days. Nice to see some people still care about the old 'uns. Know your way?'

I said I did and turned to battle through *I am the very model of a modern Major-General,* then halted.

'Three?'

'Pardon?'

'Three visits in three days, you said.'

She looked at the book again. 'Yeah, that's right.'

'Can I see?' She handed me the book. My signature was there beside Saturday's date, but on Friday Geordie Harris had had a different caller: the signature was that of Lizzy White.

I knocked on his door and thought I ought to wait to be invited in although I was bursting with questions.

'What is it now, come in.' He sounded grumpy. 'Oh it's you, bonny lad. Thought it was the carer again. Come on in.' He picked up the television remote control and silenced a minor celebrity who was about to win a small windfall for his chosen charity by naming three colours of the rainbow.

'I've got your rum, Geordie. This one's on me, for all the help you're giving me.'

'Ay, that's generous of you. There's no need you know, I may be old, and a bit decrepit, but I'm not penniless quite yet.' He laughed. 'Might have to take it a bit easy today, though. I had a bit of a head after our session yesterday. I think the nurse is beginning to suspect something. One won't hurt, though.'

The glasses were still on the windowsill from yesterday, although I noted they had been rinsed. He levered himself up with an unsteady hand, wobbled and slumped back down in the old armchair again.

'Bugger. Do you mind getting them. Joints aren't working well today. Probably that din downstairs.'

'Not keen on Gilbert and Sullivan, then Geordie? The nice young lady on reception seems to be enjoying it.'

'The blonde? Doreen from Dagenham? She's a sweet little thing, isn't she?'

'Is that her name? She showed me the visitors' book. Seems I'm your third in as many days. You didn't mention yesterday that Lizzy White had been to see you on Friday.' I handed him a tumbler with an inch of rum in it and gave myself half the measure.

'Well, you didn't ask.'

'No, I guess I didn't. But we did discuss the Rother Gallery, and her name did crop up.'

He looked into his glass. 'Yes, well. Sorry about that, son. But what we talked about was private, like.'

I told him that Lizzy had disappeared. He did not seem surprised. I told him Lizzy's daughter and her brother were getting concerned, but I did not tell him I knew where she had gone.

'The brother, was that Stanley? Short-sighted podgy youth with too much to say for himself?'

'Sounds like him, he's not a youth anymore, but the rest of the description applies. The thing is, Geordie, the family say it's very out of character for Lizzy and they're concerned. In fact, I've been detailed to find her.'

He looked up at the paintings on the walls of his little room. I sensed the memory banks was slipping into rewind again. 'You might try Alderney.' I was glad he had volunteered the information. It showed we had some trust between us.

'What's the significance of Alderney, Geordie?'

'It's where her parents, John and Elle, met and where they married. I know Elle scattered his ashes there too. It was a special place for them.'

'That's exactly where she is, Geordie – and something's happened to make Lizzy go there now. Do you know what it is?'

'I think I have an idea, but, what she told me, well, it's been something of a family secret. She ought to tell you. I know she's very upset about it.'

'Has it got something to do with the War, Geordie?'

'Aye, we both served there in the War, me and John. Not together mind. I was there in '45 with the Royal Engineers 259 Field Company after the island was liberated. We were rebuilding the place after the Germans had finished with it, and we helped clear the mines. Thousands of them there were. We only lost one of the Sappers, which was a bloody miracle. What was his name?'

He slipped back into the past again, to some lost heroic and dangerous time when men faced unimaginable danger. He stared out of the window and shook his head sadly. 'I know they buried him in the church graveyard there. Never even took what was left of him back home. Onions. That was it. Sapper Onions.'

I stood up and sipped the sweet warming liquor and looked at the paintings again.

'You say John painted these while he was in Alderney?'

'I think so, yes.'

'JW.43.' Does that refer to the year? 1943?'

Geordie looked at me and nodded. I think he already knew the next question.

'But Geordie, there were no British troops in Alderney in 1943. All the islanders had been evacuated according to what I read this afternoon. The only people there were German Nazi troops and slave workers.'

Geordie swallowed the remains of his rum.

'Yes, that's right. John White was a German.'

Alderney 1943

The Germans were getting jumpy. Giselle's father had been told by one of the last civilian farm helpers brought over from Guernsey that summer that the War was going the way of the Allies. Instead of being the bombers, the Germans were now being bombed in their homeland, he'd said. The tide was turning, like it always did in island life.

There was talk of some of the slaves being shipped back to nearby France this autumn and of the four prison camps being flattened so that the English would not know what had gone on in Alderney when they did arrive. Allied commandos had already landed at night in Guernsey to liaise with the locals, the farmhand had said. An inflatable raft had been found in Corblets Bay to the north-east of Alderney, sparking rumours that a commando landing party had also put ashore there.

And David Hanlon, the Irishman who had befriended the occupiers, was deported to Guernsey after being accused of subversive activities. The Germans were over-reacting to everything.

Jens Weiss had recounted the story of the hapless Irishman to her father over cognacs one evening. It all happened, said Weiss, after two Canadian Spitfires flew low towards St Anne. The anti-aircraft guns brought down one of the planes on Longis Common, the other got away. Hanlon lived on Rue de l'Eglise, near the Convent, which was now a soldiers' home run by a formidable matron, Sister Maria. She had taken a dislike to the Irishman, complaining about the noise and smell of the chickens he kept.

She had seen Hanlon going into his backyard carrying a candle just as the Canadian planes were approaching. He claimed he was using it to find his way to the rat-infested outhouse in the dark. She claimed his was signalling to the pilots. Sister Maria insisted Hanlon was a British spy, and, while the German command thought this was laughably far-fetched, to keep the peace, the Commandant had arranged for him to leave.

Her father had roared with laughter at the story. It was the first time Giselle had heard him laugh like that in a long time. The German officer had laughed too, and for one evening at least, life in the farmhouse was happy. Father seemed to like the German, and the German seemed to like her father.

✠✠✠

11

Friday night's mayhem at Gatwick had left its mark. Seeing off Alice for her holiday in Spain amid the shuffling, pushing, shouting misery of North Terminal had hardened my conviction never to fly again from one of London's two major airports. I had done so much of it out of necessity because of my past job as a sports news reporter for a national newspaper, but now I had a choice. And I chose to come to homely little regional airports like Southampton.

The place was an oasis of relaxed efficiency even on a Monday morning. One terminal and one row of check-in desks where you could talk to a person and not a machine. There was one person in line for flight GR504 to Alderney. He did have a flat-packed giant collapsible dog kennel with him, but even that did not seem to send the process into a tailspin. He was checked in and pointed where to go with his over-sized luggage.

'You're nice and early, sir,' said the attendant looking at my booking on her screen. 'The flight's not for another ninety minutes. Just so as you know for next time, there's no need to check in until forty-five minutes before departure time.'

She handed me a boarding card. 'I ought to tell you,

it's pretty windy out in the Channel today. We hope to be able to get you down in Alderney. There is, however, a slight chance we might have to divert to Guernsey. The crew will keep you informed.'

With that reassuring thought in mind, I settled down by my departure gate with a large cup of what masqueraded as coffee and set about finishing Sunday's crossword. *4 Down. Strip show for soldiers? (8,2,6).* I filled in the squares: *Privates on Parade.*

Outside, a slim yellow tube with two whirling propellers either side taxied across the apron and came to a halt a few yards away. A young man with a clip board wandered over. 'Flight to Alderney?' I nodded and handed him my boarding card. He ticked off something on his clipboard, handed me back the boarding card and said: 'Boarding in ten minutes'. He then did the same with the couple sitting opposite me.

Sure enough, ten minutes later we were wandering across the tarmac to stoop inside the Dornier twin-prop. It had eight seats down each side, but that was more than enough for the ten people boarding today. As we got on, the pilot popped his head out of the cockpit ahead of us.

'Morning folks. How are we all today?' He did not really wait for an answer. 'We should be pushing back in a few minutes. Our flight time to Alderney today will be about forty minutes. You may have heard, because of the tail-end of Storm Jasper, we only just got out of the island this morning with the winds picking up to twenty-five knots, which is about the limit for these planes. The forecast is it will be about the same when we return, so I will keep you advised. We'll try our utmost to get you in, but we may have to look for alternatives if the approach is too lumpy.'

A slightly nervous murmur went around the cabin. 'Don't worry, we'll look after you,' he said. 'I take it you've all seen the safety video. Sit back, enjoy the flight.'

As promised, about forty minutes later, the little plane with its now silent human cargo started its descent, juddering as it banked sharply through the clouds. Light flooded in through the porthole windows as we dropped below the dense cloud cover and I got my first glimpse of Alderney down below. I hoped it would not be my last.

As we descended over the rocky eastern tip of the island, the Dornier bucked as a gust caught it and the child behind me started to cry. The fields below dotted with sheep and cattle appeared to be coming up to meet us at an alarming rate. The aircraft jolted again as the undercarriage was lowered. And then we were down, with a squeal of rubber on tarmac and the roar of the turbo-props being pushed into reverse thrust as the plane shuddered to a halt at the end of a runway that seemed barely wider than a dual-carriageway.

The pilot put his head out of the cockpit again. 'Welcome to Alderney, folks. Sorry if that was a bit bumpy, but I guessed you'd all rather be here than stuck in Guernsey. Sit tight, we'll have you off-loaded in a couple of minutes.'

The terminal was a glorified hut. Passengers were invited to help themselves to their bags that had been loaded on to a small trailer behind a car. I slung my weekend holdall over my shoulder just as the rain started to fall.

'Are there any taxis?' I asked the luggage handler.

'Sometimes there are, if not there's a phone inside to call one. But you can stroll to town from here. It's only about a ten-minute walk.' He pointed at a church spire. 'That's St Anne. Only place on the island.' He looked up at the murky clouds racing in over the wild sea from the west. 'On the other hand, walking might not be a good idea.'

I waited in the terminal café making another cup of dubious coffee last thirty minutes having left a message on the taxi answering service. The outside door opened, letting a gale whistle through, and a familiar face looked in. 'Taxi's here.'

It was the luggage handler. He showed me to a blue Skoda parked outside, opened the passenger door, put my bag on the back seat and got in the driver's side.

'Are you the same man or his twin brother?'

'Same man, sir. Just finished my shift at the airport. Now, where to?'

Mark was his name, and very helpful he seemed too. 'Do you get to see most of the people who arrive here?' He said he did, so I described Lizzy, saying I thought she had come to Alderney on Saturday.

'Ah, that's my day off, I'm afraid. Monty may know, though. We share the driving.' He picked up his mobile and keyed in a number. A short conversation later, he related that a lady of Lizzy's description had been dropped off at the tourist information office in the centre of St Anne on Saturday.

'Better take me there, then, Mark. And I'd better have your number, I may be needing you again.'

For such a small island, it took a long time to reach the centre of the capital and sole town. This was partly due to Mark needing to pass the time of day with almost every other driver we met on the way and the fact that the narrow main road through St Anne was one-way and had to be approached from the other side of the island.

He stopped outside the tourist office blocking the road, seemingly oblivious to the van behind. In London, this would have caused a major urban incident. In St Anne, the van driver simply started reading his newspaper while I thanked and paid Mark as he got my bag off the back seat.

'Any time,' he said, handing me back two crumpled green £1 notes. He saw me study them with suspicion. 'Local currency. Perfectly legal. And if you're looking for somewhere to stay, the Braye View may still have some rooms. Tell my sister Emma I sent you.'

The Skoda bounced away across the wet cobbles followed by the van as I stood on the pavement, the cold rain soaking through my inadequate linen jacket. I cursed my foolishness at not bringing my walking coat.

The door of the tourist office rattled open and a young couple with vast backpacks came out, the male holding the door open for me.

'Thanks,' I said, stepping inside. At least it was somewhere to start and it was dry. The front room had a giant 3-D map of the island covering almost all of one wall showing Alderney's rolling contours and steep cliffs. A coastal path was depicted in yellow around the edge of the green landmass, which was criss-crossed with other paths in blue. White squares denoted the sites of fortifications left behind by, first the Victorians, and then the Germans during the Second World War.

'If you need any help, just ask,' an earnest looking man with Julian on a lapel badge said over my shoulder. 'Not a great day for walking, but the coastal path can be glorious, especially around Trois Vaux Bay and Telegraph Bay.'

'Telegraph Bay?'

'Yes, in the south-west corner there,' he pointed to the map on the wall. 'Just beyond the end of the airstrip. If you flew here, you'd have nearly fallen into it.' He laughed, so I joined in.

'The bird colonies out there are spectacular, some of the largest in Europe. Here take these, they're free.' He handed me two pamphlets, one on the coastal path, the other on Alderney's wildlife.

'If you're interested in our World War Two fortifications, take this one.' Another pamphlet. 'A lot of people come here to see the huge amount of military defences around the island, and the sites of the concentration camps.'

'Concentration camps. Really?'

'Well, only one to be exact, that was Lager Sylt run by the SS, just by Telegraph Bay again,' he pointed to the map. 'The other three were more prisoner camps for the thousands of east Europeans brought here as slaves to do the work for the Nazis. Here, here and here.' He pointed again.

'They're just fields now but there are a few signs of the horrible things that happened. There are still some entrance posts standing, and stone works. If you want to know more about the War years, we have some very good DVD films we can show you in the study room upstairs. There's one about the evacuation, one about the occupation and one about the resettlement.'

'What exactly happened here?'

'Well, I'm not the historical expert, you want to go to the museum for that, but in June 1940, with the Nazis about to invade, the UK Government evacuated everyone – all 1,400 of the inhabitants – to the mainland. They couldn't do that on Guernsey and Jersey because there were too many people. The Germans then moved in for five years until the end of the War basically. They say thousands of the prisoners died here because of the barbaric treatment, but figures do vary. Have a look at the films.'

'I can't stop right now but I will come back. Were you here on Saturday by any chance?'

'Saturday? Yes, I was, only in the morning though. Why?'

I spun him a yarn about planning a surprise party for Lizzy but had lost the name of her accommodation and was trying to track her down. Even with a description of her, he could not recall her visit to the office. He did, though, give me directions to Braye View, which was at the lower end of town, so I set off to find a bed for the night.

Taxi driver Mark's sister Emma did indeed have a spare room. A small single with shared bathroom on the landing. I was lucky to get that in high season, she said, so I took it. I didn't expect to be there for more than two nights, three at the most. I quickly checked through her guests' register for Saturday's arrivals but there was no L. White signed in. That would have been too much of a coincidence.

As the name said, the guest house on the Rue de Braye, did have fine views of Braye Bay and the harbour, but only if you ventured into the guests' lounge at the rear. My pokey single had a narrow sash window overlooking the steep hill which ran from the harbour into town.

'I've arrived.' I had keyed in Zoe's mobile number. 'It feels a very small place, just one town with a couple of main roads in it although I guess there are properties dotted around the island.'

'Have you tried the police station?'

'I did, on my way to the guest house. There was no-one there. I'll go back this afternoon, but I suspect they might be wary of passing on any details. I should have thought of this before I left, could you email me a photo of your Mum so I can show people I ask?'

'Will do.'

'How are Stan and Ollie?' I heard a giggle at the other end. 'Have they decided whether to stay or go back to Wales?'

'They're staying for the time being, and have moved from the hotel into the cottage, partly I think to keep an eye on the gallery. It is, after all, Stanley's inheritance too. They're upstairs at the moment re-arranging what was my bedroom.' She sounded indignant.

'Has Stanley said anything more about Alderney or your grandparents? Or the paintings?'

'No. Not a dickie-bird. He seems pretty worried by it, though. I'm sure there's something he's not … oh, they're here.' Her voice dropped. 'I'll tell you later – and I'll send that photo.' She hung up.

I laid the pamphlets from the tourist office on the single bed as I waited for the little plastic kettle to boil. I could do the Coastal Path walk in a day comfortably, perhaps tomorrow if the forecast was OK and I had no leads on where Lizzy might be. There was every reason to go to Telegraph Bay, the subject of the painting on the wall in the gallery that apparently meant a lot to her and her mother.

Geordie Harris's revelation that Lizzy's father, John White, had been part of the Nazi occupying force in Alderney was still troubling. Was the old man rambling? Was it the rum causing a short-circuit in the over-stacked memory banks somewhere? I didn't think so. For all his years, Geordie was still lucid and very aware of what was going on. There was also the 'Nazi Scum' graffiti at the gallery, and the delivery of the Iron Cross in its own odorous bubble-wrap. There was surely a link there?

I poured the boiling water into the mug and the teabag floated to the surface surrounded by a dusty film. A splash of long-life milk from the plastic carton failed to make it look more appealing.

My phone pinged. Zoe's email with j-peg attachment had arrived. It was a head and shoulders of Lizzy as promised. She beamed out of the picture from underneath her tousled mop of hair seemingly without a care in the world. The tea was disgusting. I poured it on to a sad-looking plant on the windowsill, folded the maps and set off into town in search initially of a shop that sold coats that could withstand the wettest of westerlies.

Obviously there was plenty of demand for stout waterproof windproof clothing on Alderney. For such a small place, the Outward Bound shop had a surprisingly wide range of walking, hiking and biking gear. It came at a premium though. Island prices were considerably higher than those on the mainland.

'Don't you get undercut by mail-order these days?' I asked the shop owner as she processed my credit card for the all-weather North Face jacket.

'If you look in the small print on Amazon, you'll see the words "not available in the Channel Islands" on a load of goods. The shipping costs exclude most items. That's where we step in. I take it you don't want this wrapped?' She was looking out of the plate glass window as virtually horizontal rain battered pedestrians into submission.

Victoria Street led regally and loyally to Queen Elizabeth II Street, where the police station and court house stood opposite a small swing gate into the churchyard of the Parish Church of St Anne, an imposingly sturdy edifice that towered over the rest of the buildings in the town.

This time the police station was manned by one of the island's three officers. Friendly but unhelpful is the phrase, I think. Constable Squires had, indeed, spoken to Lizzy White on Saturday afternoon. She had answered all his questions satisfactorily and convinced him that she was not about to leap off Hanging Rock. He said he understood the family's concern, but was not at liberty to divulge where she was staying. He added that he thought she was still on the island, and wished me a happy stay.

Standing in Queen Elizabeth II Street again outside the police station with my back to the rain, I remembered what Geordie Harris had said about one of his old army comrades who died during the clearing of the mines. He had been buried in a local graveyard. There was more than one church in St Anne, but the one opposite was as good a place to start as any.

It did not take long to find what I was looking for amid the rows of immaculately kept graves and headstones. Beside the path leading down the slope to the church's front door was a white marble grave. The name on it was the one Geordie had remembered.

Written in memory of
Sapper Onions, G. E.
2 Platoon 259 Field Coy., Royal Engineers, B.L.A.

The epitaph read:

> In honour of a great man. No, not a political leader or a statesman, just an ordinary sapper. He died a hero's death not fighting but clearing mines from the fields and beaches in the Channel Islands. To those who read this, say a silent prayer for the equally silent men of the Royal Engineers. Their work in the War is not yet finished.

Judging by the fresh flowers on Sapper Onions' grave, his sacrifice clearly still meant a lot to the islanders. I shivered. Graveyards are cold places, even on the balmiest of summer's days, and this certainly was not one of those.

The path had been turned into a rivulet, sending flower petals and grass cuttings cascading towards the church porch. My new coat's claim to be 'storm-proof' was getting a thorough test. I needed somewhere warm and dry to wring out some decisions.

The bar of The Georgian was welcoming enough, and the sign invited guests to log on to the pub's wi-fi. I ordered tea and Welsh rarebit, found a corner table and hung my dripping coat on the back of a chair. The list of accommodation on the island on the tourist board website was not long. I discounted the caravan park and self-catering, and on one side of a paper napkin wrote the names of the hotels, pubs and guest houses with their contact details.

'Welsh rarebit, sir?' The waitress beamed and waited for me to clear away the napkin before putting down the plate.

'A friend of mine has just arrived on the island, but I've lost the address she gave me. She's not booked in here by any chance is she? The name's White.'

'I don't know, I'll check at reception, sir. Be back in a minute.'

She was as good as her word, but when she returned she looked crestfallen at not being able to help. She shook her head sadly. No Ms White at the inn. I put a line through The Georgian on my napkin and the Braye View Guest House, where I was staying.

As I steadily reduced the size of the rarebit, so I also reduced the options for where Lizzy might be holed up. By the time I had finished, only two of the nine on my list were unscathed. Five had lines through while two had question marks beside them because the person who had answered the telephone had refused to respond to my question or had not understood. The other two had rung out into answering machines. I was beginning to wonder if Lizzy had hired a tent and was wild camping.

The waitress collected the plate. 'Would you like to see the dessert menu?'

'No thank you. Tell me, do you know if there other guest houses on the island that are not listed by the tourist board here?' I held up the defaced napkin for her to read.

She squinted at the scrawl and crossings out. 'There are a few places that put people up that aren't there, yes. I'm sure there's a place at White Gates and out near Longy Villas. Down on the estate at Newtown there are some B&Bs too, they get the people who've just come off the boats.'

I thanked her and paid. The rain had just about stopped. Newtown was a bit misleading, I thought as I studied the map. It looked little more than a cluster of houses by the beach road that led to Braye Harbour. At least it was downhill from here.

The steep hill back past my own accommodation led down to Braye Street and a large, out-of-place hotel that sprawled beside the sandy beach. It had already been crossed off my list. The harbour echoed with the clanging of containers being loaded off a small freight ship but otherwise it was devoted to small craft: fishing boats and private yachts. Even in the summer, the waves were pounding the giant breakwater with deep soft thuds, each one followed by plumes of spray breaking over the top of the deserted walkway. The small boats clustered behind the wall for safety, lashed to heavy metal rings, refusing to go out to play in such conditions.

Crouched at the foot of the breakwater and sunk behind grassy embankments was Fort Grosnez, with gun placements overlooking the harbour and Braye Bay to the east and Crabby Bay to the west. The plaque said the Victorian strongpoint, called Josephsberg by the Germans, had been greatly adapted by them for modern warfare with flak guns and searchlights, now long gone.

The harbour was an incongruous mixture of the quaint – pretty, painted fishing boats and lobster pots – the derelict: the footings of a stone crushing machine and old railway lines – and the historic remnants of warring times across the last two centuries.

The rusty railway lines embedded in the concrete quay did not stop at the entrance to the harbour, carrying on across the modern road to a grass verge where a wooden hut bore the sign 'Braye Road Station' painted in the style of the London Underground. The August timetable behind a plastic sheet screwed to the wall said the trains to Mannez ran on Saturdays and Sundays at 2.30pm and 3.30pm. The single line left the station and weaved eastwards through the clutch of modern houses that was Newtown. I found three with accommodation signs swinging in the wind, but no-one claimed to have a Ms White living under their roof.

I traipsed along the railway track secure in the knowledge I was not about to get mown down by an HS2 express. The rain had returned by the time I had left the estate behind and reached an overgrown German gun nest, its squat concrete entrance barred by wire screwed into the thick walls beside the viewing slits, which were also covered in mesh. The coastal road had re-joined the railway track here. On one side, the ground rose gently towards a quarry in the hillside. On the other, it dipped through vibrant yellow gorse bushes to a strip of cropped grass, which fell away down a sandy bank to the beach. High to the right was another imposing grey angular fortification. The map identified it as The Arsenal and beyond that, Fort Albert. Despite my 'storm-proof' protection, I was getting wet again. It was time to head back to the warmth of my lodgings.

By my reckoning there were seven pubs and bars in St Anne, from the harbour side through to the top of town in Marais Square. As much as a pub crawl went against the grain, Lizzy White had to get out and eat at some time, so that was my arduous task for the evening ahead. I decided an afternoon nap was the best preparation and set the alarm on my mobile phone for six o'clock.

Lizzy White resurfaced like a submarine in an old war-time movie to send a message to concerned colleagues before slipping deftly beneath the waves again with barely a ripple. She might have been in the next room for all I knew, or on a different island altogether.

The contact had been made with Zoe, whose tea time call woke me long before my alarm had had the chance.

'It was just a text message, Tom, a few minutes ago. I'll read it to you: "I'm OK. Try not to worry but please don't open the gallery. Be back soon. Sorry for the mystery. Mum." That's all it says.'

'She must have turned her phone on to send that, have you tried ringing back?'

'Of course, I did that immediately, but it just rang out into the answering service. So I sent a text back begging her to ring because there's something else.'

'Something else?'

'Yes.' Her voiced wavered. I thought she might be about to cry. 'I was tidying up in the gallery this morning, emptying the wastepaper basket beside the desk when I found something horrible. Like a threat ....'

'Zoe, what is it?'

'It was a screwed up piece of paper, which I thought was odd because Mum always tears up letters she doesn't want. Half go in the wastepaper basket, half in the bin in the kitchen. It's just something she does for security. This bit, though, was just screwed into a tight ball.'

'So what was on it?'

'Hang on, I've got it here.' There was a pause and a rustle of paper. 'It says: "I know your past and I can prove it. Shut your gallery and get out of Rye Harbour if you want your sordid secret kept quiet. Now." The last word is written in capital letters and underlined. What's it all mean, Tom?'

'I've no idea. I assume it's not signed?'

'No. It's odd, it's written in charcoal on a piece of paper torn out of an exercise book by the look of it. And there's a sign at the end, like a funny stickman.'

'Stickman? Can you send me a photo of the letter, the whole thing?'

'Yes. Tom – I don't know what to do? Why has Mum run away like this?'

'What does Stanley say – I take it he's still there?'

'Yes, he is. He didn't say much really. He thought it was best we keep the gallery shut for now. I showed him the threatening note, but all he said was we'd better keep this to ourselves.'

'Have you told him about the text message?'

'Yes. He didn't say much about that either. It's odd, he's very quiet, almost evasive. It's not like him, he normally has an opinion about everything. What's happening in Alderney?'

I told Zoe about my trawl through my list of hotels and guest houses and my plans for an evening of pub visits in the hope of bumping into her mother. 'It's such a small place, there must be a fair chance,' I added for justification.

While I was talking my mobile vibrated softly to alert me of an incoming email. It was from Zoe, a photograph of the threatening letter attached. 'Hang on, your email has just dropped. I'll read it quickly.'

After a pause she asked: 'Well, what do you think, Tom?'

'It's clear enough, but I don't understand what it's about or why.'

'And the funny symbol at the end? Is that anything?'

'Doesn't mean a thing to me, Zoe. Look, I know it's easy to say this but try not to worry. As Stanley and Olivia are staying there, why don't you go back to your flat? Haven't you got work in the morning?'

'That's exactly what Uncle Stanley said. I suppose I should. Please ring me if you find out anything, though. Any time.'

I promised I would and ended the call. I opened the emailed photograph again and re-read the note. The writing was deliberate, well-spaced with no joined up letters, as if the sender was trying to disguise his or her hand. The symbol at the end had been written with some force as the paper had been torn slightly by its ugly outline.

It was a swastika. A symbol of divinity and spirituality in many cultures but most widely recognised as the hated emblem of the Aryan race during the Nazi regime of the Second World War.

It was badly drawn. I could see why Zoe might think it looked like a childlike stickman. But I recognised it instantly. I had not told her what Geordie Harris had said about her grandfather being German. Perhaps she didn't know; after all, there was no reason for her to know. She had never met him. He had died twelve years before she was born. If she didn't know, it was not my place to tell her of the family's past. Stanley had clearly not said anything to her, but it was possible he too didn't know about his father's background either.

Anyway, it might be totally unconnected to this threat to Lizzy, although I doubted it. There was only one way to find out.

The rain had at last relented as I headed back down the hill from the guest house to Braye Bay, past the island's only school, over the railway line to the Divers Inn, a cosy bar built into the back of the large hotel overlooking the beach. I started with a pint and sat next to deep-sea diving costume which was propped up, lifelike, on a seat by a table. He did not have much to say for himself so

I opened up the newspaper and found the crossword. *1 Across. Every worker's playing cards. Help! (3,5,2,4).*

There was very little help from my helmeted companion so I folded the paper and finished my pint. On the way out I showed Lizzy's photograph on my phone to the barman. He shook his head.

The Moorings was only a few steps along Braye Street at the other end of the hotel complex. It was more of a restaurant than a pub, with a large decking area for diners beside the sand dunes. This was more Lizzy's sort of place. A few brave souls huddled in cagoules were outside eating, the parasols over the tables swaying precariously in the sea breeze. Inside was cosier, and to my great surprise, the waitress who had taken my drinks order hesitated over the photograph I had shown her.

'Yes. I'm sure that's the lady who was in at lunch time. She had a bowl of soup outside, but then the rain started again and she brought it in, except she forgot her garlic bread and I made her some fresh. She was ever so nice.'

'I don't suppose she mentioned where she was staying?'

The waitress shook her head. 'Sorry. Now, it was just the glass of pinot was it?'

Lunch time. I had been down by the harbour that afternoon. We might have almost walked past each other. At least I knew she was on the island.

Alderney 1943

Weiss had announced his arrival that morning by banging his fists on the thick farmhouse door, yelling Giselle's name. The dog started barking furiously as she rushed from her bedroom wondering if there was a fire or a bombing raid, but all she found standing outside was a breathless, red-faced Weiss in trousers, braces and undervest.

'Your father's been arrested – accused of sabotage,' he said as he collapsed into the armchair. 'I've just run from the town. He's in the old jail. I don't know why, but the Field Police brought him in last night. Do you know if he has been doing anything he shouldn't have?'

Giselle shook her head. 'Will they shoot him?'

'I don't know. You'd better come, we'll try to talk to him and the police commander.'

'I can't. If father's not here I must milk the cows alone.'

'Can't that wait, Giselle?'

She shook her head again. 'I can come after milking.'

'Do you know how to get into the town safely?'

'Yes, of course. I go every week. Your soldiers never see me. They're so stupid.'

Weiss ignored the slur on his countrymen partly because he knew it to be true. 'Come to my office when you can, I'm upstairs in the big white building in Connaught Square. Do you know it?'

'I do. It's very close to my old school. We used to play games in the square.'

He sensed the resentment in her voice. 'As soon as you can, then.'

Weiss got up to leave. 'And try not to worry. I'll talk to the police, I'm sure it's a mistake. Unless you know something you should be telling me about?'

She shook her head again and he left.

Giselle arrived in the High Street around mid-morning. She could not be sure because the clock in the old church tower no longer worked. The road was busy with important-looking Germans on big black horses, and trucks shuttling to and fro. A ship had arrived in the harbour. One truck with wooden barrels roped together was parked at the church entrance, a relay of men passing the booty down a line into the dark interior. The coolness of the church made for the ideal wine store. Sacks of grain and potatoes also passed down the human line when another truck arrived. They were too busy to notice a slight girl with a blue headband and yellow summer dress.

When she entered Jens Weiss' office she was surprised to find he was not alone. Another sterner looking older man was sitting at a desk opposite the only German she had ever spoken to.

'Giselle, come.' Weiss beckoned.

'Who's this, Weiss?'

'It's Giselle Sparrow, daughter of Edward Sparrow, our farmer friend incarcerated in the old jail.'

'It's not safe for her here. Not now, not with the departure being planned.'

Giselle looked at the two officers. She had not understood a word that had passed between them except when they mentioned her and her father's name.

'Sorry, Giselle,' said Weiss in English. 'Herr List here was just saying he was worried about your presence. I told him not to be. Come. Let's go to the jail, we can use the back exit and take the alley by the bakery.'

The Old Jail was in New Street, built with thick stone walls into the back of the Court House and Police Station. Before the war, it had housed the occasional smuggler and cattle rustler, but its main use had been to give rowdy workers somewhere to sleep off their Saturday night excesses. Now the German Police ran the place and the twelve cells were divided into nationalities. Half were kept for their own military personnel found guilty of minor theft, fighting or drunkenness. Three were allocated to civilian workers from Guernsey, France and Spain, most of whom had either been found pilfering or had ignored orders. One man was there for possessing a radio, another for possessing propaganda pamphlets dropped by the RAF. Another was accused of stealing fuel from the harbour store for his boat. And then there was Edward Sparrow, in a bare cell on his own, a dark angry bruise on the right side of his face, a patch of clotted blood in his matted grey hair.

The SS jailer had been reluctant to let them in until Weiss had produced two packets of French cigarettes.

'What's he accused of doing?' asked Weiss.

'Setting man-traps in the grass at the airport for the pilots. He was caught red-handed last night with at least six of them,' said the jailer, pocketing the cigarettes and unlocking the door into the inner courtyard. 'Be quick. No more than five minutes. No touching.'

Weiss nodded and gently pushed Giselle ahead of him. 'Cell twelve, at the end there.' He hurriedly translated what the SS guard had said about her father's alleged offences to Giselle.

She had intended to be brave, but when she saw her father's battered face at the bars she let out a short scream and started to sob.

'Giselle, what are you doing in a place like this?' He sounded angry.

'More to the point, Herr Sparrow, is what have you been doing?' said Weiss. 'Anyway, her presence convinced the guard that our visit was more humanitarian than devious.'

'Father, what have they done to you?'

'Don't worry, Giselle. It probably looks worse than it is. Just some Nazi thug who didn't understand English.'

'So, Herr Sparrow. What were you doing with wire traps at the airstrip in the middle of the night?'

'Catching fu….' He stopped himself from swearing in front of his daughter. 'Catching bloomin' rabbits, of course. The wires were rabbit snares. Use them all the time. Good tasty food do rabbits make. The airport and the Giffoine is over-run with the things.'

'Rabbit snares!' Weiss laughed. Then the farmer joined in and so did Giselle.

'What's going on?' The guard poked a suspicious head around the courtyard door. 'Come on, time's up.'

'Don't worry, Herr Sparrow. I'll speak to the Commandant. We'll have you out of here before afternoon milking,' said Weiss. 'Come, Giselle. I have some chocolate in my office.'

Giselle sat on the desk, her legs dangling, as she looked at the map of the island on the wall with its neat lines of red and yellow crosses, munching on her last cube of chocolate, the first she had tasted for three years.

'You should not really be looking at that, Giselle,' said Weiss. They were alone as List had taken himself off to the inn in Marais Square.

'Why?'

'It's where we have laid mines. You see?' He pointed with an ink-stained forefinger. 'That's your farm and there, the red crosses show the mines laid down near the shoreline. We need to know where they are, but no-one else does.'

'So when you leave, no-one will know where they are? They'll step on them and get blown to bits. That's horrible.'

'Who said we're going to leave, Giselle? Anyway, that's not for you to worry about.' He was keen to change the subject. 'Tell me, Giselle. Those lovely paints you use to do your paintings. Where do you get them?'

'Why?'

'Well, I like to draw – and paint – myself.' He pulled open the middle drawer of the desk and opened an exercise book. 'This one is of Telegraph Bay'. He started turning the pages. 'There's your farm from near Fort Tourgis. That's Crabby Bay – it rained that day, that's why it's so streaked. That's the harbour from near Fort Albert. There's one I did of your dog from memory. But I'm not very good at animals.'

She took the book from him and studied the drawings more closely. 'They're lovely. But the dog does look a bit cross-eyed!' She laughed and handed the book back.

'I only have pencils to sketch with, I'd love to have some paints and do proper paintings, with colour on bigger pieces of paper. I wondered, are there more from where you got yours?'

'Loads,' she said. She liked the German. He had been

kind. He made father laugh and now he had promised to get father out of jail. 'I'll show you tomorrow, when father's home and safe.'

'It's a deal.' He lifted her down from the desk. 'You should go now.'

'Mr Weiss, were you at Telegraph Bay when they shot a slave?'

He nodded. 'Come. Time to go. No more questions.'

✠✠✠

12

The name on the screen read trouble. It actually read 'Katie' but in my world, the two words were never far apart.

My ex-wife never telephoned with good news or to pass the time of day. Usually I was to blame for whatever had gone wrong in her life. The fact that we had not lived under the same roof for more than two years did not appear to alter that fact.

'Hello, Katie. How are you?'

'There's been no word from Alice, Tom. I knew this bloody holiday was a mistake. It was your decision that she should go, I hope you remember that.'

'Whoa there, Katie. She left on Friday, today is Tuesday.' I squinted at the electronic bedside clock just to make sure I had not missed a day after last night's tour of Alderney's finest hostelries. 'That's what? Only three whole days since she arrived in Spain.'

'Only? I must have sent her six WhatsApp messages in those three days and she's not replied to any. There's no answer from her phone either. You'll have to go out there.'

'What? Go where?'

'Spain, of bloody course. Where else?'

'Don't be daft. She'll be all right, she's probably having

a great time and not bothered to check her phone.'

'Even for you, that's one of the most dumb-witted comments. She's never off the screen, you know that. No, you'll have to go.'

'Have you tried ringing Beth's number, or her parents' number?'

'I don't have them, do I.'

'That's good planning.'

'You what?'

'Nothing, dear. I can't go, it's as simple as that. I'm sure she's fine.'

'What do you mean, you can't go?'

'I'm away. On business.' Katie did not need to know any more details, but even if she did, I enjoyed stretching her patience to twanging point.

'Don't make me fucking laugh. You? Away on business?'

'As a matter of fact I am. I'm overseas.'

'Overseas? Where?' She was beginning to sound increasingly exasperated with me.

'Alderney.'

'Alderney. What the fuck are you doing there?'

'Katie, your language. You'll really have to watch what you say, especially in front of the baby.'

'What sodding baby?'

'Oh sorry, isn't it public knowledge yet? It's just that Alice said you were planning to start another family in your mid-life.'

'That's really none of your business, Tom, but if you must know, it's horribly stressful. This IVF business is ghastly.' Her tone had changed dramatically. I realised I might have pushed too far. Silence fell between us as it always used to do when we rowed and one of us had said something hurtful.

I tried a conciliatory tone. 'Katie, if anything had happened to Alice, we'd have heard. No news is good news and all that.' But before I had finished the sentence, I realised that she had hung up.

I could not be bothered showering before breakfast. In fact there was no time, anyway. Emma the landlady had said breakfasts finished at 9.30am, and her tone suggested 9.31am was too late. I just made it, declined the full English and asked for coffee and toast.

'There's a note for you, by the way,' Emma said when she returned with a large cafetière and row of white bread triangles that hung limply in the rack masquerading as toast.

'Note?'

'Yes, a lady popped in to see you at about eight. I told her I thought you might be in need of a lie-in as you got in so late last night, so she left a note. It's pinned to the guests' board in the hall.'

The note was from Lizzy White. I had missed her again for the second time in less than twenty-four hours. I would never make a private detective. It read: 'Planning to walk the coastal path. Will be on the bench at Telegraph Bay around midday. Will wait there. LW.'

I finished my breakfast in a hurry although there was no need: landlady Emma had said the walk to Telegraph Bay was less than half-an-hour, twenty minutes if I strode out.

I spread the map from the tourist office on the bed.

The route looked simple enough: through St Anne to Marais Square and then turn right on to the road towards the airport. Two left turns around the end of the runway and I would arrive at an old telegraph tower, once used, said the information panel on the map, to send semaphore signals to Guernsey and Jersey, the only way Alderney had of communicating with the outside world in the 19th century. The footpath cut past the tower and alongside the cliffs that rose above Telegraph Bay and The Sisters, the ragged stacks that stuck out of the sea like giant chipped teeth.

The previous night's tour of St Anne's drinking dens had proved enjoyable if fruitless: five welcoming bars, five pints of different ales and five blank looks when I asked the bar staff if they had seen Lizzy. The only thing that did come to light was the final solution to my crossword.

The answer to *1 Across. Every worker's playing cards. Help! (3,5,2,4)* was *All hands on deck,* and I certainly felt in need of some help by the time I had wandered back down the hill and kicked over the empty milk bottles on the doorstep before wrestling the key into the yale lock of the guest house.

If I had had no success tracing Lizzy, the note from her this morning suggested that she, at least, had had no trouble finding me. I sent Zoe a text to tell her that her mother had made contact and then I phoned Stanley White.

'Well that's good news at least,' was all that Stanley said when I told him of the planned midday meeting.

'What did you make of the threatening note that Zoe found?'

'Oh, that. Not much really. Some nutter, I guess.'

'Stan, there's something you're not telling me. Your sister receives a threatening note with a swastika drawn on it, the words 'Nazi Scum' are spray-painted on the cottage wall, an Iron Cross is posted through the letter box and an old war-time German gun is found at the property. There's a theme here that you are not explaining.'

'Iron Cross did you say? Oh God.'

'Yes. You know, the Nazi war medal? It was accompanied by a bag of dog shit, too. Now I haven't said anything to Zoe because I didn't want to scare her, but I'm guessing you know something about this, Stan.'

'I haven't got a clue, old man. Like I said, just some nutter. Nothing to worry about, I'm sure. Now, I really must be going, Olivia wants to go into Rye.'

Stanley White could not wait to end the conversation. That much was obvious. So too was my headache, which two paracetamol had failed to subdue. Fresh air and exercise was almost certainly the only cure. That and a bacon roll from the bakery in Victoria Street on my way to the road to the airport.

There was a pavement all the way to the airport entrance, but it wasn't needed. Pedestrians would have been just as safe walking down the centre of the road, so absent was the traffic on Le Grand Val. A single-engine light aircraft swaying in the wind as it descended touched down. Its arrival probably doubled the number of in-bound flights this morning.

Beyond the airport entrance, the road swung away from the airstrip and then arced left in a circle so that I found myself standing a few yards from the end of the runway, the landing lights on wooden poles in the field behind me. The road became a track and the Telegraph Tower was up ahead, and just beyond that three stone pillars that bore a plaque. The pillars, read the plaque, were all that remained of the entrance to Lager Sylt, the only concentration camp built on British soil. It remembered the hundreds who had perished on this island during the Second World War.

The path sloped towards the sea and turned right as the land dipped away showing a dramatic expanse of exposed, raw coastline that plunged several hundred feet into the waves below. A stock fence prevented the sheep from wandering too near the edge, but nothing prevented human visitors from looking into the abyss. The wind barged and pushed in angry gusts as I breasted the brow of a rise to see the path sweep across the arc of the bay where a figure sat on a green wooden bench looking out to sea.

'Hello Lizzy.'

She looked around, her mane of red hair flapping frantically across her face until she peeled it aside. 'Sit down, Tom.' She patted the seat beside her.

We sat in silence for a while, the cauldron of foaming water below providing an ever-changing spectacle.

'It's fantastic, isn't it?'

I agreed it was. 'How did you find me?'

'It's a small island, Tom. The policeman told me you'd been asking, and the taxi driver – Mark, isn't it? – he told me he'd sent you to his sister's guest house. I must admit, I'm surprised you didn't find me first.'

'Where are you staying?'

'I'm renting a cute little caravan on the campsite. It's clean and handy, and I knew I wouldn't be disturbed. There's no mobile signal either. I can only get that in the town. I guess I owe you and Zoe an explanation. Come on, let's walk.'

We headed to the western tip of the island, the narrow path weaving between gorse bushes and ferns as it sloped down a gully. A twin-propeller aeroplane similar to the one that had brought me to Alderney roared overhead as it battled to take off into the westerly wind, its spinning black tyres looking almost low enough to touch before it banked to the right over the cliffs and climbed into the fluffy white clouds.

Lizzy was talking excitedly, but about everything except why she had ended up on this small piece of rocky land in the middle of the English Channel. She pointed to some white rocks just off the shore: 'That's the Garden Rocks, there's a colony of about seven thousand Northern Gannets on there.' It dawned on me that the whiteness of the stone pillars just off the headland was not the colour of the rocks, but the mass of birds crammed shoulder to shoulder on their precipitous home - and their guano.

She led the way up a bare earth slope that had been dangerously eroded by other walkers, and we were back on the tarmac road that I had walked along earlier.

'I scattered my mother's ashes back there, Tom. Where we were sitting by Telegraph Bay. What a place to finish your days, eh?' She wiped a tear from her eye and laughed as she caught me watching her. 'Don't worry, I'm not sad. It's the wind, it makes my eyes water.'

'What's this all about Lizzy? Zoe's very worried, she

found a nasty note threatening you about some secret.'

'Did she? Oh, damn. That's so stupid of me. I remember just screwing it up and throwing it in the bin. I should have burnt the blasted thing. I think I probably panicked a bit, I just packed my bag and got a taxi to the railway station. I went to stay with an old friend in Norfolk for a couple of days before coming here. I even forgot my telephone charger. I had to buy another one.'

'Even so, why didn't you contact Zoe just to reassure her?'

'I did. My phone was out of action until I got a new charger at the airport, but I sent an email when I got to Norfolk so she didn't get alarmed. I didn't go into detail, I just said I fancied a couple of days away and said she should not worry.'

'Zoe's checked her emails and not seen anything, and we've checked the gallery email address too.'

'Well it definitely went. I used my friend's laptop and it confirmed delivery.'

'Did you use your own email account or your friend's?'

'My friend's I think. Why?'

'And does Zoe know your friend, does she have her email address?'

'No, they've never met.'

'Well, I suspect then that your email is sitting in Zoe's junk mail and she's not seen it. If her laptop didn't recognise the address, it may well have diverted it into the junk folder along with the other unwanted mail.'

'Oh, I never thought of that. Poor Zoe, she's probably been worried sick.'

'She has been. What did you panic about back in Rye

Harbour, Lizzy?'

She looked down at her feet. 'I suppose it'll sound a bit silly now, but it was something my parents told me when I was about eleven. Something they said must remain a family secret.'

'That your father was a Nazi?'

'No, Tom.' She stopped walking and turned to look at me. 'Please don't use that word. It's such a brutal word, particularly to my generation. How did you know?'

I told her about going to see Geordie Harris originally because of his link to the *Mary Stanford* tragedy, then seeing the paintings on the wall of his room at the retirement home. 'That was the link to Rother Gallery. One thing led to another and he told me about his friendship with your father, and the fact that he was a German by birth.'

She looked down at her walking boots and shook her head.

'So, what's the story, Lizzy?'

She put her shoulders back and took a deep breath. 'He never talked about it much, but Dad did tell us he was in the German army during the War. He said he hated it, but as a young man he had little choice. You either signed up or were thrown into prison for being a conscientious objector. He served most of his time in the Channel Islands when the Germans occupied them and said he never fired a gun in anger. Alderney was his favourite of the islands.'

She stopped walking again and looked to the north across rolling fields down to the sea. 'The place meant a lot to him and Mum, and when he died, she scattered his ashes on the path by Telegraph Bay. That's why she said we must always keep that painting above the desk in the shop, it was one of Dad's and it was of Telegraph Bay. And her wish was that when she died, her ashes be scattered there too.'

'But why are you so scared of the past? Zoe doesn't seem to know anything about this.'

'No, she doesn't, Tom. Perhaps it's been wrong of me not to tell her, but she never knew her grandfather. You see, as kids, Stanley and I grew up in fear of his past becoming known. Both our parents told us we must never tell anyone. They were afraid of what might happen.'

'Why?'

'I can't remember how they met, perhaps I've never known, but I know they got married here six years after the war, a day after Mum's 21st birthday. They wanted to live here but the locals made life unbearable for them when they discovered that Dad had been here with the German army. I think they left after a couple of months. Then they lived in Weymouth for a while, because that's where the ferry to England took them.'

'Mum said it was horrible – they were renting a little flat and it was OK for about six months, but when the local people found out about Dad's past they started throwing stones through the windows, spitting at them, painting swastikas on the door, things like that. Mum had a miscarriage. Whether it was caused by the unpleasantness, I don't know. Anyway they went to London next, lived in the East End somewhere and Dad got a job on the buses as a conductor, but he got beaten up one night by a gang of youths.'

'That's when they moved to Rye Harbour, they both wanted to be near the sea and it was so remote and quiet there, I think they felt they could live very privately. They had found their little haven, they had Stan and me and life settled down, but Dad lived like a hermit really.'

'Yet he joined the lifeboat volunteers, that doesn't make much sense, Lizzy.'

'I think he wanted to give something back to the community, and his English was so good, no-one seemed to care about his odd accent. I remember if anyone asked, he'd say it was the Alderney accent, which had a mix of French in it. Life was peaceful at last, but they lived in dread of the secret coming out – that's why he swore Stanley and me to say nothing. Ever.'

'Why did you go to see Geordie Harris last Friday?'

'Well, I visit him about once a year anyway, the old devil, but what with the threats about the family's past, I wanted to find out if he knew anything more about Dad's background than I knew. He didn't really, he just kept saying Dad was a decent man who wanted to do the right thing by his family. The next day I came here. I wanted to see if I could find anything out. I don't know what I was hoping to discover, really. Perhaps I was just running away.'

We had reached a sprawling derelict building on a headland, rows of large windows open to the elements, chunks of roof missing and concrete fortifications on every corner.

'Fort Tourgis,' said Liz. 'The Victorians built it because they thought the French would invade, the Germans fortified it because they thought the British would invade, but no-one ever came. Fancy an ice-cream?' She pointed to a van in the visitors' car park.

We sat on a bench looking down the gentle hillside where the road swept around to the right towards a row of modern houses with views across a common and a sandy beach.

'You should tell Zoe all this, you know.'

'Yes. I will. Just give me time to think what I should do now and how I should do it.'

'What's there to think about Lizzy? Does it really matter if your father fought on the wrong side in the war? It's seventy-five years ago now.'

'You're right, I suppose. It's just that we grew up being told no-one must know. Even after Dad died, we felt there was a stain on his past. Our past. Perhaps that's it: I just feel ashamed that he once wore a Nazi uniform. I don't think I could face people back home if they knew. That's why I've been thinking about selling up the gallery.' She looked away and rubbed her eyes again. 'But that would be such a pity after all these years. I kept it going partly because it meant so much to Mum and Dad. It was their sanctuary.'

'After you left, there were a couple of incidents.'

'I know about the German gun, if that's what you mean. The police here questioned me about it, but I didn't know it existed until they told me. The thieves who got into the shed must have taken it. I can only assume Dad kept it in a tin on the shelves at the end of the shed as a sort of memento. It was no use to anyone.'

'No, not the gun. There was something else.'

She tossed the tip of her ice-cream cone to a waiting

gull, who caught it expertly before it touched the grass and flapped away with its prize. 'What else?'

'The night after you left, someone sprayed "Nazi Scum" on the front of the gallery.'

'Please. No. Say it isn't true.' Lizzy buried her face in her hands. This time it was not the wind causing the tears. 'You see what I mean, Tom? This is what it would be like if I went home. Everybody knows now. People are still very sensitive about the War, even after all these years.' I put an arm around her shoulder, her whole being heaving with sobs from deep within.

I decided not to tell her about the Iron Cross. That could wait. Slowly the tears subsided and she gently pulled herself away from me. 'Come on, let's get a coffee down by the harbour. I could do with something warm.'

Sitting inside Cantina Café, Lizzy spooned idly at the creamy foam on top of her coffee. Although she was physically sitting here staring at the view across Braye Bay, she was to all intents and purposes in 1960s England.

She smiled and shook her head. 'Geordie Harris. He always seemed a nice man, even when we were kids. His funny accent used to make me laugh. He'd always called me "Bonny Lass" for some reason. On a Sunday, Mum would put on her best dress and hat and go off to the church with Mrs Harris. Before she'd shut the door, she'd yell out to Dad "look after the kids." Dad's idea of looking after us was to tell us to be good, and then he'd disappear into his shed with Geordie. Stan usually went off with some mates on his bike, I just messed around with my paints: outside if it was nice, inside if it wasn't.'

She sipped her coffee and delicately wiped the foam

moustache off of her top lip with a finger. 'One Sunday, Stan came home crying with a bloody knee and a buckled wheel, he'd fallen off his bike somewhere, and Dad got into a bit of a panic. I think he thought Mum would be cross. Dad didn't seem to know what to do, but Geordie took charge. He washed Stan's knee under the water butt tap, wrapped a handkerchief around the wound and stuck it down with black tape – you know the stuff, they use it for wiring?'

'Insulating tape?'

'That's it. Insulating tape. Dad must have had some in the shed. When Mum got back, I remember she was horrified. It was one of the few times I ever heard her get cross with Dad. She made such a fuss of Stanley too, you'd have thought he was about to have his leg amputated. She always did spoil him.'

Lizzy laughed and drained her cup. 'Let's have another.'

When she came back from the counter with two more coffees, she wore a puzzled expression. 'You know, I never realised Geordie knew about Dad's past. I'm shocked Dad told anyone, but perhaps if the two of them started talking about the War over a Sunday beer, he might have felt it safe to confide in him.'

'Geordie also had a close link with this island,' I said. 'He was here immediately after the War helping to get the place fit again for the return of the inhabitants. Possibly it was Alderney which created the bond between him and your father.'

'Perhaps I should sell up and move here, too.'

'That's giving in, Lizzy, and I don't think you're a

quitter. We need to find out who's making these threats and why.'

'And I'd like to find out more about my father. If Mum and Dad were married here, there should be some sort of public record.'

Island Hall was a square grey stone three-storey building set behind railings and a sweeping drive in Connaught Square. A painting of Queen Elizabeth II smiled down on the States Office reception, from where we were directed up two flights of highly-polished stairs to the municipal records office where, we were told, a Ms Deschamps would help us.

'It was 1951, you said?' Ms Deschamps, the archivist, had her back to us as she reached for a row of identical box folders on the shelves behind her desk. 'Here it is. Births, deaths and marriage certificates.'

She put the box on her desk and slipped on white gloves before she untied the black ribbon around the fastening on the lid. 'Can't be too careful, some of these documents are getting a bit fragile.'

'I think the date we're looking for is November 6th 1951, the day after my mother turned twenty-one,' said Lizzy as the folder lid was opened and a cloud of dust particles danced in the afternoon sun shining through the window.

'Marriages … July … October, November. Here we are. Only two that month. What names did you say?'

'John White and Elle Sparrow.'

'I've got a Sparrow here, but it's not White. Could this be it?' She held out a sand coloured piece of paper with faint neat black italic writing filling the columns.

'It must be,' said Lizzy.

'I'll copy it for you, but I'm afraid it will cost £5. Is that all right?'

She closed the folder, winding the ribbon back around the fastener before disappearing into a side room.

'Well, is that it, Lizzy?'

'I think so, Tom. I think so. You tell me what you think.'

The archivist returned flourishing the photocopied document. We paid and Lizzy beckoned me to sit on two seats just outside the archive office on the landing. 'Look.'

The document recorded the marriage at a civil ceremony of Jens Weiss, occupation: surveyor, and Giselle Sparrow, occupation: none, on Tuesday November 6th 1951. The printed names under the signatures of two witnesses were Edward Sparrow and Anton List.

'Mum's name was always Elle, but I guess she could have been Giselle, that sounds rather French doesn't it?'

'It does, she might have wanted to change it because of the War, and Jens Weiss, well, unless I'm mistaken, that's the German equivalent of John White.'

'He was a surveyor. That would explain some of the old tools in the shed, and his love of drawing.'

I pointed to the names of the witnesses. 'Edward Sparrow, do you suppose that was her father, your grandfather?'

'I suppose it must have been, or a brother, although Mum never mentioned that she had a brother. She did have a sister, but she died when she was young during the

War, as did her mother.'

'And Anton List? That sounds a bit Germanic. It could be a friend of you father's.'

The archivist popped her head out of her door. 'I thought I heard voices. When I looked at the marriage certificate again something struck me. The name Weiss. It rings a bell, I'm sure there's something about a Weiss in the museum.'

Alderney 1943

Georgi and Petr were not sure exactly what had happened to Alexei but they had seen him escape over the wall and a few minutes later they had heard the shots. They knew he was dead, that was all. Perhaps he was now in a better place than them.

Their firm today was being led down to the harbour where the giant stone-crushing machine was devouring rocks brought in from the quarries by the railway. At one end large boulders fell into the hopper, at the other end piles of hardcore spewed out. The crusher was like a roaring prehistoric monster, discharging clouds of dust that coated everything within one kilometre.

The slaves' job today was to shovel the hardcore into barrows and wheel them up into the backs of trucks. If they slowed in their work for a minute, the pile on the quayside would get too high for the crusher to work efficiently, and the overseer would make them pay. Today's overseer was Weird Herman.

'We'll shovel, you run the barrow up the plank,' Georgi told Ivan, who, since Alexei's disappearance, had become even closer to the Roslov brothers.

It was hot, filthy work. After four hours, they would be allowed a ten-minute break for rest and water, but Ivan was not certain he could wait that long. He had been doubled up most of the night with excruciating stomach cramps, the result of eating a dead seagull they had found beside the road on their march back to Helgoland the day before. Petr had warned him. His hunger had tempted him otherwise.

After three trips up the ramp with the laden barrow, Ivan fell off attempting a fourth, the stones spilling around the back of the vehicle, the barrow crashing down beside him, buckling the wheel forks as it hit the concrete ground.

Two guards were upon him in an instant, shouting insults and hauling Ivan to his feet before Herman arrived. 'What's going on?' His Russian was poor but Ivan understood him well enough.

'I'm sorry sir, it's a sickness. Please, I think I need to shit. Urgently.'

Herman nodded and smiled, 'Ja.'

He beckoned Petr to hand over his shovel. He took it, laid it on the ground beside Ivan and pointed at the shovel head. 'Ja. You shit.'

Ivan could not have waited if he had wanted to. He just about got his trousers down before he filled the head of the shovel.

Herman pushed him to one side, picked up the shovel and inspected the contents closely. 'Das ist gut,' said the overseer sniffing. He looked at Ivan:

'Good shit.' Then he swung the shit-laden shovel at Ivan's head, sending him sprawling in the gravel, and roared with laughter as he strode away.

Georgi and Petr did not see Ivan again. His bleeding unconscious body was taken by the guards and left by the railway line. They never learned if he had survived. A Pole, who worked as an engineer on the diesel locomotives, told them that he had seen him being carried away on the back of a horse-drawn cart. Whether he was bound for the cemetery, the infirmary or Lager Sylt, he could not say. 'Best not think about it, boys,' the Pole had said in the soup queue.

'We've got to get out of this place, Petr,' Georgi said to his brother as they consumed the thin tasteless broth from their cans while sitting looking across the harbour during their brief break for lunch.

'Oh yes, brother. And were you thinking of taking the steamship or an aeroplane. I fancy England myself, they tell me it's very civilised. How about you?'

'Very funny, Petr. But it can be done. I know it can. And what have we got to lose? Drowning at sea must be better than living in hell.'

Georgi looked across Braye Bay and nodded. 'France is in that direction. It's only about twelve kilometres away apparently, but they say the currents are treacherous. There are other islands nearby but they're full of Germans too, so, yes, England is the obvious place to go.'

The boys fell silent. Their land-locked home in central Russia had not prepared them as seafarers. They had never even seen the sea until they were shipped out of St Malo on board a German prison ship bound for their captive island a year ago.

Braye Bay harbour was crowded with boats, large and small, military and civilian. The wreck of a steamer poked its stack and mast out of the water just a few yards from the jetty steps that led down to a cluster of fishing boats and dinghies.

'We'll get a chance,' said Georgi. 'I know we will. And when we do we must take it.'

✠✠✠

13

The museum was only two minutes' walk away, Ms Deschamps had explained: through a small gate in the high stone wall at the top of Connaught Square, across the old graveyard and through another gate by the clock tower. When we arrived, though, the large green door was shut. The board giving opening times said we were too late. It would be open again at 10.30 tomorrow morning.

I could sense the impatience in Lizzy. She paced up and down the yard outside the museum, every now and again re-reading the photocopied document in her hand.

'Do you think this Jens Weiss was my father – John White?'

'He has to be, Lizzy. It's your mother's name and the right date. Your father was German and that sounds like a German name. I suspect he just translated it into English to make life easier when they tried to settle in England. A German sounding name would not have been welcomed in those post-war years.'

'Yes, I'd worked that out.'

'There's nothing to be done until tomorrow. Let's have dinner and we can discuss what you're going to do over a poppadum or two. In the meantime, you really must phone Zoe.'

Every little village in England it seems has an Indian restaurant these days and St Anne on Alderney was no different. Like one of Pavlov's dogs, I had reacted to the aroma of cooked spices in the air on my first morning walking down the cobbled main street, and the restaurant did not disappoint.

Lizzy had spoken to Zoe as promised. Her daughter was happy, worried and angry in just about equal measure, she said. She had also spoken to her brother Stanley and he was just angry in one big measure.

'He's upset that you know about the German thing, he's upset that Zoe knows and he's upset that the subject of our father's past has cropped up again. He says we must sell the gallery and that I'll have to move.'

'Surely that's your decision?'

'Not entirely. He's half-owner of the property although the business is left to me. He'd kept the whole thing secret, even from Olivia. Can you imagine, not even telling your wife?'

'Well, in the case of my ex, yes I can, but I know what you mean. I can't imagine Olivia was best pleased.'

'No,' Lizzy started to laugh. 'She'll have Stanley's guts for garters.'

'Lizzy, there was something else that happened after you left, something pretty unpleasant as well as the graffiti.'

I told her about the Iron Cross delivered in its aromatic parcel. 'Do you think the medal was your father's?'

'Who else could it have belonged to?'

'It could have been a memento, like the gun. Or they

could have both been his. Keepsakes from a time he'd rather have forgotten.'

'Or rather not forgotten. Perhaps that was when he met my mother. Perhaps the War was not all bad for him if it brought them together.'

Lizzy joined me for breakfast at the guest house the next morning, which did not please the landlady. She explained that I would have to pay extra, even though my companion had only tea and toast.

We were outside the museum fifteen minutes before opening time, which was not a wise move as the rain had set in again and there was no shelter.

'My, a queue. That is unusual.' A smiling man with a large grey beard bustled into view, holding a bunch of clanking keys. 'Sorry to keep you waiting, especially in this weather.'

He turned one deadlock on the large Victorian door, then another and it swung open, sending an alarm into action with a series of short sharp beeps. 'Give me a moment to switch that blasted thing off.' He held up a hand.

When silence returned, so did he. 'Open now, in you come. We have to have the alarm, you see, there are quite a lot of firearms inside. All under lock and key, of course, but the law is very strict about these things, quite rightly I suppose, even on little old Alderney.'

The entrance passage opened up into a large long hall, with high windows and showcases in four neat rows. Arrows taped on to the floor recommended a route around the exhibits, starting with prehistoric Alderney up until the rebuilding years after the War.

The curator took off his dripping coat and dried his beard with a polka-dot handkerchief the size of a single bedspread. 'Help yourself to these little guides, they're free,' he said as we handed over the £3 entrance fee. 'And if you want any help, just ask.' He sat behind the desk and flicked on a tiny fan heater by his feet.

'Do you have much on the War years?' I asked.

'Lots, that's the centre-piece of our exhibition really. There are cabinets down the aisle depicting the mass evacuation of the inhabitants, through the occupation years and then the repatriation of the islanders.'

The story of how 1400 inhabitants had been evacuated in 1940 on a fleet of boats large and small was told in old monochrome pictures, newspaper cuttings and official documents.

About a week later, the first of the German army arrived, and cabinets were full of Nazi uniforms, weaponry and medals. Proud German officers on horseback were photographed on the cobbled streets of St Anne while a military band marched past, the Nazi flag hanging from the outside of the local Lloyds Bank. Smiling German soldiers holding bottles of wine posed beside large guns pointing out into the English Channel, their helmets dangling from the metalwork.

There were photographs of the harbour, battleships docked in the bay and cannons lined along the quay. One picture showed the portico of the Island Hall we had visited yesterday guarded by a German soldier, another showed barbed wire in front of a beach and a skull and crossbones sign with the legend *Achtung Minen*.

Another cabinet was harder to view. Abject prisoners in rags were seen being marched along a road by their German jailers. There was a photograph of a field overgrown with grass with ranks of crosses marking graves. Beside it was a piece of paper, browned and disintegrating around the edges but still clearly depicting a typed row of names under a card reading 'List of the Dead'.

In the far corner was another cabinet. Inside was a large, hazy photograph of a smiling young, fresh-faced man in open-necked shirt and baggy trousers, and in the background was a rudimentary pencil sketch of Braye Harbour.

Lizzy looked at it transfixed.

'That's my father,' she said almost in a whisper.

'What?'

'It is, look.' She pointed to a caption underneath the photograph. It read:

> Jens Weiss was a German soldier who spent much of the War stationed in Alderney. He was a draughtsman and surveyor, and, among his duties, he was given the task of plotting the minefields around the island. He was also a keen artist and produced many pictures in pencil and paint of the Alderney landscape (shown here).
>
> Before the liberation of Alderney, the German Command ordered the destruction of all the minefield plans, but Weiss made a second set at considerable risk to himself which he hid, hoping the Allies would find

> them to avoid further bloodshed when the mines were cleared. This they did, and his actions almost certainly saved many lives.'

Below the commendation was a collection of black and white sketches by Jens Weiss, all with the signature in the bottom left-hand corner: JW.43.

Lizzy's hands were clasped over her mouth and small tears ran down either cheek. She turned to look at me, her eyes glistening as she said: 'He was a hero, Tom. My father was a hero.'

We perched on the maroon-painted wall of a large oval water trough that formed the centrepiece of Marais Square. Despite the rain, Lizzy did not want to be inside. She was too full of questions and excitement to settle for more than a few moments.

As soon as she had digested the story of her father, she had gone to see the museum curator at the front desk, but he had told her he was not the one to ask about the War years. He knew the story of Jens Weiss, he said, but little more than was explained in the display. He suggested we return after 2pm when his colleague, Joan, who was more of a specialist, would be in and could take us upstairs to see the archives – for a small fee.

Lizzy looked at her watch, frowning at the tardiness of its hands, and held it to her ear to confirm it was still working. She left her perch and paced up and down.

'You checked less than two minutes ago, Lizzy.'

'Did I? Surely it was longer ago than that?' She sat down again.

I took a bite of the chicken curry pasty I had bought from the bakery and shook my head. 'No, two minutes max. Eat your sausage roll, it'll be going cold.'

She studied the greasy paper bag in her hand and nibbled at the protruding pastry. 'I can't get over it, he was a genuine hero. A good man at heart. All those years of living in fear in England and he never said anything.'

'Soldiers rarely do say much about their time in the services if my experience is anything to go by. They just want to forget. The ones who do want to talk about it are generally those who did very little and want to big themselves up.'

'But he had nothing to be ashamed of, although he was in the German Army. He took a huge risk to save British lives. If the Germans had discovered that he left the minefield plans, he'd have been shot at dawn or whatever they did to people who disobeyed orders.'

'You know, I've just remembered something Geordie said. When he was here after the War, one of his jobs was helping with the mine clearing. He said they lost only one man, which was a minor miracle. Perhaps he knew about your father's maps and what he'd done. That might have been why they became close and trusted one another.'

I screwed up my paper bag and stuffed it into a pocket. 'Come on, it's starting to rain again, I'll buy you a drink in the Marais Hall before we go back to the museum.'

By the time we got back there it was busy. Bad weather is always good for museum business. The curator was still at his station toasting his toes, but this time the seat beside him was occupied.

The lady he called Joan turned out to be the museum treasurer and specialist in war-time history. Her accent sounded French although she informed us she was born and bred on Alderney. She ushered us through a curtain marked 'staff only' and up a narrow spiral staircase with a rope as a handrail.

'It's a wonderful old building,' I said.

'It used to be the school up until the War years, they built a new one afterwards to encourage the families with children to come back, but, yes, it is a lovely old place. In here.'

She took us into a small office lined with metal racks that were stacked with books and folders. In the centre of the room was a table with two desk lamps, notepads and pencils on it.

'This is only the tip of the iceberg,' she said, noticing me look around. 'We have a lot more material next door and in the cellar. And then there's my spare room at home, and my loft … I could go on.'

She looked over the top of her glasses at the bottom shelf, where ring-binders stood to neat attention, letters inked on to their shoulders.

'Here we are. W. Weiss. Anything in particular you want to know about our modest local hero?'

I could almost sense Lizzy swelling up with pride. 'Everything really. You see, he was my father.'

Joan looked over her glasses again. 'Oh, how wonderful, I've often wondered if he had family, because the story goes that he got married here, you know, to a local girl.'

The archivist opened the ring-binder and started

leafing through plastic folders, most crammed with drawings, some with documents and maps. She pulled out a photocopy of a map of the island, with symbols and German words written on it.

'This is only a scaled down picture, you understand, but it is one of the few documents we found. It shows the road plans and tank traps, we think Jens did the original.' She offered it across the table.

'Is this the one he left secretly showing the minefields?' I asked.

'No, sadly we don't have that. What a wonderful find that would be. And these,' she offered a sheaf of sketches across the table, 'are some of his drawings. They are not all of Alderney, he did serve in Jersey and Guernsey as well before he came here, and some of the pictures are from there.'

Lizzy was entranced with the pictures, muttering her appreciation of the artwork, so I took my opportunity. 'Did you say he married a local girl?' I asked.

'Yes, but I'm not sure I have her name here or any documentation. We've mainly concentrated on the military side of his story.' Joan rifled through the ring-binder tutting to herself at her lack of proof. 'No, can't find it, which is a shame really because according to island folklore, our Jens met her during the War and returned several years later to rekindle the romance. It's all very Mills and Boon.'

'I thought there were no locals left on the island after the evacuation, or was she French?'

'No, she wasn't French as far as I know. One or two locals, much to the annoyance of the authorities, refused to leave, while a few others came back here from Guernsey to work under the German regime. I suspect she must have been one of those.'

'Her name was Giselle Sparrow,' said Lizzy, looking up from the pictures laid across the table. 'Although we thought Mum was just called Elle.'

'Sparrow? That was quite a well-known name on the island. There was a Sparrows Farm near Saline Bay, out below the airport, and I think it was where they had the last ever of the Alderney Cattle breed, which is sadly now extinct. There's a wall mural about the Alderney Cattle in the flora and fauna room downstairs if you're interested.'

Joan's knowledge did not stretch as far as knowing Jens Weiss' military record and whether he had ever received the Iron Cross. He had left the island late in 1943 and was posted back to Germany. There were no records of what happened to him after that during the conflict.

'He did come back here in about 1951, that much is known from the customs records at the port office, but we don't know when he left again.'

'He must have received a hero's welcome,' suggested Lizzy.

'Oh no, I don't suppose so. The story of him leaving plans of the minefields for the Allies to find did not become public knowledge until many years later. There was so much secrecy about the German occupation in the years immediately after the War, nothing came to light for ages. I suspect he probably had to keep a low profile on the island in the fifties with a name like Weiss.'

'Where did he leave the minefield plans?'

'That's one of stories that has been lost in the mists of

time I'm afraid. After the War, any documentation from here that remained went back to Guernsey and Jersey, some of it made its way back to the English mainland, but most of it was destroyed. The British Government wasn't proud of the fact that their Channel Islands had been occupied by the Germans, you see. What happened here during the War largely went untold on the mainland.'

'That's disappointing,' said Lizzy. 'I'd love to see what he left. How do you know the story is true?'

'It's known for certain that he left the minefield plans, that much at least was confirmed by military sources in Whitehall after so much speculation from the Allied soldiers who worked on the mine-clearing after the War. But just how he left the plans has not come to light. There are all sorts of rumours: one story is that he left the plans hidden in a bible in the church, another is that they were ferreted away in an old art cupboard here at the school, another is that he left them on the back of one of his drawings. One day we'll find out, I'm sure.'

We must have looked a morbid couple, hunched in our rain jackets going from grave to grave.

Being told her mother was originally an islander had shocked Lizzy, who wanted more proof. If Sparrow had once been a well-known name on Alderney, as the archivist had suggested, there might be more evidence of her family background.

Next to the museum was a small graveyard of a church long-ago demolished apart from its clock tower, but that offered up no headstones with the name Sparrow carved into ancient granite, so we moved on to the Parish

Church of St Anne at the hub of the town, where Sapper Onions was laid to rest.

On a 'you-take-that-row-I'll-take-this-row' basis, we weaved our way backwards and forwards covering the large graveyard on the slope down to the church's main entrance. Many of the names were of French descent, a few sounded Germanic, but there appeared to be no flock of Sparrows.

Lizzy straightened up with a groan, holding her back with both hands, shaking her head. 'No joy.' She was disappointed but not defeated. We agreed to split up to check for more graves around the large buttressed sides of the church and then meet at the rear.

We met underneath a tall slim stained-glass window depicting the Crucifixion. In front of us were yet more graves, these were spread over two grassy tiers behind the church, several of them freshly dug. 'You take the upper tier, I'll take the lower,' I suggested.

We split up again and almost immediately Lizzy shouted excitedly. 'Over here, Tom. Look.' She pointed at a plain headstone and read: 'Edward St John Sparrow. Farmer, loving husband and father. Born in 1903, died 1960, aged fifty-seven. That's no age is it?'

'Edward Sparrow – that was the name of one of the witnesses on the marriage certificate wasn't it? It must be her father – your grandfather.'

'They didn't go in for over-elaboration in those days did they? That doesn't tell us much. No names of any other family members. No other family graves here either. You wonder where his wife was buried, don't you?'

She contemplated the grave, pulling out a few long

dandelion heads from around the headstone. 'You know, I was three when he died in 1960. I don't remember ever hearing anything about it. I don't even know if Mum came to the funeral. I suppose she must have done.'

We continued the search and just as it looked as though it would be fruitless, I found a nest of Sparrow family members interred in a corner by a short flight of stone steps that led into a lane. There were four neglected graves side-by-side, small mounds of long grass and wild flowers by a thorn hedge. The inscriptions read as though two earlier generations of the family dating back to the middle of the 19th century were buried here, the headstones suggesting there might be more than one deceased in each plot.

Lizzy read through the inscriptions silently, running her fingers lightly over the lichen-mottled stone. 'How strange to think these people are probably my great-grandparents and great-great grandparents. I don't remember ever asking Mum about her family, and she never volunteered much about her past. I guess the past was back here on Alderney, and that was not something she and Dad wanted to revisit. It was something they wanted to blot out. Now, Mum and Dad are back here at Telegraph Bay and in peace.'

That evening I booked us both on the last flight back to Southampton the next day.

Alderney 1943

Father was in the shed making new rabbit snares to replace those confiscated by the German police. It was a chance to find out the time without arousing his concern. The only way of telling the time in the farmhouse was father's fob watch, which he never wore, keeping it on his bedroom dresser and winding it every night before he went to sleep. It had been a wedding present, he said, from his father.

The watch said it was just past two in the afternoon and her chores were done. Being a Saturday, she had no lessons to do. The rest of the day was hers.

Jens Weiss was waiting by the large stone cattle trough in Marais Square. It had been many years since the trough had been used by thirsty animals brought to the cobbled square on market day. It was now unloved and full of the debris of an occupying force that had installed mains drainage and running water into the town, but needed somewhere to dump the rubble.

The morning sun had disappeared and the ever-darkening clouds gathering in the west suggested more rain was on the way to this windswept, forgotten island. Weiss turned up his collar and sat on the edge of the trough. The girl had promised to be here by three. It was now five past by his watch.

She appeared from an alley beside Marais Hall, breathless and flushed. She had been running, not something to do if you wished to avoid the suspicion of the military police.

'Slow down, Giselle. The War is not about to end today.'

She sat on the low wall of the trough beside him and looked around. 'The square used to be such a fun place, you know.'

He sensed the sadness in her voice.

'Market day was always crazy,' she said. 'And the street crier used to stand over there shouting out the news,' she pointed. 'On New Year's Eve everyone came here for singing and dancing, and the fire engine used to spray the crowd with a hose.'

'When was that?'

She paused. 'I s'pose 1939 was the last time. The winter before you lot came. I was here with Martine, and mother and father.'

'How old were you then?'

'1939? I was nine then. I'll be thirteen this November. On the fifth, Bonfire Night.'

'Bonfire Night?'

'Yes. Don't you Germans celebrate November the fifth? Remember, remember, the fifth of November. Gunpowder, treason and plot,'

Weiss shook his head.

'We'd have a huge bonfire down at the cricket field, cook sausages and let off fireworks. Something to do with Guy Fawkes who tried to blow up Parliament.'

'Sounds fun. When did he do that?'

'Oh, years ago, I think. Anyway, my birthday's the same day, so it's easy to remember. And this November I become a teenager.'

'I'll try to remember to get you a present. Now, come on, you promised to let me into the secrets of your paint supply.

Let's go. We shouldn't be seen walking together so you go ahead, I'll follow.'

It had started to rain. She picked up a discarded broken umbrella from amongst the rubble in the cattle trough. After a couple of attempts, she got it to open, three of its spokes bent and sticking out with no canvas, the black material flapping in the wind.

'This will make me easy to spot.' She twirled the old brolly.

'You're enjoying this, Giselle. I can tell.'

She set off back towards the High Street, but quickly slipped into a cobbled cut that Weiss did not even know existed. She was sure-footed and quick on the slippery stones. If it had not been for the old umbrella, Weiss would have lost sight of her. He caught her up by the tree in the centre of Connaught Square.

'C'mon,' she gestured towards a granite wall. There was a narrow gap in it that led into a small graveyard by the old clock tower, which was all that remained of a church that once stood on the site.

'Round this way.' She skirted the perimeter of the graveyard and stood with her back to another stone wall, this one as tall as Weiss.

'Well?' He looked around puzzled.

She tilted her head backwards. 'In here.'

'In where?'

'Over this wall behind me'. She folded the umbrella, propped it against the wall and checked both ways. There was no-one in sight. She turned, and, picking out three well-worn gaps in the stone work, she levered herself up and over the wall. He heard her drop on the other side. 'C'mon, Jens.' It was the first time she had used his Christian name.

Likewise, he checked both ways and, feeling like the errant schoolboy of his youth who used to steal apples, he climbed over the wall with much more difficulty than the girl and dropped on the other side.

'What's this place?' He looked around a long narrow yard, with walls on three sides and an imposing building in front of them. There was a collection of faded white painted boxes on the ground at his feet. On the wall they had just climbed over were another three white lines about a metre high. On another wall he could make out a large painted shape like goalposts. The ground was littered with broken glass. The windows of the building were boarded up as were the two entrances at either end. Above one it said Filles *above the other* Garçons.

'It's the playground. This is my old school. This way.' She pointed to a sign at one end of the building that read Toilettes Filles. *Inside, she stepped on to the rim of a cracked porcelain bowl, then, using the cistern, heaved herself onto the wall which separated the cubicles. The lavatory was open air.*

She pointed to a window on the first floor. It too had been boarded up, but two planks on one side were gently swaying in the wind. Using a drainpipe bracket as a foothold, she heaved herself up again, her loose dress flapping in the wind, pushed the planks aside and nimbly rolled over the windowsill into the building.

Moments later her face appeared looking down at him. 'Your turn. It's easy.'

The grunts and grazes suggested he did not find it half as easy as she had made it look, but eventually he found himself sitting on a dusty floor amid bird droppings and scraps of paper, most, he could make out in the dim light, torn from reference books. On the wall opposite was a blackboard and on it someone had scrawled in chalk in English: 'Fuck Hitlers Vermin.'

She saw him looking at it. 'That wasn't me, by the way. This way.'

She led him into a dark corridor past another classroom then up a short flight of steps to another empty space. His eyes were now accustomed to the gloom. The two tall windows in front of them let in enough light between the planks that had been hammered over the broken panes for him to see his surroundings.

'This was the art and crafts room. That's my peg over there at the end.' She nodded towards a row of pegs. 'Art was my favourite lesson. Mrs Crabtree said I was very good at it too.'

She walked over to the row of six pegs. 'The looters didn't find this. It's about the only thing they didn't find.' She turned a dark brown wooden catch, the same colour as the wooden panelling, and the section of wall holding the pegs swung open to reveal an under-eaves cupboard.

'This was our art store. Here, have a look. There are a few paints left on the shelves, and there's a box of paper at the back. It might be all right if the rats haven't got to it.'

Weiss would have kissed her had it not been improper for a German officer of twenty-seven years of age to do such a thing.

When she reached the door of the farmhouse, Giselle could hear her father whistling. That was a good sign. He whistled only when he was happy. He was around the side of the building by the log store.

She had picked some ferns and small pink wild roses she had found growing beside a wall outside the airstrip, which was silent and seemed deserted. As he was in a good mood, she decided to tell him where she had been if he asked.

Edward Sparrow was stacking chopped lengths of wood close up to the farmhouse wall to give them as much protection from the weather as possible. Behind him, the tip of the axe was buried in the chopping block, the dog contentedly watching from a safe distance.

'What've you got there, Giselle?'

'Just some little roses, growing out near the airport of all places.'

'Where have you been then?'

'Oh, nowhere much. Just had a look at my old school. It's still there.'

'You should be careful in town, you know that. Particularly of a weekend if the civilian workers have been drinking.'

'It was OK, I was with Mr Weiss.'

The farmer stopped his stacking and stood upright. 'Weiss? Why were you with the German?' He sounded displeased.

'He's a nice man, father. He made sure they let you out of that jail. And he likes my paintings.'

'I don't know if any German can be "a nice man." You have to realise, Giselle, that while we get along with them at the moment, they're still our enemy. They took over our island and forced everyone to flee. They've built their fortresses everywhere, ruined our land – and God knows how many of the slaves have perished doing so. It's probably thousands.'

'Yes, I know father. But Mr Weiss is only here because he has been told to be here. I don't think he likes what's going

on any more than we do.'

'You may be right, but at the end of the day, he will follow orders. He's still a German. Anyway, why were you with him?'

'He likes painting but hasn't got any paints, so I showed him the cupboard in the art room at school. He was so excited. He filled his pockets, took some brushes and a roll of paper. He's promised to paint me something.'

'No harm done, I guess. But be careful Giselle. Don't get too close to him.'

✠✠✠

14

Larry Lander's phone calls were rarely succinct or dull. My old drinking partner and colleague, now occasional commissioning boss on the local newspaper, could have represented the UK had talking the hind legs off a donkey ever been recognised as an Olympic sport. With break-dancing and wall-climbing on the agenda for the next Games, there was still hope for him.

He had called during breakfast and, confronted by the glares of my fellow diners in the guest house, I had had to leave the full English half-finished to take him outside.

The 'GAP' boys had been identified, he said. Those guilty of the shed raids around Rye Harbour who left their calling card in the form of the graffiti warning 'Mind the GAP' were brothers George and Peter Clunes and pal Alex Lee. 'GAP' representing the initials of their first names.

Lander's police contact had told him they saw themselves as the local gang, but as hard men went, they were more kindergarten than Krays. They would be up before the local magistrate next week, but they were only the drones in the operation. The Queen Bee was Dawn Speed. She had flown.

What had led the police to Rookery Farm on the salt marshes in the first place was the World War Two

German Walther pistol, Lander explained. The GAP Gang panicked when they were questioned about the gun. Firearms were out of their league. They spilled the beans on Dawn Speed's garden equipment enterprise.

They were stealing to order for Speed, erstwhile partner of artist Fin McEvoy. She in turn passed the goods on to her extended family near Camber, who shifted the mowers, chainsaws and hedge-trimmers at various boot fairs. In return, the GAP Gang received a small cut, which was part of the trouble.

They thought their cut was being trimmed too much, said Lander. So they returned to Speed's home when they knew she and Fin were absent to seek retribution or recompense. They broke into the barn next to the couple's caravan where the stolen garden equipment was stored, but to their annoyance found it had already been moved on. They found nothing but Fin's artist's equipment and bits of driftwood. It was not what they were looking for, so they caused a bit of damage – as kids do, said Lander.

'And the fire at the caravan?' I asked.

'Nah, nothing to do with the little buggers after all. They're just kids, not nasty enough to set fires it seems. The fire investigation discovered that it wasn't arson as first suspected. It had been started by an electrical fault – the result of some dodgy wiring by Fin, who'd illegally tapped into a local power cable. Serves him right.'

'That's a bit harsh, Larry. They did lose a dog because of the fire.'

'And his missus. With the coppers sniffing about, she's disappeared off the scene, but it seems Fin is in the clear over the shed thefts. The police accept that he wasn't involved, although, of course, he knew the stuff was being stored in the barn.'

'Isn't he guilty of some offence then?'

'Technically, yes, but she was the brains behind the operation. I think the cops accepted that McEvoy kept quiet because he knew what was good for him. Her family can be quite heavy, by all accounts.'

'He's probably best out of it. She sounds like bad news.'

'And your vanishing lady, found her yet?'

'I have. In Alderney, of all places.'

'That's one of the Channel Islands, isn't it? What the hell's she doing out there?'

'That's a very long story, Larry, which I will regale you with over a good meal soon. Suffice to say she's fine, and we're flying home later today. By the way, are the little sods getting done by the police for threats and intimidation to Lizzy as well as the thefts? Someone or some people have been trying to warn her off and close the gallery.'

'If you mean the graffiti and the dog shit, Tom, I've not heard anything. Your gallery lady should talk to the police about that when she gets back.'

When I returned to my table, the other guests had departed and my congealing eggs were being cleared away by Emma. She did not look too happy that her breakfast had gone to waste. I decided against asking for fresh coffee. Lizzy was due in a taxi any minute and I still had to finish packing.

Mark's Skoda appeared to have carried a number of drunken late-night pick-ups, young children and take-away curries and pizzas since Monday. The taxi's carpet was stained, the odour rich and the door handles sticky.

A valet service would not have gone amiss, but the lack of many rival taxi firms on the island probably made that an unnecessary expense.

He was prompt and cheerful. That much at least was going for him, and Lizzy appeared to like his company. The trip was her idea. She wanted one last guided tour of Alderney with some local knowledge thrown in before the flight back to the mainland.

I told Lizzy about the three youths who had been arrested for the shed thefts, including the one at the gallery, and their admission to having found her father's Walther pistol before it was sold on by Dawn Speed's connections.

She shook her head. 'I don't understand, though. Why would three teenage kids send warning notes to me and do such horrible things? They probably don't know anything about the War.'

'I don't know, Lizzy. That's if it was them.'

'Who else? They found the gun. Presumably they found the Iron Cross at the same time.'

'I think you should tell the police all when we get back.'

She didn't answer. I suspected she was still uncertain about re-opening the gallery.

Mark's magical mystery tour took us through the heart of St Anne before making a short detour to show us a rather grand property behind double gates and a gravel drive where a blue plaque said that John Arlott, a much-revered cricket commentator and writer, had once lived there.

The single track road headed south, passing the end

of the runway at the airfield, twisting through fields of sheep and horses towards the sea where we stopped at a Luftwaffe radio station that had been converted into a home for the island's wildlife trust.

We skirted the tiny airstrip again and headed north, cresting a hill and looking down towards the sea again as we approached Fort Tourgis, where Lizzy and I had enjoyed an ice-cream two days previously.

'That's Saline Bay ahead,' said Mark. 'And those rough waters out there beyond, that's called The Swinge. It's pretty treacherous for small boats.'

'What a lovely property.' Lizzy was looking at a sprawling modern house set in immaculately kept grassy grounds on the hillside, with a large sun-house overlooking the coastline.

'It's one of the biggest on the island. It's been developed piecemeal since the end of the War. Some people think it has been allowed to get too large because there used to be just a simple little farmhouse there.'

'Do you know what it was called?' I asked.

'Sparrows Farm,' said Mark.

Lizzy, sitting beside me on the back seat, squeezed my hand and let out a tiny squeak of excitement.

The road swung around in front of the cliff and levelled out by the beach. Mark pulled up outside a row of indistinct modern houses, all with large picture windows facing a common, beyond which was the beach.

'This grassy area here with the picnic table used to be where Lager Helgoland was. It was one of the four prison camps on Alderney. See those two pillars there?' He pointed at a pair of five-foot high square pillars in the drive of one of the homes. 'That used to be the camp entrance.'

'There are some wild estimates about how many prisoners died on the island during the War, a lot of the bodies were just thrown into the sea, but it's generally accepted that the figure was getting on for two thousand.'

The scene of such tragedy could not have been more starkly different to the serene view today. Undulating grassland rolled down to yellow gorse and a rough track before it gave way to a white sandy beach. At one end of the common, trimmed privet hedges surrounded a tennis club, where middle-aged men and women in their whites sedately clipped the ball over the net to each other.

Mark's route took us behind the houses up a steep climb to a grassy plateau with a spectacular vista across Braye Bay. Behind us rose the tower of The Church of St Anne where we had found the graves of Lizzy's ancestors.

'This is the cricket club and down there is Crabby Bay,' said Mark, pointing to the left of the harbour. 'There was a row of little beachside villas by the bay, but the Germans flattened them so their guns had clear sight-lines. Now the island's fire and ambulance station is down there.'

And so the tour went on. Ugly, utilitarian concrete fortifications rubbing shoulders with sandy beaches and rocky cliffs. Another site of a prison camp, a common turned into a graveyard by the Germans, and memorials dotted around for the fallen of so many nationalities during the War years.

'Lager Sylt was the worst,' said Mark. 'That was run by the SS. The prisoners there were from all walks of life: common criminals, political prisoners, conscientious objectors, Jehovah's Witnesses, homosexuals – you didn't have to do much wrong in the Nazis' eyes to end up there. The regime was brutally cruel. The prisoners were worked all day, barely fed and, not surprisingly, the death rate was high. You could be executed just for stealing a loaf of bread: shot and thrown over the cliff. There are lots of books on the War years in the bookstore in town, if you're interested.'

'No thanks,' said Lizzy. She wrapped her arms around herself and shivered.

Mark's merry tour ended up back at the airstrip. He removed his taxi-driver's badge and slipped on his baggage man's high-viz jacket. He shifted our bags from the boot of the car to the scales beside the check-in counter, and then to the luggage room behind a curtain while we settled at one of the two tables in the café area, which also doubled as duty free sales.

We had two hours to wait, enough time to top up on caffeine before the airport's last departure of the day back to the mainland. While Lizzy did the honours at the counter, I returned to the crossword I had been working on at breakfast before being interrupted by Lander's call.

10 Across. Fallen lady and Roger are here and never miss a day (4,7).

Lizzy returned with the drinks. She ought to be happy but she did not look it.

'Has your trip been worthwhile, Lizzy?'

'Yes and no.'

'The yes stuff first.'

'Well, it's been wonderful to discover that my father did something good in the War. He may have worn the wrong colour uniform, but fundamentally he was just another young soldier following orders. And he broke those orders to help the British soldiers in the end. You know, Stanley and I lived in fear all through our childhood in case his secret came out. Mum loved him, I've no doubt about that, but I think they felt ashamed of their past. She must have lived here with the Germans too.'

'Well, they say children should never be burdened with the sins of their fathers, and in this case you've absolutely nothing to feel ashamed about. As you said, he was a hero in many respects. Old Geordie probably knows that, you should talk to him about it. And so what if your neighbours in Rye Harbour know your father was on the wrong side during the War? No-one will care now.'

'I hope you're right.'

The high-pitched drone of twin propellers drifted in through the open window as an arrival sped along the tarmac before juddering to a halt just before the turning circle at the end of the strip by Telegraph Bay.

'That'll be our plane back. You are going to ignore these threats about leaving the gallery, aren't you Lizzy? You shouldn't be driven out.'

'I know, you're right, but I don't think I'll be able to decide about the future until I get back. Until I know who made the threats and why, I don't imagine I'll ever feel comfortable living there again. And Stanley thinks I should sell up anyway.'

'I'm sure he does. Half the money from any sale would be his, I assume.'

She nodded. 'I think he means it for the best though. He's mentioned before about me moving to be near them in South Wales – property is so much cheaper there too.'

'What about Zoe? She wouldn't want you to move.'

'Well, I think Zoe's got other distractions at the moment, Tom'. She looked at me at smiled.

'What do you mean?'

'I reckon you know what I mean, Tom. She's had a couple of unsuccessful relationships, but you must know she's sweet on you.'

I almost dropped my coffee. 'Don't be silly, Lizzy.'

'What's silly about it? My daughter's not that bad is she?' Under her red mop, Lizzy was grinning from ear to ear.

'No, of course not, but I've never thought of her in that way. I think we're just, you know, chums like. Anyway, she's fourteen or fifteen years younger than me. She wouldn't be interested in a shop-soiled old crock.'

'You don't scrub up too bad, Mr Kidd. Anyway, I've been thinking about that. My father was fourteen years older than my mother, so perhaps it runs in our family: fancying the older man.' She giggled and nudged me with a sharp elbow.

'No, I'm sure you've got it wrong. Don't you start match-making Ms White, you hear?'

The woman behind the solitary check-in desk told us our flight was ready for boarding and ushered us through a metal-detector that failed to pick up the acute embarrassment I was smuggling on to the flight home.

The bumps and judders of the forty-minute journey through the white clouds back to England's south coast were nothing compared to the jolt I had just received in Alderney's airport café.

Alderney 1943

Georgi Roslov was convinced he and brother Petr would not survive another winter on their island of dread.

All they had to wear were the thin clothes handed out after the summer de-lousing. They had found cement bags to wear under their shirts, tearing holes in the corners to turn them into vests, but it was feeble protection against the weather. Their wooden shoes had long since disintegrated. Now all they had on their feet were bits of sacking held on by string.

The food rations had started to dwindle even further. They were lucky if they received one loaf a week. Their German captors complained about being short of food themselves and Georgi suspected them of taking some of the slaves' rations.

Summer had gone. He could tell that from the falling of the leaves from the few trees left standing. The constant wind grew colder, the rain felt touched by ice. Their guards grew ever more irritable.

This week their firm had been set to work building a resistance nest and searchlight installation near the railway line that ran around Braye Bay to the quarries in the east of the island. As tasks went, it was less demanding than some. Their German overseer was a more kindly man, too. The Orel brothers had not seen Weird Herman since the day he attempted to beat the shit out of Ivan. The word had gone around that he had been court martialled and sent to prison in France. Georgi hoped it was true.

Their work was steady and tedious. It was also exposed, the gorse bushes and ferns providing a feeble windbreak to the gusts rocking the craft behind the breakwater in Braye Bay. The four guards with their two dogs tried to find shelter beside a wooden fuel store while the slaves shifted rocks and mixed concrete under the guidance of two French civilian workers.

Further along the beach, beside the road curving up to The Arsenal Buildings, Jens Weiss sat in long grass that rolled in waves around him in the wind like the sea down below. He had a wooden board propped up on his knees on which he had stretched a piece of thick paper, held in place by a thumb tack in each corner. Even in war, the view across the bay to the harbour and the white crested waves beyond in The Swinge was beautiful. He was using only pencil to sketch, but later in his room, he would add the water colour paints Giselle had provided.

Georgi and Petr were sitting a short distance away from the other eighteen slaves in their firm during the lunch break. Their meagre cold soup had been served out of the back of a truck doing the rounds to the gangs of workers on the coast road.

'How's the foot today, brother?'

'Not so good,' said Petr stretching out his right leg. He had cut his instep on a sharp rock two days previously, the inevitable infection now setting in. Inside his sacking footwear, it was swollen and the wound was beginning to weep.

'Don't limp. The guards will shoot you as quickly as they would shoot a lame dog.'

Petr nodded.

Georgi chewed slowly trying to eke every bit of goodness out of his piece of stale bread. 'Petr, do you think you could make it down there?' He nodded at the clump of gorse at the edge of an expanse of grass that ran the other side of the coast road behind a coil of barbed wire. Beyond the bushes was a short slope that fell away to the sandy beach.

Petr looked towards the bay and then at his brother. 'I think so.'

'Well, let us take our chance. What do you say?'

'What chance is that?'

'A slim one, but I'd rather be in the hands of God than our jailers for another night longer.' Georgi finished his soup and last crust of bread. 'I've been watching the fishing boats.' He pointed discreetly. 'The two small ones nearest the shore. The blue one and the red one. See them?'

Petr squinted at the shimmering water in the middle distance. 'I think so.'

'When we started work today, they were both at the quayside where the fuel depot is. My guess is they refilled, ready for their fishing on the morning tide. If we could get out to them, and the tide is getting low which will help, we might make it. Wait for the evening tide then set sail.'

'Where for?'

'England, I guess. At least the English are our allies.'

'Two questions, Georgi: how far is it and how do we start the engine on the boat?'

'I don't know the answer to the first, but this island is part of England so it can't be far. I think we just have to head northwards. As for starting the engine, well, we both did machinery at craft school, between us we should be able to

work it out. It can't be that different from a tractor engine.'

Petr looked towards the horizon. 'OK, when?'

'The quarry train comes by about four times a shift, and sometimes it stops, either dropping something off or just because the driver is a lazy bastard. This morning, the driver even got out and had a smoke with the guards and the French overseers. They all had their backs to us – even the dogs.'

'How do you know the same thing will happen this afternoon?'

'I don't, but there's a chance. And if it doesn't, we'll be back here tomorrow and there will be another chance.'

Petr nodded and stood up, grimacing at the pain in his foot. 'Let's get back to work.'

The October afternoon sun was creating patterns of shade and light on the water that Weiss wished he could capture in his sketch, which to him looked crude and clumsy. The concrete installations down near the shoreline were a scar on the landscape that he had decided not to include in his picture.

His countrymen had turned this little island into a fortress over the past three years. He had always harboured doubts about the wisdom of the exercise, and now he knew it had been futile. He had been told they would soon be shipping the slaves back to France and destroying the prison camps. He was also expecting to be posted elsewhere. He hoped it was back to Germany.

The dusty quarry train had stopped again, its diesel engine coughing clouds of dark fumes as it ticked over. He looked back at his drawing and then refocused his eyes on the shoreline. There was movement down there. Not the movement of swaying grass or a bird, but that of two scurrying, crouched figures. Weiss knew instantly from the rags that flapped around their pathetic frames that they were slaves.

He stood and automatically felt for the pistol in its holster at his side, but his hand rested on its handle. He could not shoot them from this distance, but he could fire a warning shot to alert the guards, who he could see were chatting to the train driver, their backs to the shore. He could run down the hill and shout to the guards, but instead he sat down again and watched in silence.

He saw the runaways crawl through the strands of barbed wire and then across the open grass. Did they not know mines had been laid there? Weiss held his breath, dreading the low 'whoomp' of one of the deadly shrapnel mines buried just below the surface. He had seen them in action: one touch and the mine would be projected a metre into the air before exploding, sending more than three hundred pieces of deadly shrapnel one hundred meters in every direction.

Nothing happened. The pair had somehow found a clear path to the edge of the ten-foot drop onto the sandy beach. He watched as they stumbled onto the seaweed-covered rocks revealed by the low tide and then across wet sand, one of them limping heavily, the other trying to support him. Just as they reached the shallow water, the deep blast of the loco's horn sounded and it lurched forward, filthy plumes of smoke belching from its exhaust. The soldiers by the working party waved to the driver and turned their attention back to the working party, seemingly unaware that two of their number were missing. They've got a chance, thought Weiss.

He looked back to the bay. The two escapees were now waist deep in the water wading towards two small fishing boats moored on buoys. 'Get down before you're seen,' he was shocked to hear himself say quietly.

As if they had heard him, the two slaves slipped their shoulders under the water and started to swim agonisingly slowly towards the craft. Weiss looked back at the work detail. There was still no indication that the guards realised what had happened. He really should alert them. It was his duty. Instead, he remained sitting and watched in silence.

The slaves had reached the nearest boat, the red one. It bobbed on its rope as one of them put a hand on the buoy. With his other hand he pulled his colleague towards him and then pushed him around the stern to the other side of the craft. He then followed. A few moments later, Weiss saw the two bedraggled figures haul themselves into the back of the boat and then drop out of sight.

✠✠✠

15

Much like my phone, I was switched on to aeroplane mode for the forty-minute hop across the English Channel. Sitting in the single bucket seat with Lizzy across the aisle, I stared out of the little round window, enveloped by thought and the deafening drone of the engines. If there were any messages coming my way, I was not receiving them.

What Lizzy had said about her daughter Zoe had left me churning restlessly like the waves below. I had been so determined to keep up a cold front for weathergirl Denise Rutter in case she should get the wrong idea, that I had not noticed any warmth radiating from Zoe White.

A broken marriage and a short-lived – if exhilarating – union with a work colleague had left me alone and quite content with that state of affairs. It was far less complicated having only one person to please. On the other hand, Lizzy White had set the hares running.

Once inside the terminal at Southampton, normal service was resumed and my telephone told me I had two voice messages. The first was from Alice saying she was having a lovely time in Spain and their trip home had been put back by three days. She also apologised for the communications black-out that had so alarmed her mother. She had jumped into the swimming pool at their

Spanish villa with her shorts on and her phone in her back pocket. One of them was not so smart it seemed, but now, fully dried out in the Spanish sunshine, both were working again.

The second message was from a voice that sounded vaguely familiar but not one to which I could put a name.

'Hello, Mr Kidd. You gave me your number when you visited and you said to get in touch if I learned anything. Well, this might interest you and your newspaper. Please give.'

The message ended abruptly and incomplete. I listened again, but there was no clue as to the caller's identity. I looked at the list of numbers under calls received, but it appeared to have been from a withheld number.

It was not until after I had collected my Audi from the long-stay car park, dropped off Lizzy at the gallery promising to see her in the morning, and slid the key into my front door that my phone rang again. It was the same softly-spoken voice.

'Mr Kidd, good, got you at last. Did you get my message earlier? Sorry about that, my battery packed up on me and I've had trouble getting to a power supply, you know what it's like.'

'Sorry, who's this?'

'It's me. Fin McEvoy.'

Of course. The soft Scottish accent. 'Fin, how are you?'

'Well, so-so, you know, given the circumstances. I'm having to bunk down in the barn but my electricity has been cut off.'

'I heard about that.'

'Yes. It's not ideal. And Dawn's not coming back, although that's probably a good thing.'

'Yes. You said you had something that might be of interest to the paper?'

'Yes. Of big interest.'

'Well, what is it?' I had dumped my bag on the bed, and was sitting at the window table, pen poised over the margin of yesterday's newspaper ready to make some notes.

'I take it the paper pays for good stories.'

'That's beyond my pay-scale, Fin. I'm just an occasional freelance. You'd have to talk to the editor, Mr Lander, about that, but, to be honest, I very much doubt it. Local papers don't pay for stories. You should take your tale to the *Sun* if it's that good.'

'I don't know about that. Look, anyway, it would create a big stir around here if this story came out.'

'Well, try it out on me and we'll see.' I was trying to sound interested but all my attention was now taken up with attempting to use a corkscrew on a bottle of red wine clamped between my knees whilst holding a telephone.

'What are you doing tomorrow?'

'Tomorrow? Well, I've got a few things planned.'

'How about we meet up at the Bosun's Bite in the morning?'

'Make it midday and I could be there. I hope this is going to be worth it, Fin.'

'Oh, it will be Mr Kidd. It will be.'

The cork flew out followed by half the contents of the bottle as it slipped out of the grip of my knees and spun across the wooden flooring, red wine decorating the once-white rug in front of the sofa. 'Bugger. That's all I need.'

All I needed, too, was a meeting with an eccentric driftwood artist in the morning, but out of loyalty to Larry Lander and the *South Coast Gazette,* I felt duty bound to say yes to Fin McEvoy's proposition.

Rug in the washing machine, the remaining red wine in my glass, I settled down to finish the crossword. *10 Across. Fallen lady and Roger are here and never miss a day (4,7).* I filled in the answer that had eluded me at Alderney Airport. *Ever present.*

Rother Gallery was still not open. It was the Friday prior to the August Bank Holiday weekend. The fine weather would bring piles of visitors to Rye Harbour for the last big tourist opportunity of the year and its front door was shut while a 'Closed' sign was propped up in the window.

I went around to the back door and was surprised to see Zoe in the kitchen busying herself making drinks. I found myself looking at her in a different light following her mother's assertion that her interest in me went beyond that of being an innocent drinking companion. She was an attractive young woman, I had to admit.

'Not at work?'

'I should be, but I've taken a sickie. Family pow-wow required.'

I followed the direction of Zoe's stare. Stanley and Olivia were in the gallery front room hunched over the desk, flipping through a large book, pointing and shaking their heads.

'I'm just making a large pot of coffee, fancy one?'

'Well, I do – but if this is a family meeting, I ought to leave you all to it.'

'We feel you're very much part of the family now, Tom. It's because Mum knew that you were coming around this morning that she's called everyone together. She'll be down in a sec.'

Slightly alarmed at Zoe's assertion that I was 'part of the family,' I sat at the kitchen table. 'Has you mother said much to you about her trip to Alderney?'

Zoe nodded as she lifted the whistling kettle from the hob. 'She's told me about Grandad. It's such a pity I never got to know him. Quite an adventure the two of you had, Tom. And between you and me,' she looked around to make sure no-one was within earshot and lowered her voice conspiratorially: 'I think she's become very fond of you.'

I opened my mouth to say something but all that came out was a throttled cough.

'Oooh, I've embarrassed you.' Zoe grinned as she put the coffeepot on the table and sat surprisingly close, our knees brushing. She put a hand on my arm. 'Don't worry, Mum doesn't bite, and she looks pretty good for her age don't you think?'

I nodded over-enthusiastically as Lizzy entered the room looking cool and elegant in a floral summer dress and long silky white scarf draped around her shoulders. She was followed by Stanley and Olivia, the latter carrying the ledger they had been studying.

'Conservatory everyone,' said Lizzy, who led the way to a large round table that had clearly been set up earlier, with biscuits and cakes arranged on a centre stand.

As we took our seats, I spoke first. 'I take it you knew about your father's past, Stanley, and his rather brave act on Alderney?'

Stanley looked up from the ledger that he had buried his nose in again. 'I knew that Dad was born and grew up in Germany and that we were to keep it a family secret, but I didn't know anything about the War and what he did until Lizzy told us over breakfast,' he said. 'It all seems so remote now, but I feel kind of proud.'

All the family also now knew about the threatening letter sent to Lizzy and the Iron Cross posted through the letterbox.

'Fucking kids.' I was shocked to hear the words come from the normally prim Olivia.

'I don't know,' I said. 'It still puzzles me. The three who stole the stuff from the shed were just teenagers. What would they know or care about Nazis and the Second World War? It just doesn't seem their style.'

'Who else could it have been?' asked Stanley. 'They stole those old tins with the stuff in. Of course it was them.'

It wasn't worth arguing and Lizzy clearly felt the same. The meeting, she said, was to decide the future of the gallery; whether she re-open and carry on as before, or sell up and start afresh.

Olivia opened the ledger and pushed it towards the centre of the table. It contained lists of the art work sold at the gallery over the past five years. Beside each entry was a figure showing the price it was sold for and another figure showing the commission made. The second column contained lots of modest numbers.

'I'm surprised you make ends meet, Lizzy love.' Olivia ran a finger down the right hand column of the last page of takings that had been bolstered by my two recent purchases. 'This is more a hobby than a business.'

'It keeps me out of mischief.' Lizzy looked at me. 'Stanley and Olivia think I should sell up, Zoe wants me to stay and I want to stay. That leaves you with the casting vote, Tom.'

Four heads had turned in my direction and four pairs of eyes looked at me expectantly.

A pathetically weak voice asked: 'Me?'

The riverside moorings were already jostling with visitors while customers crammed into the little RNLI gift shop. Rye Harbour's omnipresent wind whipped small waves up the slipway where a gaggle of children lined-up to have their photographs taken beside *Hello Herbie II*, the orange-hulled rigid inflatable rescue boat resting on a trailer on the launch way. It was open day at the lifeboat house.

Fin McEvoy was sitting at one of the outside tables at the Bosun's Bite, out of the wind on the leeward side of the café for our midday appointment. He looked more than ever like a dishevelled artist. Rebellious strands of hair had escaped the rubber band around his ponytail and flapped around his face. He had several days' growth of stubble around his goatee beard, giving him an unwashed look, which was not surprising since he was sleeping rough in his barn. His terrier, tethered to a leg of the table, was sniffing around hoping to find a discarded morsel.

'I'll get the coffees, shall I?' I noticed he was sitting there with nothing in front of him.

'That would be nice. Cappuccino please, Make it a large one.'

When I returned I noted he had placed an old biscuit tin on the table. It had Huntley & Palmers scrolled in white lettering on the chipped blue container.

'No chocolate sprinkles.' He frowned at the foam on top of his coffee.

'Sorry, didn't know you wanted them.'

'No matter, I s'pose.' He sucked at the foam and then tapped the top of the tin with a forefinger. 'I've got something here that I think you'll find very interesting, Tom.' It was first name terms now.

'Go on, then Fin. Let's hear it. But, like I said, if you want payment for the story, you need to talk to the editor about that.'

'No, that doesn't matter. If you publish this, I reckon it'll be to my benefit anyway.'

He paused while I took a notebook out of my backpack and clicked the voice record button on my phone, which I slid across the table beside his coffee mug.

'I'll start at the beginning.'

'Always a good place, Fin.'

'Yes, guess so. Well, you may have heard that Dawn was involved with some local kids in robbing sheds. It was nothing to do with me, mind, I don't hold with that sort of thing.'

He put his hand over my phone. 'This won't get me into trouble, will it Tom?'

'I shouldn't think so. I know my libel laws. I wouldn't

write anything that would drop you – or me – in it.'

He nodded and removed his hand. 'Well, the bairns would hide the stuff – mowers, strimmers and the like – in the barn for a day or so before Dawn's family came to collect it. Early last week they brought in some stuff including a collection of old tins like this.' He tapped the one in front of him again.

'They opened a few and left the rest scattered on the floor. I thought I might be able to flog them, being the sort of collectables folk like these days so I checked them over.' He prised open the lid of the tin. 'And found this among other things.'

He gingerly unfolded a section of fawn paper, so fragile that it was breaking at the creases. It had closely printed type on it that I could not make out. A faded black and white head-and-shoulders photograph was stuck in the top corner and a scrawled signature could be seen in a ruled box in the middle.

I reached out to take it but Fin pulled back. 'Not so quickly, Tom. I want to know if you're interested first. How about some more coffee?'

When I returned with two more coffees – plus chocolate sprinkles on one – the lid of the tin was closed again and the old document nowhere to be seen.

'This tin, and a few others, were all taken from the shed at the Rother Art Gallery. Now, I know it's stolen property, but what's inside is more important than that,' said Fin, spooning the chocolatey foam into his mouth.

'In one of the tins, Dawn found an old gun, which her family took away to sell, but they didn't bother with the rest. I found an Iron Cross in one of them – you know what that is, don't you?'

'A German war medal.'

'Exactly. A Nazi medal. I also found these documents.' He tapped the tin again. 'I've checked them out on the computer at the library, they're World War Two ID papers. There's a ration book too, and some coupons of some sort. There's also a wee silver cross – I don't think it's real silver though – a child's hairband and a few other trinkets. They're nothing really, but what do you think of the documents, eh?'

'I don't know Fin, what do you think?'

'Well, clearly they belong to that bloody stuck-up woman White who runs the gallery. She's done her best to corner the art market in the Harbour, but I never dreamt that she was also a Nazi sympathiser. Her parents used to run the place before her, you know? Perhaps they were Nazis. I hope this ruins her business, the fucking cow.'

'Don't you think you're over-reacting, Fin? She didn't block the planning permission you wanted to open a gallery at the barn, neither did the parish council. It would have been a district council decision at least.'

'It's not just that.'

'Then what is it?'

The knuckles of his bony hands went white as he gripped the tin. 'I hate the Nazis and what they did to my family.' He spoke in a slow determined whisper. The seemingly gentle old hippy sounded like a man consumed by anger. Something had stoked a part of his past that burned him deep inside.

'What do you mean, Fin?'

'I never knew my grandparents on my mother's side.

They were Jewish and they were exterminated by Nazis in one of their death camps around 1940 I think. My mother was three at the time. I don't know exactly what happened but she said her parents handed her over to some neighbours just before they were arrested and taken away. Can you imagine that: giving away your only child in the hope of saving her?'

I shook my head.

'My mother was smuggled out of Germany and ended up in Singapore with her adopted family. Then, when the Japs arrived there, they fled again, this time to Britain. She grew up in Glasgow with them.'

'It's tragic, Fin. But it's also a long time ago. You have to let go of these things eventually.'

He looked at me. His eyes appeared to be accusing me of something heinous.

Flecks of spittle were trapped in his goatee beard.

'You just don't know.' He spat the words out with a sneer. 'My mother never got over it. Yes, her new family were good to her, and yes, she settled in Glasgow. She met my father and they had two kids but behind the apparent family bliss she was never right, never truly happy. She suffered from depression, she said she had nightmares about Germany and the gas chambers – and when I was ten she swallowed enough sleeping pills and gin to end it all. That's what the Nazis did to her, and I'll never forget that.'

I let the silence settle between us. There was nothing to say that would ease the pain gnawing at the man sitting opposite.

Finally Fin McEvoy coughed and drained the cold

coffee from his cup. He had returned to the present. 'So?' he asked.

'So, Fin. Where's the Iron Cross?' I knew the answer but I wanted to find out what he would admit to.

'Well, I don't have that right now, do I?'

'If the stuff in the tin belongs to Lizzy White, shouldn't you return it?'

'Why should I? She's never done me no favours.'

'Look, your family story is tragic, and I'm sorry your past causes you so much grief but you can't lay that at her door just because a few pieces of war memorabilia were found in her shed.'

He stared at the old tin but said nothing.

'You know, don't you, that as one member of a parish council, she could never have – probably would never have – blocked your plans for a gallery of your own? I doubt you'd ever get authority to develop a business on the salt marsh, it's a protected area. Can't you sell your work elsewhere?'

'I have to, don't I? I have to rely on boot fairs, advertising at the pubs and direct sales from the caravan to walkers. But now the caravan's gone, I won't even be able to do that.'

'So what do you expect Lizzy White to do? Does she know you have this material?'

'She might do.' He peered at me intently through the grubby lenses of his glasses. 'She ought to close up – and if your paper carried the story about a Nazi sympathiser living in the village, I reckon she'd soon lose any trade she had anyway.'

'Do you, Fin?'

'Ay, I do.' He nodded enthusiastically as I reached across and switched off the recorder on my phone.

'Well, Fin. I think I can see where this story is going.'

He leaned forward in his chair. 'On the front page?'

'Not exactly. I can see you taking this tin back to Lizzy White with all of its contents, plus a bouquet of flowers and an apology.'

His laugh was a nervous one.

'I'm not joking, Fin.'

'You fucking must be, man. This is dynamite. I've got nothing to apologise for.'

'How about the dog shit posted through her door? Or the graffiti sprayed on the outside wall? I think they rate that as criminal damage. Or the threatening letter? I'm sure that's another offence. I know you're upset, Fin. I understand your grief. But you need to make that apology and forget this Nazi business.'

By the time I had finished, McEvoy was on his feet and clasping the old tin to his chest, his eyes wide with indignation and anger. I stood up too and patted my pocket. 'And if you deny it, I have it all here recorded.'

'You bastard.'

'That's as maybe, Fin. But think about what I've said. I don't think you are a stupid man, just a rather sad and desperate one. Lizzy White is quite aware of her family's past and, in fact, she's quite proud of it. So – you've had two coffees out of me, now piss off and do the right thing.'

Michael Monday and Steve Kain were standing by the lifeboat on the slipway in their issue yellow waterproofs complete with lifejackets posing for photographs beside the boat and talking to the children about the work of the RNLI.

They had seen me sitting outside the Bosun's Bite with McEvoy and had waved me over when the artist had made his sudden departure.

'Signing up new volunteers?' I said, indicating to the excited gaggle around the powerful craft.

'You never know, a few might just get the bug like we have,' said Monday. 'How's that book of yours coming along?'

'It's not yet, but I'm definitely making a start after the Bank Holiday.'

'If you need any more help, let us know. The more people who know about our work and the sacrifices of those before us, the better.'

'Was that old Fin McEvoy you were with?' asked Steve Kain.

'It was, he was trying to flog me a non-story. That's all.'

'I think he's pretty desperate, what with the fire and this business with Dawn. She's disappeared for good you can be sure of that.'

I turned to Michael Monday. 'What about that lad who works for you at the exhaust centre, Alex Lee, wasn't it? I hear he was arrested for the spate of shed thefts.'

'Little shyster. I helped him out by giving him a job and all the time him and his mates were the ones nicking stuff. Well, he won't be working for me again, I can tell you. I hope they throw the book at the lot of 'em.'

'Probably be a slap on the wrist and a few hours'

community service if I know the magistrates around here, especially if it's their first offence,' said Kain.

When I arrived back at the gallery, the front door was open and the 'Closed' sign gone. The two display rooms were crowded with browsers. Zoe sat at the desk underneath the old watercolour of Telegraph Bay trying to look busy but failing.

'Business good?'

'Uh-ah. Lots of footfall but very few sales, apart from a few postcards. Still, at least we're open again.'

I looked over her head at the one picture in the room that was not for sale. 'That was your mother's meeting place for us on Alderney – a bench over-looking that wild piece of coast.'

Zoe craned her neck to look around. 'It's been here so long, that I've never really paid it much attention, you know. It just seemed part of the furniture. Something Mum had. I suppose it's quite nice, but, even if it is Grandad's work, it's not my cup of tea.'

'Did Lizzy tell you your grandparents' ashes are scattered along the cliff walk there. The place must have meant a lot to them.'

'Yes she did.'

There was a crash and tinkle of something breaking in the gallery room where the pottery was displayed. 'Oh no, I'd better go. Mum's serving teas out back if you want to see her.'

Lizzy was in the garden, but sitting on a bench seat underneath the shady strands of a small willow tree rather than waiting on the tables in the conservatory café.

'Don't get the wrong idea, Tom. This is just a five-minute lull before the tea-time rush. It's been pretty hectic since we opened at midday.'

'I'm glad you decided to stay and open up again. Stanley and Olivia gone?'

'They have. I think they were rather disappointed with you not seeing things their way and not backing up their proposal to sell the place.'

'It wasn't my position to make a decision either way, Lizzy. It had to be between the four of you, and as this is also your home as well as your business, I think it was only right that you had the casting vote.'

She tapped me on the knee and pointed to the shed. 'Have a look in there. The strangest thing has happened. I'd better go – some thirsty punters have just arrived.'

The new shed door had been fixed, its bright fresh pine standing out starkly against the dark brown stain on the rest the overlap wood. It was shut, but not locked. Inside everything was in its place. The old tins were stacked in rows on the shelves at the far end in the gloom. Tools were on hooks or in tea chests under the counter. Empty picture frames were leaning against one another in order of size in the corner. Garden equipment was pushed under the work surface on the window side, which was clear of clutter apart from a battered blue tin that had Huntley & Palmers printed on it.

I prised the slightly bent lid off the tin that Fin McEvoy had kept out of my reach on the café table and emptied its contents into the sunshine on the work bench.

The German Army ID papers that McEvoy had held up as though they were his passport to a wealthy future were there. The faded head-and-shoulders photograph of a young man was overlaid by official ink stamps bearing swastikas, and the signature underneath was still clear enough: Jens Weiss. Opposite was listed his name, his date of birth – 05-07-1916 – and place of birth – Hanover. There was his army number, and other information I could not translate, but the names of his parents at the bottom were clear.

There were coupons that appeared to be for rations, an old train ticket, a collection of small pencils and what looked like a thin school notebook, its stapled spine rusty and frayed.

I gingerly turned the pages. They contained child-like drawings of a small house in woods by the sea or a lake. There were several attempts at a dog's face, a couple of them scribbled over as if the artist was unhappy with his efforts. There was a rather good portrait of a young man, but it did not look like Jens Weiss. Underneath the word 'Hans' was written.

At the bottom of the tin were a faded blue and silver headband and the little silver cross McEvoy had mentioned. There was also a rusted piece of wire, made into a loop just about big enough to go around a man's fist. There was a pale green German passport. It belonged to Jens Weiss. I flicked through the pages that were largely blank, but near the end there it was: a stamp from 1950 showing he had entered the Bailiwick of Guernsey and Alderney. On the next page was a stamp from immigration at the Port of Weymouth marked 1952.

I packed the papers back inside, snapped the lid shut and carried the tin to the end of the shed where there was just space enough for it to resume its rightful place in the world.

Lizzy's perspiring face was at the door. 'Did you find it?'

'The old tin? Yes. Where did it come from?'

'It was left on the front step sometime early this afternoon. Neither of us saw who left it, we were busy inside.'

'Have you looked inside the tin?'

'I had a quick glance, but didn't have time to go through it carefully. It looks like some of my father's old stuff.'

'It's his past in a biscuit tin, Lizzy. Now you look like you could do with some help. Need a washer-up?'

I picked up Lizzy from the gallery at six as promised. Her hair, still damp from the shower, was tied back in a topknot and she wore a man's white shirt with tails over denim jeans. She smelled of something expensive as she got into the front seat of my less than fragrant Audi.

We stopped at the village stores briefly before heading towards the windfarms in the east and the tranquil flatness of Romney Marsh that was criss-crossed by the power lines stretching from the coastal power station.

Lizzy had rummaged through the CDs crammed into the glove compartment and stuffed into the pocket in her door. She had chosen Bruce Springsteen and we were heading down 'Thunder Road', windows rolled down, the low sun dancing off the sea.

The jigsaw of Lizzy's past was still incomplete. Several pieces had been slotted into place in Alderney, and she had cast off the fear of her father's background being discovered. In fact, in some ways, because of what he did in Alderney, she almost wanted the truth to come out. She also wanted to find out all that Geordie Harris knew about her father.

A different day meant a different doorkeeper. The ever-changing face on the front desk of the Green Leaves Retirement Home suggested they could not keep their staff or had a work rota chosen by the blindfold-and-pin method.

They all knew the routine, though. Print name, sign in with date and time. Car registration if applicable. The young man, who said he was from Hastings and had started only this week, insisted on showing us the way to the day room and pointing out Geordie Harris, who was slumped in a chair by the window, chin on chest, eyes closed, an arm hanging limply by his side.

The local evening news was blaring out of the giant screen. Sue Lander, looking as sophisticated as ever, was cheerfully confirming that more rail chaos was expected over the bank holiday weekend because of engineering works on the main line to London.

'Mr Harris,' the nurse shouted in his ear and gently rocked a shoulder. 'You've got visitors.'

When Geordie's eyes did not open, a jolt of alarm hit the pit of my stomach, but his curse reassured me. 'Blasted sunshine, it wasn't here when I dozed off.' He squinted up at us and rubbed his watery eyes. 'Who is it? Not the bloody undertakers yet?'

The walk up the corridor to Geordie's room was slow and laborious. The old man refused a helping hand, determined to make his own way, gripping his stick tightly in one hand and using the other to lean on the wall whenever he needed a breather.

'I am privileged, two of you together.' He eyed Lizzy and me, perched side by side on the edge of his bed wearing almost identical clothing of white shirts hanging loosely over jeans. 'And a fine pair you make too.'

'Thought you might appreciate this, Geordie.' I fished a full-sized bottle of navy rum out of my backpack, and the old man's eyes lit up.

'Cracking. Good lad. I ran out of the stuff last night.'

Lizzy told him about her trip to Alderney: the story of her father's war on the island and the secret mine map, his subsequent marriage to Giselle Sparrow and the Sparrow family graves in the cemetery at the Parish Church of St Anne. Geordie listened in silence, sipping and savouring the dark liquid I had poured into his glass.

She also told him about the theft at the gallery: the discovery of the World War II German pistol, the Iron Cross, the graffiti and the subsequent threats she had received.

He held up a wrinkled hand. 'You can blame me in part for that. The Walther was mine originally. I brought it back from the War as a souvenir. I got it decommissioned by a local blacksmith, but my wife was still unhappy about it being in the house. Eventually I asked your father to look after it for me. I'd forgotten all about its existence, to be honest.'

'What about the Iron Cross?' I asked.

'I think that was John's. He said they were handed out to lots of mid-ranking soldiers towards the end of the war, a sort of morale-boosting exercise. He wasn't proud of it or ashamed of it. I think he just accepted it.'

Geordie tilted an empty glass in my direction. I poured him a refill and topped up my own tumbler. Lizzy had declined a drink, saying she would drive the Audi back to Rye Harbour.

'He was a good man, your Dad. I didn't care about him being a German. He had been a soldier in the War just like us Sappers. We both took orders and didn't question them. That was how it was, you see.'

'Did you know the story of the mine map?' I asked him. 'The one Jens left behind for the Allies to find.'

'At the time, no. We just followed instructions of where to clear the mines. The German prisoners did most of the dangerous work to be honest, a few of them died doing it too. Like I told you before, we only lost the one. But there were rumours among the men that the officers had found some sort of map left behind by the Krauts because our work was so successful.'

'Do you think it was the one left by my Dad?'

'Yes, my love, I do. We had a company re-union ten years after the War and the officers there were talking to us, treating us like equals now the fighting was all over. Well, one of them did say they'd used a map secretly left behind by a German officer. Reckoned it saved plenty of lives, too, he did.'

Lizzy beamed. She hurriedly brushed away a small tear as it rolled down her cheek. This was what she had hoped to hear: vindication of her love for her father, proof to her that he was a good man inside a uniform that represented evil.

'I just wish his story had come out before he died. He should have been proud of what he did, not scared of what people might say,' she said.

'I told your father the same thing, but he said it was too complicated to talk about. Some British people, even into the 1970s when he died, resented the Germans for what they did in the War. You know, some people were so bitter they wouldn't even buy a German car.'

He took a swig from his glass. 'But I think by then he was more worried about reprisals from Nazi sympathisers. There were still some around, you see, small groups of war survivors who believed in the cause, younger blokes who glorified Hitler's regime. If it had come out that your Dad had tried to help the Allies and save British lives, they'd have branded him a traitor. He genuinely feared they might go after him and his family – your Ma, you and Stanley.'

'Surely not?'

Geordie nodded. 'That was only thirty years after the War. Memories were still fresh for a lot of folk. It's different now, thank God.' He rocked back into his armchair having been perched forward to tell his tale. The effort, and perhaps the rum, was beginning to take effect. He rested his head back and closed his eyes. I put a finger to my lips to hush Lizzy's next question.

We stood up. Lizzy studied her father's paintings of Alderney hanging on the walls of the little room. I looked out of the window listening to the old man's soft, slow breathing. A rich and full life, no doubt a brave one, would be coming to an end soon, but not too soon, I hoped.

It was Geordie who broke the silence. 'You can have them when I'm gone.'

Lizzy looked around. 'Oh, I wasn't hinting at that Geordie. I was just looking at them in a different light now, having visited Alderney and knowing the significance of them. This one here with the boats, it looks like Braye Harbour.'

She moved to the wall behind the bed. 'And this one of the fort on the hill, I think that's Fort Tourgis.' She turned and looked at the painting behind the armchair. 'I can't be sure about that, but I think that might be the farm where mother grew up. The coastline reminds me of Saline Bay.'

'Did John ever tell you how he and Elle met?' I looked at the old man as I topped up his glass.

'She was just a kid when they first met. It was during the War. He was in his mid-twenties, I guess; and she was twelve, according to John.'

'Why was she still on Alderney? All the locals were meant to have been evacuated before the occupation.'

'John said Elle's father refused to go after his wife and another daughter were killed having just been evacuated to Guernsey. They were caught in a bombing raid but Elle survived. He stayed on Alderney, looked after Elle and his herd of cows. They got by, selling milk and eggs to the Germans, who left them in peace, pretty much.'

Lizzy had taken a piece of paper and a pen out of her bag and was doing some maths. 'If Mum was twelve, that was 1943. Dad would have been twenty seven.' There was disbelief in her voice.

'Don't get the wrong idea, Lizzy. I don't think anything

wrong happened then,' said Geordie. 'John said they formed an innocent friendship during the War because of their love of drawing and painting. But when he left the island with the rest of the troops, he said he couldn't help wondering what had happened to her. He eventually went back seven years later, found her still working on the farm with her father.'

'And a romance started?'

'It must have. A year or so later they got married. I don't think her father was too happy about it, mind, so John said they waited until after her twenty-first birthday, so he could not object. Then they moved to England.'

'They waited just the one day after her twenty-first,' said Lizzy. 'We've seen the marriage certificate, but her father was there so he must have come around to the idea.'

'When did you last see John, Geordie?' I offered to top up his glass but he put his hand over the top of it and shook his head.

'About a week before he died. We had one of our regular Sunday morning get-togethers. He seemed fine. Next thing I hear is he's keeled over with a heart attack. Poor bloke.'

'You went to the funeral, didn't you?'

'Aye, I did. Not many of us there, sadly.'

'Stanley said there was a German at the funeral. Do you remember that, Lizzy?'

She shook her head.

'That's right,' said Geordie. He paused to thumb through the dusty files in his memory bank. 'Fellow didn't speak good English, like John. Seemed nice enough though.' He fell silent again. He'd found the file marked 1975 and was checking it through. 'Anton. That was his name. Buggered if I can remember his surname though. Said he'd been with John on Alderney during the War and even remembered meeting your mother then when she was a girl.'

'Anton List,' said Lizzy.

'List. That's it. You do remember him from the funeral.'

'Not really, if I'm honest. But his name is on the marriage certificate. He was one of the witnesses.'

Alderney 1943

The smoke from the charred remains of Lager Helgoland still drifted across Crabby Bay and an acrid stench hung in the autumnal air. The Germans had torched the huts, the canteen, the hospital, and the guards' quarters. Even the Chief of Camp's bungalow was gone. The barbed wire was being hauled away by a mobile crane and the steam road-roller was attempting to pulverise all signs of the camp's barbaric past into the Alderney hillside. When Churchill's troops arrived, it would seem as if the atrocities had never happened. That, at least, was the plan of German High Command.

The prisoners had been moved, some into the three remaining prison camps on the island, others onto ships to be ferried to France and an uncertain future.

The road was blocked by the military units conducting the work so Jens Weiss had been forced to turn around and take the long route to Sparrows Farm back through the town and past the airstrip, which had also been made unusable for fear of RAF planes landing there.

He arrived late afternoon. It was already getting dark and he could see the warm glow of a candle in the kitchen as he walked up the muddy path, his satchel over his shoulder, a large square parcel wrapped in brown paper and string under his arm.

'Herr Weiss, to what do we owe the pleasure?' Edward Sparrow was in the shed and had heard the car pull up.

'Edward, good evening. I hope I am not disturbing you.'

The farmer showed him two bloodied hands. 'Just skinning a rabbit. Will you stay for supper?'

Weiss hesitated. 'Yes, that would be excellent. Thank you. And I come bearing gifts.' He held aloft the square parcel.

'Go inside, Giselle is there. I'll be in in a minute.'

The kitchen was warm and the collie was in his familiar place curled up by the stove, which crackled with burning wood. Giselle was at the sink chopping a swede. On the table he could see she had already prepared onions and something green and leafy.

'Better draw the curtain, Giselle. Don't want the Military Police to see the light after black-out.'

She looked up. She had been so engrossed in her work, she had not heard him come in. 'Oh Jens. How nice to see you again. It's been a few weeks.'

The farmer came in with the headless torso of a skinned rabbit, its belly gaping and innards removed. 'He's ready for the pot, Giselle,' he said, putting the dead animal on the wooden surface next to the stove, which immediately aroused the interest of the dog.

Giselle put the dirty dishes in the sink and the dog sulked as she shovelled the bare carcass into the stove.

'Come and sit down Giselle, I have something to tell you both,' said Weiss.

When she was seated, he reached behind him for the parcel and his satchel, which were propped against the one armchair in the room.

'I'm leaving this weekend. I've been summoned back to Germany like a lot of us here. I wouldn't be surprised if

we're all gone by the end of next year, although I shouldn't be telling you that.'

'Is that why Helgoland's been flattened?' asked the farmer.

'It is. The other camps will all be destroyed too. Command are worried about being accused of crimes against the prisoners. I don't know how they expect it to all stay secret, though.'

'You'll be leaving behind a bloody fortress and thousands of mines. The island will never be the same. I don't suppose the island folk who left will ever want to come back now they're settled on the mainland.'

'I don't know, Edward. We'll at least be leaving behind a good sewage system, and piped water and an electricity supply. You didn't have that before we arrived.'

'We still don't here at the farm.'

'No, that's true. Anyway, I wanted to thank you both for making my stay on Alderney more enjoyable.' He reached into the satchel. 'For you Edward, a bottle of that fine cognac, and for you Giselle, here are some paints I never used.'

The farmer and daughter looked at the gifts on the table, then at the large paper parcel resting against the German's knee. He had a broad smile on his face.

'And this,' he said lifting up the parcel, 'is also for you, for your thirteenth birthday next week.'

Giselle let out an excited 'Oh' as she reached across for the parcel.

'Manners, Giselle,' said her father.

'Oh yes, of course. Thank you Jens. I've never had such a big present. May I open it?'

'Of course. I hope you like it, but I'm not sure it's up to your standard.'

Giselle tugged at the well-tied string with no success. She jumped up to the sink to fetch a knife and sliced the parcel free of its bonds. She laid the parcel on the table and started to unpeel the paper.

Beneath was a glowing watercolour picture of the sea and jagged rocks, illuminated by a setting sun casting stark shadows on a cliff.

'It's beautiful. Truly beautiful. And the frame!'

'Ah yes, that is rather good isn't it, but I can take no credit. I got one of the carpenters to make it out of a packing case. He has even sanded it down.'

Giselle propped up the picture on the broad windowsill and placed two candles in front of it.

'It is lovely. I shall treasure it. Is it Telegraph Bay?'

Weiss smiled. 'You recognise it. Good. Yes, it's from the sketch I showed you in my office last summer. Keep it safe – and when the English troops arrive, make sure you show them. Tell them to study the whole picture. Tell them to look beyond the waves.'

✠✠✠

16

The English south coast, one month later

The late-afternoon rain, driven in by a chilling wind straight from the Baltic, was pounding out a tattoo on the double-glazed window beside the dining table, which doubled up as a work-desk. It was perfect writing weather. It was also suitably atmospheric for my attempts to capture the scene of seventeen brave souls launching themselves into a hellish storm in a vain attempt to save lives. The *Mary Stanford* story was beginning to take shape.

Writing was always a chore when the sun shone and the day invited you out to play. On days like today, the words flowed and the time flew. The meteorological gods had, in fact, been smiling on me for most of the month, driving the holiday-makers away from Rye Harbour and me inside to my laptop. I had also decided to make September a dry month, which appeared to have had a great effect on my output of words as well as my ability to get up in the mornings.

Something else that had dried up had been work for the *South Coast Gazette*, but I was not sorry, even though the wheezing remains of my redundancy pay-off were in need of a defibrillator. Whatever my pecuniary state, I was determined to see it through this time and produce a book, although the manuscript was still very much in its infancy and still nameless.

The only contact I'd had with Larry Lander, the editor of the *SCG*, since the 'The Great Shed Robberies' had been at a party to celebrate his wife Sue's birthday at their house. They had told me the news that Denise Rutter had fallen head over heels for a former Olympic gymnast, who was now making a name for himself as a celebrity chef on television. *From vault to velouté* in one bound, was the favourite gag of the TV show's chubby bald presenter.

Zoe and her mother Lizzy had been inviting me out for dinner with them both at least once a week in the past month, but I was never quite sure who was doing the match-making. We alternated between the Grenadiers and the Nelson, each of the women giving me knowing smiles whenever the other disappeared to the loo or the bar. I never gave encouragement, but had to admit I enjoyed the game.

Tonight was one of those dinner dates. I was to meet them at the gallery. Lizzy was more enthusiastic about the art business than ever and was making room for new artists to exhibit their work before the Christmas trade picked up. She had never discovered who left the biscuit tin containing her father's war-time memorabilia on the doorstep, and I did not intend to enlighten her as Fin McEvoy appeared to have done a runner.

Despite my insistence on sticking to alcohol-free lager for the month, Steve Kain had become a regular drinking companion, particularly since I had proved my mettle to him in a terrifying experience to which I had committed myself one evening in the Grenadiers. Seeking to find out exactly what it was like answering an emergency call on the lifeboat and ploughing into the unknown on the high seas, I had idiotically accepted a challenge that Kain had thrown down.

I was to join one of their training exercises – as the victim. Clad in layers of old clothing and the latest life-jacket, I was dumped in the freezing Channel with another regular member of the crew. We bobbed about like discarded corks before the rescue craft circled around and plucked us out of the sea. For some reason, they found the whole exercise hilarious.

It all fed into my burgeoning manuscript, which Sue Lander had promised to read when complete to see if it was worthy of presenting as an idea for the television station's weekly local arts programme.

I reluctantly closed the lid of the lap-top after I spotted I was already late for that evening's dinner date(s). The Audi refused to start, as it had all the previous week, so I had no option but to leg it to the gallery, imagining myself as an ancient mariner on a storm-tossed night battling my way to a safe haven, or a warm pub at least.

I need not have worried about being late. When I arrived at the gallery, my two dining companions were clearly far from ready for the short trip to the Admiral Nelson. Both women had headscarves around their manes of red hair and were wearing dungarees. Lizzy was on a stepladder adjusting the channel lighting, Zoe was collecting the artwork off the walls and piling it up in bubble-wrap in the café area at the rear.

'Just the man,' said Lizzy, looking down from her perch. 'Tom, we can't shift the screws on those shelves over there, can you put your muscles to good use. The screwdrivers are in the tool box there on the floor.'

'Ah, ladies, have you forgotten something?'

'Dinner? No we haven't, Tom,' said Zoe as she returned. 'Rye's best Indian is delivering a banquet for three at eight, and we have plenty of booze, both alcohol-free and regular, in the fridge.'

'What's going on?'

'Spring cleaning – or rather, autumn cleaning,' said Lizzy climbing down the steps. 'With September virtually over, I've decided now is as good a time as any to sort this place out, get rid of some of the stuff that won't shift and give it a lick of paint before the new exhibits arrive.'

'And you want me to provide the masculine know-how. Fair enough.'

'Well, you could come in useful. Starting with those shelves, and then help Zoe shift the desk. I'm not sure my back is up to carting that old thing around.'

The shelves came down after an initial struggle with a screwdriver, and then I helped Zoe heave the oak desk through the narrow doorway into the café while her mother cleared the highly-priced paintings off another wall.

'Just Dad's old watercolour to go,' she said. 'Tom, can you hand it down, you'll need the steps to reach it.'

The old wooden frame was riddled with woodworm holes and felt as though it might buckle at any moment as I lifted the picture gingerly and felt behind to release the hanging wire from the hook.

'Here we go.' I handed it down to Lizzy who, just as she reached up to take it, screamed and lurched back as a large hairy house spider appeared from the rear of the frame, clearly unimpressed at being evicted from his cosy cranny. As the spider made a dash for the dark confines of her armpit, Lizzy tumbled backwards, I stumbled off the steps and the painting was airborne heading for the unlit fireplace.

It landed on the edge of the stone hearth, the corner angle of the frame splintering and then cracking open to release the painting from its mount and the hardboard backing board. The picture coiled up on itself and rolled to a halt by the grate.

Zoe's immediate concern was her mother. Her mother's immediate concern was the painting. No-one seemed too bothered about me or the fate of the spider.

While Zoe helped Lizzy to her feet, I carefully picked up the painting of Telegraph Bay which meant so much to the family and laid it on the dust sheet covering the floor, before rolling it out flat.

'No damage done it seems. Picture looks fine, and the old frame will make good kindling.'

The two women came over and kneeled down beside me. Lizzy ran her hand over the painting, barely touching its faded colours. 'Thank goodness, yes, it looks undamaged. I'd have hated to have ruined it after all these years – all for a stupid spider.'

'Let's put it away somewhere safe, we can sort out a new frame later.' I let the painting roll loosely back on itself and noticed some marks on the back of it. 'What's this?'

I laid the painting face down and slowly unfurled it so that it was flat again. The markings on the back were faint but Lizzy slowly traced a finger around what appeared to be an outline of a shape.

'That's a map of Alderney.'

Around the coastline were neat blocks of shaded areas and a straight line from each block led to the centre of the island where there was written one word. *Minen.*

Present day. Orel, Central Russia

'Just one, you understand, as it's a special day.'

'Make it a large one, Olga, there's a good girl, it can't do us any harm now.' The old man picked up his glass of clear liquor and tilted it at the matronly figure in the tight blue uniform as she started to fill a second glass on the low table beside the imitation coal fire which flickered red.

'All right, but only this once Georgi. I suppose it's not every day you reach your ninety-fifth birthday. But don't you be thinking you can flatter me by calling me a girl.'

'And my brother Petr, don't leave him out. Just because he cannot see, doesn't mean he doesn't know how much vodka is in the glass.'

'You pair will get me in trouble,' she grumbled, but they knew she did not mean it. She led Petr's trembling hand to the glass, which he raised to his lips and smelled.

'Good stuff, Olga, Good stuff.'

He raised the glass in the direction of where he knew the other man was sitting. 'Happy birthday, brother, and thank you. We have come a long way together.'

✠✠✠

Afterword

In Alderney Museum there is a cabinet dedicated to Conrad Gries, a German soldier based on the island during the Second World War.

Gries, pictured on the back cover, was a military draughtsman and surveyor given the task of plotting the mines laid across the island. He was also a keen artist, painting and sketching many pictures of the island's landscape.

Before leaving Alderney, he defied orders to destroy all plans, and secretly left a second map showing the minefields in the hope of avoiding more bloodshed. His action almost certainly saved many lives when the mines were cleared.

The exact details of how and where he left his secret map remain a matter of speculation. One story suggests he hid the plans in a bible in the church, another says they were found in the old school building. Yet another says he drew them on the back of one of his paintings.

In 1990 the Alderney Society made contact with Conrad Gries, and he donated much of his artwork and letters to the Museum. He died in 2006.

During the German occupation, two men escaped from Alderney on a fishing boat. When they arrived in mainland Britain and recounted the atrocities happening on the island, they were not believed.

The stories of the lives of the slave workforce in this novel are taken from authentic accounts of those who survived. The official inquiry after the War estimated that between 1500 and 2000 prisoners died on Alderney although that figure continues to be disputed to this day.

While the island's population was evacuated a few days before the Nazi occupation, a handful of them returned to work the land and co-exist with the Germans. The pure breed of Alderney Cattle died out during the War.

Sapper Onions' grave can be found in the churchyard of the Parish Church of St Anne on Alderney.

The story of the 1928 *Mary Stanford* Lifeboat tragedy is true.

Thank you…

I am indebted to Ken Baker from the Alderney Society for opening the island's museum solely for me on a filthy day in March 2019, and for arranging for archivist Giulia Hempel to be there too. Their help in piecing together the inspiring story of Conrad Gries was invaluable.

The photograph of Gries on the back cover was tracked down with the guidance of artist James Colmer, and is used courtesy of Alderney Museum.

Thanks also to Andrew Pantcheff, whose father Major 'Bunny' Pantcheff conducted the official enquiry into the German occupation of Alderney and who wrote the definitive account of what happened on the island between 1940–45. *'Alderney. Fortress Island'* by T. X. H. Pantcheff was one of the books used to ensure the details of the war years on Alderney in this novel are accurate.

Another was *Island of Dread* by Brian Bonnard, a book based on the letters of Georgi Kondakov, who was fifteen when the Germans took him from his home in Orel, Central Russia, and imprisoned him as a slave worker on Alderney in 1941.

Other books referenced were *The Alderney Story 1939–49* by Michael St.J. Packe & Maurice Dreyfus, *Living with the Enemy* by Roy McLoughlin, and *Festung Alderney* by Trevor Davenport.

My gratitude also goes to my guinea-pig readers, David and Hilary Llewellyn, Sabina Knees and the ladies of the St Leonards book club for their eagle eyes and astute feedback.

Once again Amanda Helm has provided her expertise and guidance in editing this, the second of Tom Kidd's escapades, while my wife Brenda has been a source of never-ending support and cups of strong coffee.

About the Author

Colin J. Bateman has spent his working life as a newspaper journalist, first in the West Country and then on the national press based in London. He has also dabbled in magazine, radio and television work. He has written three other books and this is his second venture into fiction, continuing Tom Kidd's story which began in *A Dreadful Trade*. He and his wife live in Kent.